THE TAKINGS

A Psychological Thriller

Sandie Will

Awards and Praise for
The Takings

2020 Florida Writers Association
Royal Palm Literary Award Finalist
in Blended Fiction

"The Takings is a twisted psychological thriller that will take your mind and emotions on a suspenseful journey that will leave your heart pounding as you race through the pages to see what will happen next. The reader is kept in suspense throughout the book and taken on a dark ride into the mind and life of a pathological character that leaves the reader's mind reeling."

~Amazon Review

"This was definitely an edge of your seat, heart in your throat, psychological thriller."

~Amazon Review

"The Takings by Sandie Will immediately pulled me into the story. It was mysterious, dark, and suspenseful to the very end. The author was also extremely talented at writing descriptive, vivid imagery that put me in the book with the characters. At times, I felt trapped in the swamp and Adrian's visions as well. In addition, I also felt some sort of sympathy and empathy for the villain. I was so conflicted as you clearly should root for good over evil but sometimes you can't help feeling a bit too much when you come across some great writing. The Takings by Sandie Will is definitely a great mystery to read on your vacation this year."

~Shannon Winings for Readers' Favorite

Also by Sandie Will

The Replacings

The Caging at Deadwater Manor

For Michael

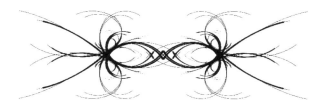

Sometimes, in the haste of a day, one does not stop to reflect on the unexplained. The shadows that exist in small corners, for instance, tend to be ignored. Sudden movements seen in the blink of an eye are disregarded. Moans carried by the wind are not investigated.

We all forget about the spaces that we have come to ignore. Those spaces that hold secrets from daylight. Those spaces that, if entered, could change one for an entire lifetime.

Such was the case for Mr. Adrian Webster.

CHAPTER

1

The light from Wyatt's bike jounces through the woods as he races along the path he knows well. He swerves around the tree roots that protrude from the earthen trail, skidding on a few in his haste. Long strands of tree moss brush against his shoulders as he plunges through them, leaving behind a wake of spiraling locks. Wyatt knows he's in for it. A pink glow is already reflecting off the wetland waters, letting him know that nightfall will be upon him soon.

Too soon.

He still has another twenty-minute ride through Green Swamp, which leads to the backyard of his house in Davenport. There's no way he's going to make it home before dark, and his dad has little patience for rules not being followed. Wyatt winces with the thought of his dad's anger the last time he came home late: how he was red in the face and yelling; how he barely stopped himself from hitting Wyatt with a belt. He cringes at the thought of his dad losing control even worse this time. He pushes back the lump in his throat when he thinks about his mom's fatal car accident and how his dad hasn't been the same. He now regrets not leaving earlier, but that last game of Mario Kart had held him prisoner and beating his friend Colton just felt too sweet.

Wyatt stands up on his bike pedals to pump them harder, watching the trail more intently as the night envelopes the sky. Chattering crickets bring the day to a close, their legs moving faster and faster, just like Wyatt's. The pungent smell of organic muck surrounds him, making Wyatt wrinkle his nose in protest. He's completely surrounded in darkness as he rides farther down the winding trail, the only light being the one on his handlebars. Sweat begins to cluster on his forehead, the fatigue slowing him down. The woods are solemn now, too quiet even, and for the first time since starting these routine visits a year ago, Wyatt's feeling a twinge of nervousness. He hears the familiar clanking of the bike chain echoing off the trees as he passes by, but something just doesn't feel right. He tries not to think about the things that frighten him, like the gators, or the spiders, or getting lost, or the dark emptiness between the trees, but the more he rides, the more bothersome these thoughts become.

An old barred owl announces itself with a boisterous hoot, causing Wyatt to glance toward the top of the trees a second too long. His front tire slams against a tree root, jerking his front wheel to the left and ejecting Wyatt out of his seat and over the handlebars. He lands hard on a cypress knee sticking up from the ground, wrenching his leg backward. He groans from the pain that's searing through his torso as he cradles his leg in the middle of the path. Blood is pooling in his mouth, some of which he feels dripping onto his chin from a split in his lip. He opens his eyes. His bike is lying on its side. The front wheel looks bent, and a cloud of dust lingers in the glow of the bike light, swirling around like a mini tornado. He thinks about how much trouble he's in. It'll take him forever to ride back home with a broken bike. Not to mention, his dad is going to be mad about spending more money on repairs. He decides to fix it on his own and pedal home with his good leg.

Wyatt slowly sits up to assess his situation, causing a second wave of pain to shoot through his leg. He screams out and rolls back and forth on his side. The sound of footsteps crunching through the twigs and leaves interrupts Wyatt's focus on his distress. They are coming closer from behind. Wyatt quiets to a whimper and listens, his chest rising and falling rapidly. Then, just as quickly as they came, the footsteps stop. Wyatt lies in the path for a while, questioning whether he should face whoever's behind him. He finally tells himself he has to be brave and musters the nerve to turn around. All he sees is his bike light and his front tire. Wyatt relaxes his body, then carefully sits up again, not wanting any further pain. He hears more footsteps and jerks his head to the left.

There, just beyond his bike, Wyatt sees the silhouette of a man standing in the pathway.

Wyatt stares at him for a couple of seconds, his heart racing. The man is tall, like his dad, but his shoulders seem broader.

The man immediately starts running in his direction. Wyatt jumps up using his good leg and hobbles down the path. He sees the man getting closer from behind. He leaps toward the bushes to hide, but before he reaches them, the man catches Wyatt and drags him to the ground. Wyatt tries to get up and run again, but his leg is too painful. The man's work boots are directly in front of him. Trembling, Wyatt peers up at the man's face, but the bike light is so intense, he can't see any features. "Dad?" he asks.

Instead of an answer, the arm of a blue jacket plunges through the light toward Wyatt. A large hand grabs him by his shirt and turns him face down on the trail. Wyatt is dazed, unsure of what is happening. He now knows this man cannot be his dad, so who is it? He hunches himself up onto his forearms and tries to crawl away, screaming for help and kicking his legs despite the agony.

But the stranger's strength is too great.

The man grabs his arms, easily pulling each behind his back. Wyatt jerks his body, trying to free himself from the man's grasp. A rope is flopped onto his shoulders, some of it falling near Wyatt's face. He screams out, "No!" as he fights against his wrists being bound. He begs the man to stop, but within seconds, he senses rope being wrapped around his ankles. Footsteps shuffle forward until the man's boots are straddling Wyatt's head. Wyatt cries, his wild eyes moving side to side. He hears a long screech followed by a tearing sound and his forehead is forced upward. A strip of gray duct tape is pushed against his mouth and eyes, then wound around his head. He can't imagine why this man is tying him up.

Wyatt is in complete darkness. His heart is pounding. Every sound becomes accentuated, making him flail his head back and forth, fearful of the man's next move. The tape inadvertently slips down too close to his nostrils, causing him to have difficulty breathing. Wyatt exhales heavily, hoping to move the tape, but it doesn't budge. He squirms, afraid of suffocating. Within seconds, he feels the man's fingers on his face, pulling the tape away from his nose. He draws in a deep earthy odor, which calms him a little until he smells the man's breath.

"Why are you out here by yourself, Wyatt?" a voice whispers in Wyatt's ear—one he doesn't recognize.

Wyatt jerks back when he realizes that the man's face is right next to his. He asks the man why he's doing this to him, but the tape mumbles his speech.

"Look at you. You're bleeding from your mouth, and you've hurt your leg." The man sighs. "You should be kept safe at all times. I guess I'm the only one who can make sure of that."

Muffled screams escape Wyatt's throat, partly from pain and partly from terror. He wonders if the man is going to kill him.

"All I want is for you to be safe, Wyatt. I'm doing this for your own good."

Wyatt feels hands around his waist. He tries to wiggle out of the man's stronghold, but within seconds, he's swung up onto the man's shoulder. Razor stubble prickles his side. His arms are dangling down the man's back. His lip is throbbing. He sucks in a deep breath at the stab of pain coming from the jostling of his injured leg.

The man leans sideways, then resumes walking. Wyatt can hear his bike chain rattling alongside them. Wyatt surmises he's removing the evidence, making him more worried.

He hears a sloshing sound from below and quickly realizes that the man is walking into the wetland water. He shudders. One time, Wyatt slipped into the water by accident during the wintertime and swore he'd never let that happen again. A chill shoots through his body as the bite from the cold moves up his legs with every step. He kicks his feet violently until he can no longer stand the pain and slams his fists against the stranger's back.

But the man continues to carry him into the water.

Seconds later, Wyatt feels himself being lowered from the man's shoulder. Wyatt panics. He doesn't want to die. He thinks about how he's only nine and has never done anything seriously wrong or made any enemies, even at school. How he always opens the door for old ladies and saves people from bending over when they drop their car keys. How he still needs to finish his math homework to keep his grades up. How he wishes his mom was still alive. How he misses her.

The man holds Wyatt steady. Wyatt takes a deep breath and braces himself in case the man attempts to drown him. He learned how to hold his breath for a long time at swim camp last summer, but he's not sure if he can hold it long enough tonight. Wyatt thrashes around as the man lowers him onto his back, and to Wyatt's surprise, he feels a flat surface beneath him. He then hears a scraping noise as something is slid beside him. The smell of rubber lets Wyatt know that it has to be his bike. Wyatt becomes hysterical, relieved that he didn't die but petrified of what's ahead. He tries to assess what is happening but is distracted by a rocking sensation. It seems to him that he's on a boat. He hears water dripping, then footsteps coming toward him. Wyatt tugs erratically at the rope around his wrists, but it's too tight. He pushes his tongue against the tape that's covering his mouth and manages to open a small hole below his bottom lip. He screams for help but immediately feels a hand pushing the tape back into place, stopping his pleas.

"Now, now, Wyatt. Settle down," the man whispers. "You'll be home soon enough, and then you can scream all you want."

Wyatt's tears gather in the crinkles of the tape, trapping the moisture and burning his eyes. He writhes around until he hears the rhythmic creaking of the oars and water lapping up against the side of the boat.

The boat's moving.

Wyatt's mind races about what will happen next. He tries to convince himself that the man will eventually let him go, but deep down, he knows he's kidding himself. This is not a good man. This is a bad man—a bad man who might do bad things.

Wyatt wonders where the stranger is taking him, then wails when he realizes he must be rowing him deeper into the depths of Green Swamp.

CHAPTER

2

Bacon jerks and crackles in the steaming frying pan as Adrian's girlfriend quickly stabs at it with a fork to avoid being splattered with oil. Blueberry pancake batter dots the griddle and sausage gravy simmers in one of his mom's old pots. Adrian breathes in deeply, enjoying the aroma from the country breakfast Lorelei is cooking. He's not sure why, but there's a comfort in watching Lorelei prepare all the fixin's, knowing she's painstakingly making sure everything stays hot enough to serve at the same time.

"Stop staring at my ass," Lorelei says without turning around. He can't see if she's smiling, but the slight exaggeration in her steps lets him know she's kidding.

Adrian draws coffee from his mug and places it back on the breakfast bar. "Well, if you'd let me help you, I wouldn't have to stare at your ass."

"Oh, no, Mister. You stay right over there. I've got this completely under control." The bacon grease snaps. Lorelei flinches and jerks her arm back.

Adrian chuckles under his breath.

"Besides, I want this to be a nice breakfast to celebrate the first day of your new job." She hurries over with the plates, placing one in front of him and one at her spot. She passes him the pancakes, which are stacked in a neat pile with a dollop of sweet butter on top and maple syrup cascading over the sides. Then she slides another plate toward him, one brimming with crisp bacon and biscuits slathered in gravy.

He smiles at her as she takes the stool next to him. Her arm touches his, and he bends over to give her a peck on the cheek. "See, you're a master chef. I knew it."

"Uh, huh. Well, we'll see once you taste it."

Adrian takes a bite and sits back to savor this rarity. Though a good cook, he knows Lorelei would rather be anywhere else than in the kitchen. It's not that it's a horrible kitchen; it's just that she doesn't enjoy staying cooped up in it for very long. She's more of a nature girl at heart and would rather be outside, despite the ungodly humid summers in Central Florida. Having to wear waders in snake-infested waters has never kept her from her research.

"So, are you nervous about your first day at the engineering firm?"

"Who, me? Nah. I know what I'm doing," Adrian replies.

Lorelei notices his leg shaking. She gets up and gently massages the back of his neck and shoulders. "It'll be fine. Maybe your first project will be wetland-related, and we can talk about it for hours."

"Oh, God. No," Adrian says, choking on the last bit of pancake that is now stuck to the roof of his mouth. "I'm an engineer not a scientist. They'd better not give me a wetlands project."

"Oh, but there's engineering involved with wetlands. Maybe designing a full-scale wetland treatment system would be a good project. This *is* an environmental engineering firm you're working for, after all. Just imagine the stench of rotted wood and decaying leaves for hours on end," she says with a smirk.

"I'll quit. What the hell good are wetlands anyway?" Adrian teases.

"I'm going to laugh my ass off when you're traipsing around Green Swamp someday, just like me. But, at least, it'll be convenient." Lorelei gives a nod in the direction of the woods behind their home.

"Over my dead body. I want to be in the office designing, not getting chewed up by mosquitoes and gnats. Why do you love your job again?"

"Because I just do," Lorelei says, putting her arms around him and giving him a "good luck" squeeze.

"Hey, no wrinkling the tie," Adrian says with an eyebrow up. Lorelei gives him an extra squeeze. "So, are you going out in the field again today?"

Lorelei rolls her eyes and sits back into her stool. "Yes, just like every Monday for the past year."

"Where are you going to be?"

"Oh, come on. This day is about you, not me."

"I want to know." Adrian turns toward Lorelei. "You're always out there by yourself in the middle of nowhere. What if something were to happen to you?"

"You worry too much. I'll be fine. I'm a big girl, and I've

been doing this for a long time." Lorelei resumes eating her breakfast.

"Just let me know where you're going."

"Fine," Lorelei says with a sigh. "I'll be working in Colt Creek Park all week and probably next, but you don't need to constantly worry about me. If I die out there, I'll be doing what I love." Lorelei regrets her words as soon as she says them.

Adrian stops chewing and closes his eyes.

"I'm sorry. What was I thinking? I'll be fine. I promise."

Adrian nods and continues eating until he finally says, "Please don't use the word death and yourself in the same sentence. I'd be sick if something happened to you."

"Yeah, I get it." She leans in toward him and whispers, "I love you."

"Yeah. Me, too," he replies with half a smile.

"Now, get out of here and go impress those bosses. Between both of our jobs, we'll be financially set for the rest of our lives together."

"For the rest of our lives?"

Lorelei places her fork down onto her plate. "Oh, Adrian. I wasn't talking about getting married tomorrow or anything, but we should talk about it. We're not getting any younger. You're already twenty-five and I'm nearing twenty-seven."

"I know how old we are."

Lorelei nods. "Well, then, you know I'm running out of time to have kids. After thirty-two, the chances of having problems with your first pregnancy go up."

Adrian stabs at his pancake. "Well, you know how I feel about it. I don't think I'm the marrying kind."

"Fine. Forget it." Lorelei fiddles with a slice of bacon.

"You say I know how you feel, but I really don't. I wish you'd talk to me more."

"Well, just let me get through today. Now is not a good time to be talking about this. I've got enough pressure just trying to get through my first day."

"We can talk later then?" she asks with those brown eyes Adrian has never been able to resist.

"I suppose, but—"

"Good. We need to get this settled."

Adrian arrives at work twenty minutes early. The Graystone Group is located in Davenport, just a few miles from his home. He sits in his truck for a few minutes to relax before entering the multi-story glass building, talking to himself to calm his nerves. Soon, he exits the truck, hurries through a cold January wind to the front entrance doors, and enters the building. Inside, the space is warm and open with a well-maintained atrium in the center. Adrian peers up and sees three balconies stacked above him. He finds the stairs and climbs them to the second floor, peering out into the atrium as he passes by. He spies the Graystone entrance and opens the door.

Sitting behind a mahogany desk is a receptionist. He almost didn't see her with all the business cards and brochures aligned along the front of her desk. She's young, maybe twenty, and has an earpiece in one ear attached to a small microphone angled toward her mouth. She pulls herself away from the computer monitor to greet him. With a smile and glance at his suit, she says, "Welcome to the

Graystone Group. Can I help you?"

"Yes, ma'am. I'm Adrian Webster. I was told to be here at nine today to start my new job."

"Yeah, that was me who called ya. Just have a seat. Someone will be here to take you back in a few. I'm Rebecca, in case you were wonderin'."

"Okay, thanks." Adrian turns around and takes a seat directly in front of the receptionist's desk. A green and blue company sign with a logo that resembles a babbling creek is on the wall at the opposite side of the room where it boasts about being voted the best environmental engineering firm in Central Florida. The waiting room is small with a handful of cushioned chairs and side tables with lamps, the glow from which makes the room feel warm. The floor is covered with variegated blue carpet tiles and the walls are painted stark white. Behind the receptionist, the wall opens to a hallway with a narrow table holding silk flowers of white and blue.

Adrian notices his hands are shaking, so he sits on them.

"It should only be a few more minutes," Rebecca says.

Adrian clears his throat. "Oh, that's fine. I'm good."

He calms his nerves by taking a few deep breaths and grabs his phone. As he scans through the apps, he thinks he sees someone coming toward him. He glances up, but no one is there. Adrian turns toward Rebecca and asks, "Was someone just here?"

She stretches back in her chair to see down the hallway. "No, not yet."

Adrian frowns and peers over to the opposite side of the room again. "Oh, thought I saw someone go by."

"You might have, actually. Staff are always walking

through the hallway." Rebecca smiles at him and continues typing on her keyboard.

Adrian closes his eyes for a few seconds and takes another breath, concerned that he is already making a bad impression.

"Didn't sleep well last night?"

Adrian's eyes fly open to see a tall, well-built man who appears to be in his forties standing in front of him. He's wearing pleated khakis and a white polo shirt with the company name embroidered on the left side of his chest.

"No, I—"

"You must be Adrian." The man reaches his hand toward him. "Welcome to our group. I'm Sherman, one of the owners."

Adrian shakes his hand. "Nice to meet you. Thank you for the opportunity."

"Glad to have you here. Follow me, and I'll show you to your office. I'm sure you're going to really like it here."

"Yes, sir. I'm glad to be here, too."

Sherman escorts Adrian through a maze of hallways while he rattles on about working at the company. He pauses at a doorway and gestures for Adrian to enter. "Well, here's your office."

Adrian walks into his office. The morning sun is shining across the room through two windows on the far side. The office is rather small, fitting an l-shaped wooden desk to his left and a couple of bookshelves to his right with a chair for guests. He's not concerned with the size. He's just happy he has an office with a door.

"Someone will be by to get your orientation started. In the meantime, I put a report on your desk for you to review. Just make yourself comfortable." Sherman turns to leave, then says, "And lose the tie, young man. We're pretty casual around here. I'd keep it handy in case you have to go see a client, but most of the time, you won't need it."

When Sherman leaves, Adrian exhales and loosens his tie. He slips it from his neck and hangs it on an umbrella stand next to the door, along with his suit jacket. As he unbuttons his sleeves, he scans his office. He sits at the desk chair and adjusts its height, then wiggles the mouse and watches the monitor come to life. He can't sign in yet, so he leans back in his chair to get used to his space until he notices the engineering report Sherman mentioned. He reaches for it and flips through a few pages.

Holy hell. Is this written in a foreign language?

A voice interrupts his thought. "Hey, buddy. You're the new guy, right?"

Adrian sees a man's face peering around the corner of the doorway with a chunky mustache and sunglasses pulled up on his balding head. Crow's feet spread out from the corners of his eyes as he smiles. His skin has a pink tinge on his neck, forearms, and nose.

"Ah, yeah. Just started today."

He stands in the doorway with his arms crossed against his gray company polo. Heavy arms. Ones that have done manual work for most of his life. "I think I'm supposed to take you into the field at some point this week. Maybe Wednesday. I'm not sure since the schedule is still on the old shrew's desk."

Adrian's mouth drops open, shocked by the insult toward a female coworker.

"Oh, sorry. Guess I should be more specific. I meant Fossie, short for Fossylyn. Have you met her yet?"

"Ah, no."

"She's the administrative assistant that should have retired five years ago and resents every day she has to work. We call her 'fossil.' You'll see why soon."

Adrian shifts in his chair, unsure of what his response should be since this conversation is completely inappropriate. Not to mention, he hasn't heard anything from Sherman about going into the field yet.

"Oh, I'm sorry. I'm Clark, one of the environmental scientists here. Been here for a quarter of a century, back when the company first started. They've always treated me good, so I stayed since it's probably not better anywhere else."

Adrian nods but doesn't answer.

Clark glances at Adrian's shirt, then to the jacket and tie hanging next to the door. "Anyways, I wouldn't wear a suit on Wednesday since you'll be knee-high in wetland muck. We've got a new project in Green Swamp we need to investigate. It's for some police case."

"So, we'll be helping with forensics sampling on a case? I read that Graystone assists the police sometimes. Sounds serious."

"Yeah. We could be sampling for a dead body. It's rare for us to get involved, but maybe we gotta collect some soil and water samples or something. I need to check the work order from the forensics lab. They run the show. We just help." Clark turns to walk out of the office, then pauses. "Oh, you don't mind being outside, do you? You know, in the elements? I know you engineer-types don't usually like it, but we're short-staffed."

Adrian forces himself to smile. "Yeah, sure. I'm used to it."

"Good. Oh, yeah—here's some background information for the sampling job on Wednesday." Clark places a file on Adrian's desk. "Read through it beforehand, and don't forget to bring bug spray."

On the way home, Adrian's stomach churns. He made it through the first day on the new job but now remembers the conversation he told Lorelei they could have tonight. If there's one thing he knows about her, it's that she's stubborn and persistent. These qualities are great when it comes to being successful with her job but a different story when it comes to relationship talk. He knows she wants to get married and have kids, but he's not sure he can handle it. It's all fine when everything is going great, but when it's not, would he lose her?

He pulls up into the driveway in front of his garage and turns the headlights off, giving himself a few minutes to think. The sky is pink from the setting sun.

I'm happy here. It's safe, the house is beautiful, and it's close to work. So, why can't I take the next step?

Adrian thinks back to when he first met Lorelei. It was in the campus library at the University of South Florida. He had gone there to do some serious studying for a physics final around ten at night and took the elevator to the top floor, hoping to get some alone time. He found a private spot near a window that overlooked a parking lot and Cooper Hall, the Arts and Sciences building he had just come from. Adrian settled into the carrel desk that surrounded him with enough room to open his book and notebook, yet provided enough privacy to keep out the distractions. That was, until he smelled Lorelei's perfume. It made him curious to see who was wearing it, and he saw a girl sitting a few spots down. She flung her long, brown hair back, letting it settle every which way while she studied until it cascaded around her face and she repeated it again. There was something extremely attractive about her movement and the way she studied. He watched her for a few minutes until he decided he had to meet her. So, he gathered his books and moved to a desk that was right behind her. Lorelei called him out on it immediately, of course. And right away, Adrian knew she was the one.

Adrian shuts his eyes, smiling back at the memory.

She is *the one. So, what's wrong with you?*

He tries to envision himself waiting for Lorelei as she walks down the aisle in her flowing gown and lace veil with organ music playing in the background, but immediately, his hands start to shake and his breathing becomes shallow. He thinks about saying the vows but has to stop. Beads of sweat emerge on his forehead when he remembers the last line… "until death do us part."

Adrian opens his eyes and sighs.

I can't do this, and I can't let her know or I'll lose her. What am I going to—

He jerks his head to the right when he sees a black streak shift into the corner of his eye. His senses take over as he listens for anything outside of the truck for a second. Hearing nothing but his own rapid breathing, he reaches for the door handle, barrels out of the truck, and runs on the pavement to the passenger side.

No one is there. All he hears is the breeze rustling through the palm trees and a few birds chirping nearby.

He whips around as another streak flies by, his hand landing on the truck window to steady himself.

What the hell was that?

He waits for another streak, but there are no more. After a minute, he opens the passenger door, grabs his work files, and sprints toward the house. On his way, he pauses for a moment to peer back toward the truck.

He still sees no one around.

Shaking his head, he thinks, *maybe I'm losing it.*

CHAPTER

3

Lorelei greets him at the front door as he breezes by her. "I was just coming out to check on you. What was taking so long?"

"Nothing. Thought I saw someone outside of the truck. Kind of freaked me out. I checked around, but there wasn't anyone there."

Lorelei peers into the front yard, then closes the door. "Are you sure? Do I need to call the police?"

"No, no. It's fine. It was probably just a tree branch or something." Adrian puts his papers on the table and flings his suit jacket over the back of the dining room chair. He kisses Lorelei. "I missed you."

"Missed you, too," Lorelei says with a grin and follows him into the kitchen.

Adrian opens the refrigerator door. "Do you want to eat the leftovers from last night?"

"Sure. Sounds good."

He grabs two containers and starts the microwave, keeping his back to Lorelei. He's thinking maybe if he can avoid eye contact, she won't force him into engaging in the marriage conversation.

Lorelei joins him in the kitchen. "So, how was your day?"

"Well, you know. Same old, same old."

Lorelei laughs and grabs him by his waist to cuddle. "Now, come on. Spill it."

Adrian turns around and hugs her. "The people are great, the office is great, but the homework is not so great," he says, nodding toward the papers on the table. He rambles on for a few minutes until he confesses that he'll be doing wetlands work in a couple of days.

"What? Are you serious?" asks Lorelei. "Did you quit?"

With a smirk, he says, "No."

"Well, in that case, I guess we need to do your homework together tonight. It'll be like we're back in college again."

"Funny, I was just thinking about that." Adrian squeezes Lorelei's hand, then turns around and grabs the meals from the microwave. They both sit at the dining room table to eat. Adrian, despite not wanting to admit it, enjoys watching Lorelei become animated about her work. She tells him how she spent the day in Colt Creek Park as she planned, almost getting stung by wasps and nearly drowning as she sunk into the center of one of the wetlands where the bottom must have dropped into a sinkhole. Adrian cringes.

"So, let's see here," Lorelei says as she scans through the papers. "What type of work is this going to be?"

"I have no clue. One of the scientists, I think his name

was Clark…or maybe it was Mark…I don't know, but he said we're going to be sampling in Green Swamp on Wednesday. It's something to do with a police case," Adrian explains, but at this point, he's really more interested in his macaroni and cheese and his brew of the evening—a Samichlaus Classic.

Lorelei picks up her phone to search through the news. "Okay, yeah. Here's an article about it."

"Let's look at it later. I just want to relax right now." Adrian leans back in the chair and takes a swig of beer.

"Sure," Lorelei says, but the headline grabs her attention. Her eyes grow wide as she continues reading. "Adrian, look at this!"

Adrian takes Lorelei's phone and reads the article out loud. "Davenport News Digest from yesterday. Missing nine-year-old boy. Deputies have deployed a massive search for Wyatt Corringer in the Green Swamp area."

"Isn't that Jeremy's kid?"

Adrian leans forward and glances up at Lorelei, then back to her phone when he sees a photo of Wyatt. "Yeah, it is. Apparently, he's been missing since yesterday." Adrian frowns as he reads more. "Polk County authorities have advised that he was last seen riding his bike in his neighborhood near Davenport. He was wearing a black jacket, red Spiderman shirt, and blue jeans. He is Caucasian and has brown hair and brown eyes. Anyone who has possibly seen Wyatt should contact their local authorities."

"My God. I hope he's okay," Lorelei says.

"Why in the hell didn't Jeremy call us?" Adrian's face is red. He rubs his temples, trying to keep calm. "This cannot be happening to him." He hands Lorelei her phone then picks up his own. He calls Jeremy, but there's no answer.

He scoots the chair out. "I gotta go over there."

"Okay, I'll get my shoes on." Lorelei runs down the hallway toward their master suite.

Adrian heads out the front door with his coat and rushes to his pick-up truck. He opens the door, jumps in, and turns on the ignition. He waits a few seconds for Lorelei, but grows impatient and decides to leave without her. He knows she'll be pissed, but truthfully, he doesn't want to share this with her right now. He's got to be there for his long-time friend without any distractions. He's known Jeremy since they were kids, back when they lived in the same neighborhood in Indiana. Adrian's mom even referred to Jeremy as her son.

Adrian backs the truck out of the driveway and squeals his wheels as he accelerates down the street. He turns left onto County Road 27, cutting off another car. The man inside flashes his high beams in protest, but Adrian ignores him and moves on.

After a few miles, he takes another left onto West Meadow Street. Polk County police cars are parked along the roadway in front of Jeremy's house. It's a typical Florida home—a split-plan ranch with attached garage surrounded by scrub oaks with a splattering of palms and crepe myrtles. Adrian parks along the street behind the police cars and exits his truck. He hears muffled conversations from a group of policemen who are gathered in the driveway. They watch him walk into the yard but don't stop him from heading toward the house.

Adrian's heart is beating out of his chest when he reaches the garage, concerned about how Jeremy's reacting. It's going to be tough to see his best friend break down. Adrian has known Wyatt since he was born, too, making this whole situation even harder. His mind wanders to his own loss several years back, but he pushes back at the memory. He knows he can't get lost in that right now.

Adrian rounds the corner of the garage and pauses for a second as he makes eye contact with Jeremy, who's standing inside next to a few police officers in blue uniforms and shiny badges. The three-car garage is cool with the typical gasoline smell from the riding lawnmower which takes up most of one bay, and the weed-whacker, edger, and various other small-engine lawn equipment hung up along the wall. He spies the fishing poles in the corner that the two swore they'd use every week but never had the time for anymore.

Jeremy quickly excuses himself and walks toward Adrian. Adrian can see the dark circles under Jeremy's eyes almost immediately. Jeremy's lips are drawn downward and his expression is blank, like he's stunned. Usually Jeremy is a clean-shaven, handsome man, despite the scar along his jawline. But the person Adrian sees before him now is unshaven with greasy hair that's sticking out in all directions. He has food stains dripped on his white t-shirt and remnants in the corner of his mouth. A strong body odor confirms he hasn't showered lately. Jeremy greets Adrian with their brother handshake and half a hug.

"What happened, man? Why didn't you call me?" asks Adrian.

"It's been a roller coaster ride. The police have been everywhere. They're interviewing everyone, questioning neighbors, wanting pictures of...Wyatt."

"So sorry this has happened. I saw it in the news. Any luck yet?"

"No." Jeremy wipes the wetness from his cheeks with the side of his thumb. "He was riding his bike back from his friend's house and never made it. You remember Wyatt talking about his friend, Colin, right?"

Adrian nods.

"He's gone to his place by himself a thousand times, so it's not like he would have gotten lost. I hope he's not hurt…or worse. Ever since Shelly passed away, Wyatt has been acting out. He doesn't talk about it, but I know he misses his mom. His teachers have been calling me from school, complaining that he hasn't been getting his homework done on time. Maybe he hasn't been telling me everything. I don't know."

"It's going to be okay. It has to be. I'm sure he misses her, but he loves you, man. You know that."

Jeremy stares at the concrete floor.

"And you and I didn't always get our homework in on time, either, right?"

Jeremy rubs his eyes. "Yeah. I remember. I'm probably blowing this all out of proportion."

"No, you're not. I'd be doing the same thing." Adrian watches Jeremy for a few seconds. "Are you going to be okay?"

Jeremy shifts his weight. "Yeah, they just need to find my boy."

"Well, I want to help. Which way does he normally go?"

"He usually goes to Colin's through the woods out back. See the path over there?" Jeremy points to a clearing in the woods at the back of the property line. "It takes you along the outer rim of the swamp and leads straight to the apartments. It had to happen on his way home because Colin's mom said Wyatt left their place after playing video games around five the night before last. I called the police around eight when he didn't show up. He never comes home after dark. The police are already out in the woods with the…cadaver dogs," Jeremy says, his eyes red with tears flowing down his cheeks.

Adrian holds back the lump in his throat. Watching his friend like this is torture. "Hey, hey. I'm sure that's just routine. Do you want me to search, too?"

"Sure. The more people the better. My neighbors are already searching the swamp. Check with the police first, though, because they have everything organized."

Adrian stops one of the police officers walking by and asks if he can help. "We already have search parties deployed today. Stop by tomorrow morning by five, and we'll let you know if we'll be doing another search."

"Sorry, man," Adrian says to Jeremy. "Can I do anything else?"

"Maybe just stick around to help me in case they find him."

"They're going to find him, and he's going to be alive."

Adrian arrives home around midnight to find Lorelei sleeping on the couch with a wetlands book on her lap. He moves the book to the side table and carries her to bed, slipping the covers over her and kissing her cheek. He changes into comfortable pants and slides into bed next to her, hoping for a reprieve from having to hear her gripe about the way he left earlier. Sometimes he just needs space to handle things on his own.

He tries to relax but is too wired from the day. Thoughts

of Wyatt sadden him to the point where he can't sleep. His mind races until he finally sits up and glances over to his alarm clock. It's one in the morning.

Adrian gets up to go to the bathroom. He lectures himself on not letting the old memories back in. This is about Jeremy, not himself. He flushes the toilet and returns to the bedroom. Lorelei's eyes are open, and she's motionless. Adrian leans in, unsure if she's awake.

She flinches.

"Jesus, Lorelei. You scared me. I thought you were dead for a second."

"Oh, and you would care?"

Here we go.

Adrian rolls his eyes and lies down, scrunching up his pillow to make himself more comfortable.

"I can't believe you just left me like that."

"Look. I can't handle you and this situation with Jeremy at the same time," Adrian replies with his back to Lorelei.

"What's that supposed to mean?"

Adrian sighs. "The pressure. I can't handle the pressure. My priority is to Jeremy right now. I'm sorry if this doesn't fit into your plans."

"Plans. Plans? What plans are you referring to? The ones where I'm there for you, supporting you?"

Adrian groans in frustration. "No. Of course not. I...can't handle the relationship part." He winces at the harshness of his words.

Lorelei flops backward. "Well, guess that says it all. My worst fear has always been that I'll live with you for ten years, and you're still not going to want to get married or have kids. Not that I live and breathe by that, but I want to have a family someday."

They lie in silence together for a few minutes, both of them staring into space.

"Argh! I hate myself!" Adrian jumps out of bed and faces Lorelei. "I'm the most pathetic failure of a man. I wish I wasn't this way. I wish I could give you what you want. I wish I didn't worry about you every time you step foot out of this house. I wish I didn't constantly think there was going to be some catastrophe waiting right outside, or around every bend, or around every building. If I can't handle you, how in the world would I possibly handle kids? It's so much responsibility. I wish I were—" Adrian stops for a second and then whispers, "dead."

Lorelei moves toward Adrian, but he gestures for her to stay away. It's too hard for him to let anyone close right now. He's afraid of totally losing it. He feels like he's always on the verge of insanity.

"You don't understand. You'll never understand. I should have died that day, too. My little brother died right before my eyes, and I could do nothing. Do you know what this does to your head?"

She grabs for him. "Please don't shut me out, Adrian. Maybe some therapy would help."

He gathers himself quickly and says, "No. That's not what I need. I just need to find Wyatt."

"But the police are on it. That's not your responsibility."

Adrian pulls away from Lorelei. "Yes, it is. I don't know why, but it is. Just let me have time to think."

He walks out of the bedroom, down the hallway, and into the kitchen. He flicks the light on and sits on a stool, grabbing his head in his hands. He knows he's going to have to figure things out with Lorelei, but for now, he wants to concentrate on getting Wyatt back. He'll make sure he's at Jeremy's tomorrow as early as possible to join in the search party before going to work.

He stares at the clock on the oven as he thinks about his situation until he's distracted by a black shadow that suddenly creeps into his peripheral vision. It lingers there for a couple of seconds. He can't tell if it's male or female, but it definitely appears to be shaped like a human. Then it slides out of his view and scurries into the family room. Adrian immediately leaps from the stool, knocking it over, and stops in front of the entrance to the room. It's dark, with the exception of the kitchen light that's reflecting off the windows. The leather couches are in place with no disturbance to the floor rug or lamp shades. He can see that the couches are empty, but he can't see if anyone is hiding behind them.

"Somebody there?" he asks, moving forward. "You better get your ass out here now, before I come and get you out."

He feels a hand touch his arm and spins around with a clenched fist. Luckily, he instantly sees that it's Lorelei. Adrian bends at his waist to catch his breath. "Don't do that! I almost punched you."

"Wow, this is not like you," she says.

Adrian puts his finger to his mouth and whispers, "I think there's someone in the house."

Lorelei's eyes grow wide. She snatches her keys off the counter and stands behind him, glancing behind her.

He pushes the light switch up to illuminate the family room, but there are still areas that are pitch black. He listens for the intruder, but all he hears is the ticking of his dad's wall clock hung above the mantle and Lorelei's rapid breathing. Adrian grabs a stool and rushes straight for the darkest corner of the family room. Another dark shadow shoots by to his left, and he swings the stool at it, barely missing the television.

"Did you see that?" he asks Lorelei with wide eyes.

"No, I didn't see anything."

His eyes are wild as he scans the room for more shadows, but no one is there. He stands with the stool in his hands for a minute, then lowers it to the floor.

"Are you sure you saw someone?"

"I saw shadows about the size of a person but not an actual person."

Lorelei frowns. "Well, I guess they're playing tricks on you because there's no one here. Christ, you scared the livin' shit out of me."

Adrian plops on the couch. "What the hell is going on with me? This is the third time I saw something move out of the corner of my eye today."

"When did you see the other two?" Lorelei asks as she sits next to him.

"The first time was when I arrived at work, and the second time was outside after I pulled into the driveway earlier, remember? That's why it took so long for me to come in." Adrian stands up. "I'm going to bed."

"Hey, wait. That's it? You drop this news on me, and then you just wanna go to sleep? I'm worried about you."

Adrian sighs. "I'm fine, Lorelei. It's probably just all the stress I'm under. New job, Jeremy's kid is gone—"

"Oh, yeah, and don't forget me. All the pressure I'm putting on you."

"I didn't say that."

Lorelei smooths her hair back into a ponytail and grabs an elastic off the end table to wrap it in place. "I'm not the bad guy here. I just want to know we have a future."

"You've made that abundantly clear. Now, can we go to bed?"

"What's wrong with you?"

"Never mind me. I'm just tired. We're good, right?" Adrian holds his hand out for Lorelei.

"No. You're being an asshole."

"Look, all this shit is freaking me out."

A black shadow zips by Adrian again and disappears into a dark corner next to the couch. He shudders but tries to hide it from Lorelei. "I mean it. Let's go to bed."

The shadow starts to move outward from the corner. Adrian reaches for Lorelei's hand and yanks her up off the couch, readying himself to run.

"What's wrong? Are you seeing something else?"

He blinks and the shadow disappears. Adrian closes his eyes in relief and exhales. "I think I'm just overtired. Come on. Let's go to bed."

CHAPTER

4

Adrian arrives at Jeremy's at five in the morning the next day. He's assuming Wyatt is still missing since Jeremy didn't call him. Numerous vehicles are lined up along West Meadow Street. He nestles his truck between two bushes near the driveway—a spot he has parked in for years. He steps out of his truck and hears the palm fronds rustle from the cool breeze. Adrian takes in a deep breath and approaches Jeremy's house. A part of him wants to get back in his truck and flee, not because he doesn't want to help find Wyatt, but because he wants to run away from the tragedy that happened so long ago, especially losing his brother. A flash of the desperate look on Jonathan's face when he slipped from Adrian's grip pops into his mind. He stops walking and closes his eyes, taking a moment to push back the memories.

He resumes walking and sees a white glow stretching

onto the driveway from the garage. Once he rounds the corner, he sees several officers inside surrounded by about twenty volunteers. It appears to him like they've already started to hand out assignments, so he proceeds straight to the sign-up table. The officer hands him a map, picture of Wyatt, flashlight, and sheriff contact information in the event Wyatt is found. Since Adrian has convinced himself he will be the one to find Wyatt, he stores the contact phone numbers in his cell phone. He finds out that his group will soon be led by one of the deputies, and he paces in front of the garage. Waiting has never been his strength.

Several minutes go by and the police officers lead the way to the trail behind Jeremy's house. Adrian pulls out his phone to find the Davenport News article and remind himself of Wyatt's clothing. It's still dark, so all Adrian can see is the person in front of him, beams from the flashlights jetting around ahead of him, and the tree moss that occasionally interrupts the view. They stop at their designated location about a mile in. The woods sound like they're starting to come to life with the chirping sounds from the various birds surrounding him. The morning air smells like mildew but is still cold and feels refreshing to Adrian, energizing him. The sun is rising now and streaming through the trees. Soon they'll have daylight to work under.

The deputy explains the drill, advising them to stand shoulder-to-shoulder as they move across the woods. It takes several minutes for the officer to set up a grid system to keep track of their steps, but before long, the group of twenty is on their quest. They search back and forth along the grid under the supervision of the police officers who are standing at opposite ends, several hundred feet apart, and jotting notes down on their clipboards. At first, the group is chatty, excited about the possibility of finding Wyatt. In time, though, many grow quiet, some hanging their heads in disappointment.

Not Adrian. The sun is up, and he's still energetic, sure that every step will lead him closer to a happy, healthy Wyatt. Adrian glances at his watch. He can walk for only another half an hour before having to leave for work, so he encourages the group to keep going. He's sure the rustling of the branches and leaves along the ground and desperate calls will wake up Wyatt, and he'll coming running across the woods.

But a half an hour goes by with no sign of him.

Adrian circles back to the garage with his group and sees the next group preparing to search for Wyatt. To his right, he sees Jeremy round the check-in table and dash toward him. What starts as a look of hope on Jeremy's face quickly dissipates into a look of despair. He slows his pace until he reaches Adrian who's standing with his hands in his pockets. "They're not going to find my boy, are they?"

"Don't say that. They'll find him. If they don't, I will. If I hadn't started this new job yesterday, I'd still be out there, too."

Adrian contemplates whether or not he should tell Jeremy about the sampling event tomorrow with work but quickly decides not to since he's not even sure if they'll be sampling for evidence related Wyatt's disappearance.

"Guess the police don't want me out there in case Wyatt shows up at home. They've been asking me strange questions now like about my whereabouts when Wyatt disappeared and if we had a fight. I think they suspect me. You know I would never harm my boy, right? Just the thought of him—"

"Of course. They're idiots for thinking it would be something you did to him. They don't know you like I do," Adrian says. "It's probably just part of their protocol, so don't worry about that. Does Wyatt have any kind of fort or hangout back there?"

"Not that I know of," Jeremy replies. "I should have never let him go alone in those woods." Jeremy has a dazed look on his face—a look Adrian saw on his own face years ago after the accident. He understands Jeremy and the gnawing need to hold his loved one again—the relentless craving for them, especially a child. A cold sweat breaks out on Adrian's chest, and his arm begins to ache.

Adrian gives Jeremy their brotherhood handshake. "Man, let me know if you hear anything. I wish I didn't have to leave."

"Hey, it's okay, bro. Don't sweat it. That's a mighty fine job you got yourself, so go. There are so many people here that we've got it covered."

"Call me if you hear anything."

Adrian gives Jeremy a pat on his shoulder and returns to his truck. As he backs up out of the driveway, he sees Jeremy standing outside of the garage. Adrian pauses to watch him in his rearview mirror for a few seconds, wishing he could stay to help. Anger boils up in him when he thinks about how this has to be affecting Jeremy. No one should have to endure this kind of worry. He drives off and throws on some metal music to distract himself from the flood of memories that want to return.

You cannot go there, Adrian. Do not go there.

Light flickers through the canopy of trees as he drives. He tries hard to concentrate on the rising sun. He reminds himself that the daylight will keep Wyatt safe for now. He'll be able to see his way home. If not, Adrian will do every-thing he can to find him later tonight. He won't stop until he finds him. If he can't, at least he'll be able to help with the sampling if it's actually for Wyatt's case. He needs to find out.

He arrives at the office just before eight and he's sweat-ing profusely. Fighting off the grief from his own loss is al-most a daily occurrence for him since the accident ten years ago, and he knows that he's losing ground. He opens the glovebox and flips through its contents until he lays his hand on some deodorant. He freshens up, hops out of the truck, and enters the building. Rebecca greets him when he opens the office door and nods him on. He proceeds to his office, unloads his backpack, and logs into his computer, anxious to start his workday.

Get back on track, Adrian.

Despite the stress of the second day on the job and Wy-att's disappearance, Adrian somehow gets his mind on work and reads report after report until he can hardly think anymore. The projects range from collecting water level measurements in wells to checking remediation systems to updating contamination action plans. Several coworkers stop by to greet him, most wanting to pawn their work off on him. They say they're kidding, but he knows they're not.

A petite, gray-haired woman pops in and asks, "You ready to help me count pages?"

Adrian squirms in his chair, unsure of how to respond. "Count pages?"

"Yeah. We need help counting pages to make sure we ain't missin' any in the reports we got goin' out. You in?"

Adrian replies hesitantly, "I guess."

"Well, come on then before time slaps you in the ass!"

She didn't introduce herself, but Adrian assumes this is Fossie by the way she's ordering everyone out of their offices and into the library as she marches down the hallway. Her skirt is flapping back and forth as she moves quickly past each one.

Just before they enter the library, Adrian hears Clark yelling from the other end of the hallway. "Hey, Fossil! Where are you taking my boy? I need him to help me prepare my sample bottles for tomorrow."

Fossie takes Adrian's arm and nudges him toward the office library, ignoring Clark. Inside, there are two long tables with binders opened at each seat. The room is lit with fluorescent lighting and the walls of the room are covered in bookshelves holding stacks of environmental books and magazines. "Sit in any chair you want, and don't move, no matter what that old crow says. Got it? I don't have enough people to check these reports, and they've got to be sent out today. Whatever Clark has you working on can wait."

"But I think it's related to the police case, so—"

"Oh, he has sampled a million times. He doesn't need help. Besides, this is easy billable work. Trust me, you want as many billable hours as you can get, otherwise, you'll end up canned."

Adrian picks a seat.

Clark enters the library. His face is flushed, and he starts to raise his finger toward Fossie. "I'm not going to allow you to use an engineer to count pages at his billable rate. That's ridiculous!"

Fossie pays him no mind and gathers more staff around the table. She advises them to let her know if there are any pages missing. She announces page one of three hundred and fifty, and the counting begins.

"Fossil, I swear. You are the most stubborn, arrogant admin I've ever met."

"Two of three hundred and fifty."

Everyone turns the page in their respective binders. The rhythmic counting and page turning becomes mesmerizing to Adrian.

"Five of three hundred and fifty."

"Fine," Clark says as he turns on his heel and exits. "Guess I'll have to prepare the sample bottles myself."

Half an hour later, the professional page counters are on page two-hundred-and-sixty-eight, and Fossie announces there's an extra binder of appendices that will also need to be counted.

Adrian sighs. "Can we take a break between binders?"

"What's the matter, Adrian? This work isn't good enough for an engineer?"

"I need to go to the restroom."

"Oh. Well, we can take a break now. You all better return though."

Adrian scoots his chair away from the table and proceeds down the hallway to find Clark. He sees Rebecca who directs him to the equipment room. He races in and sees Clark sitting in front of a table to his left, his reading glasses halfway down his nose. He's working on some instruments with probes, which Adrian surmises are probably the sampling meters. Several coolers are stacked along the opposite wall to his right—the forty-eight-quart kind with the flip lid. A tall metal shelving unit is located in between and filled with various equipment including peristaltic pumps, thin tubing, marine batteries, and boxes of latex gloves. The room has a chemical smell to it, kind of reminding Adrian of the old chemistry laboratory in high school.

Clark laughs as soon as he sees Adrian. "She let you leave already?"

"Just a bathroom break. Can I hide in here?"

"You can, but once she finds you, she'll rip your head off. She's a tough old broad." Clark gets up to peer up and down the hallway, then shuts the door.

"Isn't this work billable, too?"

"Sure is." Clark sits in a chair at a table set up on one side of the room. He pours pH calibration fluid into a cup and checks the accuracy of the sampling meter with a probe. "All of the pH fluids are calibrating perfectly." Clark stands and gestures to Adrian to sit down. "Here, why don't you calibrate the conductivity."

"Me? I haven't calibrated a meter before."

"Give it a try. The directions are in the manual right there next to it."

Adrian sits down at the table and opens the manual while Clark begins preparing the sampling bottle labels. Adrian fumbles around with the sampling meter for a few minutes, reading directions and trying to figure out the display.

"No, no. Here, let me help you. Didn't they teach you this stuff in school?" Clark asks.

"No. Why would they? I didn't take many science classes."

"Guess that's true."

Clark shows Adrian how to calibrate the sampling meter, then opens a cooler filled with plastic sample bottles and glass vials on the floor next to him. Clark picks up one of the vials and says, "Guess they want us to sample for organics. Here's a chain-of-custody packet. Fill in the top of the form with our company name and contact information while I take a look at the analyses they ordered."

Adrian starts filling out the form. "So, we are sampling for the police case tomorrow?"

"Looks that way. I'm waiting for the final word from Sherman, the owner of the company. Have you met him?"

"Yes, yesterday. Will we sample for DNA also?"

"Probably not. That will most likely be handled by the forensics team, though we may assist them. When we get there, do everything exactly as they tell you. They only hired us because they're short-staffed right now, and we want to keep them happy so they'll hire us again. Got it?"

"Yeah, got it."

"The lab dropped off all the sample bottles here in the equipment room. We'll be going out into the field tomorrow. Come dressed in jeans. Oh, and..." Clark swivels his chair around and pulls two polo shirts from a cardboard box on a metal shelf above the table. "Wear one of these company shirts. You'll probably want to wear rubber boots, also. If you don't have any, see Rebecca."

"I've got some."

"Good. Now, see all those coolers along the wall?"

Adrian nods.

"All of the sample bottles are inside of them. I need you to take the coolers down to our work van as well as a couple boxes of latex gloves, all the sampling meters and these boxes of pumps and various tools, tubing and other stuff I need," Clark says, pointing to the boxes on the bottom of the shelving unit. "Less than glamorous, I know. Would you rather be counting now?"

"Hell, no."

"Good."

"So, where are we going tomorrow?"

"On a bike path along Green Swamp, not too far from here."

It has to be near Jeremy's. Adrian feels sick to his stomach, but refrains from telling Clark that he knows the missing person. He's fearful they'll think it's a conflict of interest and won't let him sample.

"Hey, are you okay?" asks Clark.

"Oh. Yeah, sure. Why?"

"You turned a little pale."

"I did? Oh, well, maybe it was something I ate this morning."

"Or maybe it's the thought of sampling for a dead person?"

Adrian closes his eyes, then gathers himself. "Well, they don't really know that the person is dead, right? That's why they're sampling. The person is missing?"

"Yeah, well, if that makes you feel better, go ahead and think that way."

Clark slaps Adrian on the shoulder and grabs a plastic file holder. "I'll drop off the sampling forms in the van on my way out. I was just down there cleaning out the back to make room for the coolers, so it's unlocked. Here are the keys. Lock it up when you're done and put the keys back on the hook here near the door."

Adrian nods as he takes the keys.

"See you in the morning. I'm going to go find the old shrew and tell her to leave you alone."

As soon as the door shuts Adrian gets up and stands in front of the coolers for a while, staring at them. He opens a cooler to see the sample bottles—the bottles that will be used to sample for signs of Wyatt. Sweat drips from his nose and his breathing becomes labored.

Adrian, quit. Relax. Don't think about it. Get yourself together. Wyatt is not dead.

He closes his eyes and concentrates on slowing down his breathing.

You cannot lose control. Not here.

CHAPTER

5

After filling the work van with the coolers and sampling supplies, Adrian climbs into his truck and drives home. His thoughts quickly turn to Wyatt since he plans on heading over to Jeremy's house tonight after he changes his clothes and grabs dinner. He picks up his phone and calls Jeremy to check on the status of the search.

"Hey, Adrian," Jeremy says, his voice breaking.

"What's up? Any news?" Adrian asks, rushing through traffic only to be slowed to a crawl as he nears County Road 27.

"There's no sign of Wyatt. He's gone…or he's hurt."

"Don't say that. Have the police given up yet?"

"No."

"Well, if they haven't given up, then you shouldn't, either."

"I can see the gloom on their faces, though. What started as a pretty hopeful day is now turning into dread. The searchers hardly look at me anymore when they come out of the woods. I can tell they don't want to disappoint me."

"Yeah, but that's normal. They just want to find him. I'm running home for an hour or so, and then I'll be on my way there. The police told me I need to be there at six tonight to help with the next shift. Need me to bring you some dinner?"

"No, my sister has been taking care of that. I'm grateful to have her. With Shelly gone, dinners have been mostly takeout. I wish she were here. I miss her so much," Jeremy says, barely audible.

"I know. I'm sorry, man." Adrian runs a red light that would have surely slowed him down, but is quickly reduced to a crawl again, so he takes a side street.

"I don't think I can take losing Wyatt, too," Jeremy continues, sobbing. "After Shelly's car accident, I've just been in father mode, trying to do the best I can for him. He misses her, too. Maybe if she were here, he'd come home. I don't know. Maybe he ran away because he can't take the pain anymore or maybe he just gave up. I know sometimes I feel that way."

"He's only nine, man. He didn't give up. If he ran away, then you can get him counseling. I'm sure it'll be okay, though. I'm going to find him when I get there, so hang on."

"I hope you're right."

"I am."

After finally getting through the traffic mess, Adrian speeds down Emerald Avenue and into his development. He winds into his driveway and hurries into the house. He doesn't have a lot of time to get ready to make it over to Jeremy's by six during rush-hour traffic. Lorelei is not home yet, so Adrian fries up a few burgers and sticks some fries in the oven for both of them. He also makes extra for leftovers in case he needs to search the next night as well.

An hour later, Lorelei arrives home. Adrian is sitting at the dining room table eating dinner. Lorelei greets Adrian with a peck on the lips. He tries to kiss her longer, but Lorelei pulls away too quickly. He knows she probably wants to talk about their future, but right now, he's not in the mood. He avoids eye contact.

"How was your day?" she asks.

Adrian relaxes.

"Okay, I guess. I had the opportunity to count pages of a report."

"What?"

"Yeah, that's me. Professional page counter. It was some kind of report they had to get out today and our demanding admin made sure everyone in the office spent time counting pages to verify they were all there."

Lorelei laughs and sits down at the table where Adrian left her dinner.

"Sorry. It might be cold now. Want me to warm it up?"

"No. I don't care. You have no idea how hungry I am right now. No breakfast or lunch. I've gotta plan meals better."

"All day at Colt Creek, huh? Get the assessment done?"

"Nope. I'll be back there tomorrow."

"Okay. Well, I gotta go back to Jeremy's tonight. They didn't find Wyatt today."

Lorelei's cheeks flush. "I'm sorry, Adrian. They aren't giving up yet, are they?"

"No. I'll find him tonight. In the meantime, I've been helping with getting sample bottles together at work. You won't believe this, but I get to help sample for Wyatt's remains tomorrow."

"What? No way! Are you kidding me?" Lorelei spouts. "Can't you just tell them you can't? Maybe due to a conflict of interest?"

"No, I didn't tell them that I know the person they're searching for. I want to be involved with the sampling so I can stay close to the situation. Besides, I already said I'd do it. At least it'll get me out there, and I'll feel like I'm doing something."

"But—" Lorelei protests.

Adrian gets up from the table. "It'll be fine. I'm going to find him tonight anyway."

"Adrian, are you just rushing out of here because we never had our talk? You know we need to—"

He doesn't give her a chance to finish her sentence. He grabs his keys and leaves without acknowledging her question. Adrian jumps into his truck and backs out of the driveway, turning up the volume of the music to drown out the pressures facing him. He can barely deal with the possibility of Jeremy's loss much less a discussion on marriage. Adrian complains to himself until he realizes that his breathing has changed and feels a trickle of sweat running down his face along his sideburn.

All right, Adrian, keep calm. You'll find the kid.

Traffic has thinned on the roadways, and he rounds the corner onto County Road 27 when he sees a black shadow outside the passenger seat window from the corner of his eye. It's similar to yesterday's encounter but the shadow is more well-defined. It's a person. It happened so fast though, he couldn't tell if it was a male or a female.

"What the hell?" Adrian says out loud.

Adrian slams on the brakes. His truck skids and his work papers fly forward. They flutter and settle onto the floor mat. Luckily, no one is behind him. He pulls over, jumps out of his truck, and races to see if anyone is on the side of the roadway.

He finds no one.

Panting, he runs back to the truck and slams the door shut.

What is wrong with me? There was something there, I know it. I didn't imagine this. And it wasn't just a shadow this time.

Chest heaving, he tries to calm his nerves.

There has to be some logical explanation for this.

Pressure suddenly strangles the back of his eye sockets followed by a piercing pain. Adrian grabs his head and rubs his temples. After a few minutes, the pain lessens, and Adrian continues to Jeremy's.

Once he arrives, he finds Jeremy standing in the driveway. "Hey. Glad you're here." Jeremy doesn't notice Adrian's distress at first due to the darkness.

Adrian clears his throat and drinks from his water bottle as they walk toward the garage. He wipes the sweat from his brow with back of his hand. "Yeah. Me, too. Looking forward to finding Wyatt tonight."

"If you make that happen, I'll buy you a beer every day for the rest of your life. I can't tell you—" Jeremy stops talking once he sees Adrian's face in the garage light. "Hey, bro. You okay?"

"Yeah. Why?"

"Your eyes. They're bloodshot. What happened? You haven't been drinking have you?"

"No," Adrian says with surprise. "What do you mean they're bloodshot?"

"Just like I said. Come over here."

Adrian proceeds over to a mirror on the wall of the garage and jerks backward when he sees two red eyes staring back at him. They're not just bloodshot. The entire whites of his eyes are a crimson red. "Holy fuck!"

"You feel okay? Can you see?"

"Yeah. I feel fine. Just stressed."

"Damn, you look freaky. Well, maybe you ought to go see a doctor. You need to get that checked out."

"I'll go tomorrow. Right now, I'm going to go find Wyatt."

Four hours later, Adrian returns home feeling defeated, unable to find Wyatt. He turns on the truck's cabin light and checks his eyes in the rearview mirror. They're still red. Luckily, no one but Jeremy noticed them during the search since it was dark outside. Lorelei will surely notice, though.

Adrian exits the truck. A black shadow flies into the corner of his eye, then vanishes. "Leave me alone!" he yells and hurries to the front door. He struggles to find his keys in his pocket.

"Hey," Lorelei says.

Adrian lowers his eyes. "Hey. Thanks for getting the door."

"Got your hands full or something?"

"No." Adrian slides past her and enters the foyer.

"Key problem?"

"Nope. Eye problem, apparently."

"What do you mean?" Lorelei says to the back of his head.

"You don't want to see, Lorelei. I look like a freak."

Lorelei grabs Adrian's arm to turn him toward her. "Oh, I'm sure you don't look like a—" She stops mid-sentence once she sees that the whites of Adrian's eyes are blood red. Her forehead crinkles, examining him closer. "Holy shit! You feel okay?"

"Yes, damn it. I'm fine. I just have red eyes."

"Adrian, we need to get you to the eye doctor."

"I have to go to work tomorrow. This is my first week at my new job, remember? Besides, I need to go sampling to help find Wyatt. I didn't find him tonight."

"That cannot be healthy," Lorelei says, still staring at his eyes. "Maybe we should go to an emergency walk-in clinic tonight. Hopefully, you'll still be able to go to work tomorrow."

"It's probably just stress." Another dark shadow zips by his left side. He jerks his head to the left and lurches toward it until Lorelei stops him.

"Adrian, what is it?"

"Nothing." Adrian stares at a dark corner in the living room.

"Are you seeing shadows again?"

Adrian pauses.

"They're everywhere," he whispers.

CHAPTER

6

Look to your right."

Adrian looks to his right.

"Look to your left."

Adrian looks to his left.

"Up and down."

Adrian follows the instructions from Dr. Calvin Reyes, an optician recommended by a friend of Lorelei's. Dr. Reyes turns off the light to his ophthalmoscope and moves the rest of the equipment out of the way. Adrian relaxes back in the chair, feeling the warmth from the soft glow in the room. An illuminated eye chart is hanging on the wall in front of him.

"Hmm. So, you're sure you haven't had any eye trauma or blood pressure issues in the past?"

"Not that I know of."

"Huh." Dr. Reyes sits back on his stool and rolls it over

to his side table. He flips through Adrian's test results and sighs. "Well, I've gotta admit. You've got me stumped on what's going on here. Your eye vessels are broken, but you have none of the usual causes. Your scans are clear, except for a couple of anomalies that are most likely floaters. These probably explain the shadows you're seeing but not why the sclera of both of your eyes are showing subconjunctival hemorrhages at the same time. Are you under a lot of stress these days?"

"Guess you could say that. I also had pain behind my eyes when it happened, but it went away quickly. I didn't notice the redness until someone pointed it out to me a few minutes later. What are these floaters you're talking about?"

"Floaters are collagen that has built up in your eye—kind of like small flecks that move around your eye and can affect your vision. They usually occur later in life, but I've seen a few cases of them in younger people, especially following eye trauma. What do the shadows look like?"

"Super fast-moving dark shadows that I see in the corner of my eye. They seem human-like in shape sometimes."

"One eye?"

"No, both, but not at the same time."

"Well, I only see the floaters in one eye, but maybe they're not showing up on the scan in the other eye. Since you don't seem to have any health risks, I'd say to reduce your stress level. Perhaps some pressure change to your eyes is causing the blood vessels to break. Unfortunately, there's really no treatment. The hemorrhages will go away on their own in a week or two."

"Oh, man. You're kidding me. I can't walk around like this."

"Try wearing sunglasses as much as you can to hide them. That's about it. If the redness isn't gone in two weeks, give me a call back, and I'll do a follow-up exam. Okay?"

"Yeah, I guess."

Dr. Reyes opens the door and shows Adrian out.

"Hey, doc. I really appreciate you coming in early to see me today."

"Oh, it's fine. I'm an early riser anyway."

Lorelei races up to meet Adrian at the checkout desk. "So?"

"Floaters. Nothing to worry about," Adrian replies.

"Oh, thank God. I'm so relieved it's not something worse."

"Yeah, I'm relieved it's nothing worse too, except I have to get used to seeing the shadows. That part sucks. I've gotta learn to ignore them." Adrian shakes his head. "Not sure how I'm gonna do that."

Adrian arrives at work a few minutes before seven and walks over to the work van sitting in the parking lot. The air is cool and less humid than normal. He sees Clark sitting behind the driver's side of the van. Adrian slides on his sunglasses to hide his eyes, hoping that Clark won't ask why he has them on when it's dark outside.

Adrian opens the passenger van door and hops in. Clark is writing on a sheet of paper attached to a clipboard that's resting on the steering wheel.

"Morning," Adrian says, pulling on the seatbelt and clicking it in place.

"So, why the sunglasses when it's dark out?"

Adrian quickly thinks of an excuse. "Oh, I don't know. Just didn't want to forget them." He flips them onto his head and rubs his eyes.

"Smart thinkin'" Clark replies. "So, every morning, you always want to start your day with a log sheet and record everything that happens. See, I have written the time and that we're leaving the office."

Adrian reviews the sheet but doesn't look at Clark.

"What, you don't want to look at my ugly face in the morning?"

"No, I…the van light is just bright."

"Good one." Clark drops the clipboard onto the floor next to him, turns off the interior light, and backs up out of the parking spot. He speeds up to the entrance, rolls through the stop sign, and hits the curb, jerking everything including Adrian inside the van.

Adrian shakes his head and looks over to Clark.

Clark laughs out loud. "See, I knew I could get you to look at this old decrepit face early in the mornin'. Stop being so timid."

"What's the big deal?"

"Nothing. It's just rude."

Adrian slides his sunglasses back on and turns toward Clark. "Happy?"

"You're a fuck, you know that?"

Adrian laughs. "I've been called worse." He quiets down when he notices where Clark is taking them.

We're going to Jeremy's. I was right.

Clark drives down East Meadow Street and pulls the work van in the driveway. Three white box trucks are parked in front of the garage. There's a blue stripe across the side with the words "Forensic Services Unit" marked across it. Adrian presses his finger against the frame in the middle of his sunglasses and pushes them farther up his nose. There are multiple police vehicles around, but only one officer in the garage. They head over to talk with him and he instructs them to go down the trail until they see the rest of the unit. Adrian searches for Jeremy but sees no sign of him.

"I'm going to go down first and get things started. You stay here and I'll text you to let you know what equipment to bring. It'll help with running back and forth and wasting trips."

"Sounds good."

Clark grabs a cooler and hurries through the backyard and over to the trail. The air is still cool, sending chills up Adrian's body. The sun is rising, and the woods are already active with butterflies fluttering about and squirrels darting up a nearby tree, chattering to each other. Who knew that such a serene place would be the focus of such a disturbing event. A raindrop lands on Adrian's shoulder. Another lands on his boot. Adrian lifts his eyes and sees rain moving through the yard.

Great.

About fifteen minutes later, it's pouring and Adrian is sitting in the van. He receives a text from Clark that says to bring another cooler, nothing else. Adrian replies that it's raining, but doesn't hear back from Clark.

Adrian jerks his head back onto the headrest. *You can't be serious.*

He flings the door open and runs to the back of the van. He picks up a cooler and runs through the backyard, slipping on the grass a few times before reaching the trail.

Water is pounding off the top of the cooler and his clothes are getting drenched. Luckily, once on the trail, the trees block some of the rain from falling on him. About a mile in, he sees yellow tape tied around several areas of the wet-lands, one strip of which is strung across the path. A police officer dressed in yellow rain gear and a large brimmed hat eyes him when he reaches the tape.

"This area is off limits," the officer announces.

Adrian sees Clark squatting near the wetland shoreline, filling a sample bottle with wetland water. Forensics labor-atory personnel are on the scene, one of which is holding an umbrella over Clark's shoulder to shield the bottle from the downpour. Adrian notices that Clark is wearing special sampling gear that's similar to the getup actors wear in out-break-type movies.

"I'm one of the samplers with him." Adrian points in the direction of Clark. He adjusts his sunglasses to make sure the officer doesn't see his red eyes.

The officer waves one of the forensics investigators over. "He says he's part of the sampling team."

A middle-aged woman walks over, wearing the full sampling gear. She tugs at the hoodie and lets it hang down her back. A few strands are hanging loose from her pony-tail. "I think we got it," she replies. "We're not going to need any more help since I'm not sure how many samples we'll collect with the rain, and the dogs have identified a smaller area than we thought."

"But—"

"You heard the lady. Go back to your office." The of-ficer steps in front of the forensics investigator, shoulders wide.

She resumes sampling behind the officer.

Adrian feels the blood drain from his face. "I'm here to train with Clark, though. Can I at least tell him I'm here?" Adrian is feeling panicked that he won't be able to assist with the project.

The officer furrows his forehead. "Don't you have a phone?"

Adrian glances over to Clark. "I don't think he's going to answer."

The officer studies Adrian for a minute. "Say, weren't you part of the search crew—"

"Yeah, I'm a neighbor. I've been trying to help out."

The officer watches him for a second. "So, you're a neighbor *and* work with the sampling crew? That's odd."

"Officer! Officer! It's okay. He's with me," Clark yells from the shoreline. "He's in training. I need him to help with the coolers."

The officer glances back at the female forensic sampler again.

She rolls her eyes and gets back up. "I don't need all the interruptions right now, but all right." She glares at Adrian and waves him in, squinting from the rain. "Hurry up."

The officer moves out of the way, and Adrian ducks under the tape.

"Hold on. First, you need to put on some gear," she says. She grabs a sealed plastic bag from a table and hands it to him. Adrian sees the word "Tyvek" on the outside of it. She helps him put the suit on as well as the booties, mask, and gloves.

"We have special areas marked where you can step. Follow me and don't veer off by yourself or you could ruin this entire investigation. Got it?" she asks.

"Got it," Adrian replies and follows her to the shoreline

to meet up with Clark. He can hear the rain pounding on the outside of his suit.

"Hey, sorry. They had me start right away," Clark yells once Adrian is nearby.

"Not a problem, except I forgot the cooler up there," Adrian yells through the rain, pointing back to the trail.

"Well, just follow me to the next sampling location for now. We can get the other cooler later. We're taking the water samples first, then we'll join the forensics team to collect the soil samples. Do exactly as they tell you. Remember, we are working for them, not the other way around."

"So you've said ten times now." Adrian squats next to Clark and slips on a pair of goggles over his sunglasses.

"Are we sampling for DNA?"

"Not right now. The forensics team will do that. We're sampling for volatile organics, so we'll be using these vials."

"Why do they test for volatile organics?"

"They'll be watching for specific types as indicators of decomposition. So, between the DNA, organic volatiles, and other evidence collected, they might be able to put together what happened. It's a difficult investigation without a body, though, from what I understand. And the rain keeps washing away the evidence."

Adrian swallows hard. "Wow. No sign of the missing person yet?"

"No. The police said they searched for a boy all night. I overheard that the dogs have been having a hard time picking up his scent because it rained the night he disappeared. They think they've narrowed down the crime scene to the area up on the trail to this area near the water. Sounds like there might have been some blood on the trail, which they've already sent to the forensics lab. They were taking other samples from the trail also. It seems like they think the kid might have been taken down to the shoreline. I hope it wasn't a gator." Clark prepares the next set of sample bottles. "Sorry to say, it's not looking good for the boy."

Adrian tries not to envision Wyatt being dragged into the water by a gator. He's heard of it happening before, but mostly to toddlers and dogs. He pulls up the news report. "Wait. If that's the case, his bike would still be here. It doesn't make sense for it to be a gator."

"How did you know he had a bike?"

"I'm reading the news report on my phone."

"Yeah. I guess you're right. A gator wouldn't eat a bike."

Adrian cringes at the thought of the gator's mouth. "God, I hope not at least."

"You seem very interested in this case. Something you want to tell me?"

"Tell you? No. I'm just reading the news report."

Clark studies Adrian's expression for a moment, then decides to get back to work. He leans forward to grab another set of vials and says, "Okay, Adrian. Now put that away. It's not the time to be on your phone and besides, it's getting wet. Let's get to the sampling."

Clark teaches Adrian how to collect the water samples and fill out the appropriate paperwork that will accompany them to the forensics laboratory. After a couple of sampling locations are completed, Adrian is able to continue on his own with a forensics escort while Clark steps away to catch up on his office voicemail.

A detective stops by to check up on the progress. "Moving along okay? Everything going good?" His nametag identifies him as Detective Vic Mortensen.

"Yes, sir," the forensics scientist replies. "It'll probably take a while, but we'll get everything collected today."

"Good news," the detective replies. "Say, aren't you on the search team?"

Adrian gazes over to the trail to make sure Clark is still out of earshot. "Yeah, I've been trying to help all I can. Do you know where the boy's father is? Jeremy?"

"Yeah, they took him down to the station. He should be back soon."

"They're questioning him?"

"Got a problem with that?"

"I can vouch for him. I've known him a long time, and there's no way he'd ever hurt his son, Wyatt. He lost his wife not too long ago and has been a single parent since then. This whole thing is killing him."

The deputy crosses his arms and pushes down on a rather large gut. "Well, how about you let us take care of our police work and you take care of your science work. If we need a statement about Jeremy's integrity, I'll let you know."

"Sorry, didn't mean to—" Adrian stops to concentrate. A movement out of the corner of his eye distracts him, but when he turns toward it, it's gone.

The officer squints his eyes as he watches Adrian.

Another movement from the corner of his eye in the opposite direction causes Adrian to peer out into the woods, but once again, there's no sign of it once he turns toward it. Adrian stands up and knocks over a water bottle. His breathing becomes heavier.

"Are you okay?" the detective asks.

"Yes, I'm just—"

More movements streak across Adrian's peripheral vision to the right, like shadows are flying out of the woods from between the trees.

Floaters. These are only floaters, he assures himself.

Adrian looks away, but when his eyes return to the detective, he sees a human-like shadow lurking right behind him.

"Sir!" Adrian yells. The detective jumps backward and loses his balance.

After seeing that no one was near him, the detective says, "What the hell are you trying to pull, young man? Are you fucking with me?"

Adrian pulls his attention away from the silhouette of a figure standing next to the officer for a few seconds to respond, but he can only mouth to him to "watch out."

The detective ducks and scans the woods, only to find an empty space. He turns back toward Adrian. His face is red. "You pull that shit again, and I'll be taking you in for questioning, too."

Adrian stutters that he's sorry and that he's been having some eye problems. Inside, though, he's panicking. He hopes the detective doesn't tell Clark that there could be a conflict of interest with being a sampler and knowing Wyatt.

Clark returns and the detective storms off.

"What was that all about?" asks Clark.

"I seemed to have pissed him off. Just thought I saw something."

"Uh huh," replies Clark, repositioning the sample bottles. "Well, you probably shouldn't piss off the police. They're our client, you know."

"Yeah. I get it." Adrian takes off his sunglasses and rubs

his eyes.

Clark's jaw drops. "Holy hell, Adrian. What happened to you?" He backs up when Adrian peers up at him.

"It's not contagious. It's just broken blood vessels. They'll get better in a week or so."

"Well, it's no wonder you're seeing shit. All that blood blocked up in there has got to be affecting your vision. Next time, tell me when you're having a health problem. Don't just hide behind sunglasses. Can you see well enough to do this sampling?"

"Yeah, I'm good."

"Okay," Clark says hesitantly. "Let's get a move on."

Adrian slides his sunglasses back on and helps Clark collect the samples. He tries hard not to pay attention to the shadows that are interfering with his peripheral vision, some so vivid he swears he can make out a face if he saw them closer. Some fly by in front of him, causing Adrian to jerk backward. Others appear opaque to his side, standing watch. Adrian grows more concerned since he has no way of knowing which direction they'll come from next. His heart rate grows rapid, and he can't help but breathe from his mouth. He wipes his brow with his sleeve, unsure if the droplets on his face are from the rain or sheer panic. He sees that Clark is watching him and hopes his eye condition will keep his co-worker from judging him too harshly. A shadow dashes by again, causing Adrian to spill portions of the sample bottle.

"You need to keep yourself steady or you're going to lose all of the sample water."

"Sorry," Adrian replies.

The sampling continues slowly since Adrian has a difficult time concentrating. A half an hour later, though, the shadows disappear and Adrian gets himself into a routine and completes the sampling. He knows he needs to catch up if they want to finish tonight.

At nine in the evening, Adrian and Clark place the bundles of sample bottles into coolers and pack them in ice for the trip to the laboratory. The rain continues as they both carry the coolers out of the woods and toward Jeremy's house. A scant number of police officers are conversing in the lighted garage.

"Clark, let's stop in for a minute," Adrian says, nodding toward the garage. "I want to check in to see if they need anything else from us."

Clark huffs from the fatigue. "You go without me. I'll get my cooler in the van and come back for yours. I need a break." Adrian places his cooler on the concrete, and Clark hurries through the rain to the van with his cooler.

The officers abruptly discontinue their discussion and focus on Adrian who's now approaching them.

"Hey. I was just wondering if Jeremy was back yet."

Two of the officers glance at the third. It's Mortensen. He replies, "Not yet."

"He's still down at the station?"

"Looks that way."

Adrian shakes his head. "He's not guilty of anything. He loves that kid."

"Then, he has nothing to worry about, does he?" the detective replies.

"No, he doesn't," Adrian answers with a challenging tone.

Detective Mortensen smirks and the other two take a step forward.

Adrian changes his tone. "How about Wyatt? Are you

guys still searching for him?"

"We've quit for the evening. There'll be another search party in the morning."

"Okay, I'll be back then. Hopefully, Jeremy will be back, too."

"How long have you known him?" Detective Mortensen asks.

"We grew up together. Maybe twenty years."

"He's been sad over his wife, huh? How did she die?"

"Car accident. He was driving, so the guilt has been insane. He hit a guardrail on her side of the car on the interstate. The impact threw her through the windshield."

No way am I telling them that Jeremy and Shelly were fighting that night.

"He said she grabbed the wheel, making the car spin out of control."

"Wow. Any history of domestic violence charges against Jeremy?"

"No, but there should have been some against *her*. She used to punch him a lot. He just took the abuse. He never lashed out."

"Huh. That didn't show up on any criminal history reports."

"Well, maybe he didn't press charges. I tried to stay out of it. All I know is Jeremy's a good guy and loves his kid."

The detective studies Adrian for a few seconds and lights up a cigarette, exhaling through his nose. He writes down Adrian's story in his pad.

"They always say it's the wife's fault," Detective Mortensen says.

"Who does?"

"The abusive husband."

"Well, I can hardly believe that Jeremy was abusive toward anyone, much less Shelly. He's been broken up about her death since she's been gone."

"I'm sure he has." He nods at the other officers and they head toward their cruisers. "So, what's up with wearing sunglasses at night?"

"Oh, I just didn't want to forget them."

"Okay. Well, have a good night, sir. Come back in the morning. I'm sure Mr. Corringer will be back then. Oh, and if you think of anything else, here's my card."

Adrian takes his card and sees that the detective's name is Victor Eugene Mortensen. "Sure, Vic. Is that what they call you?"

The officer smirks. "To you, I'm Detective Mortensen."

"Yeah, sure."

Clark is back, ready to pick up the last cooler. They walk to the work van at the end of the driveway, both carrying a handle on each end. The air is brisk with a slight breeze coming in from the west. The rain is down to a sprinkle. Adrian thinks about the detective's comment regarding abusive husbands, but he's convinced Jeremy would never have hurt Shelly. He remembers spats between the two, but generally, they seemed fine. There was the one incident where Shelly had a broken wrist, but she never hinted that Jeremy was to blame. Adrian never heard much about the situation. Jeremy seemed embarrassed whenever Adrian would bring it up.

A shadow streaks across the back of one of the police cruisers, blocking the backlights as it passes by. Adrian stops walking. Clark stops too. He can see the silhouette of a man standing next to the trunk, seemingly watching him.

"What is it?"

"Not sure," Adrian replies. "Do you see someone in front of the police car?"

"No, why?"

Adrian gazes back at the police car. The shadow hasn't moved.

Floater. Just blink.

Adrian closes his eyes a few times and the shadow disappears. Relief calms his bloodstream, and Adrian once again resumes carrying his side of the cooler.

"Let's get out of here," Adrian says.

"Right," Clark replies, watching Adrian's concerned expression. "Are you sure you're okay?"

"Yeah. Just can't wait until my eyes go back to normal."

CHAPTER

7

Steam rises from the scrambled eggs piled high on Lorelei's plate, and Adrian whistles through his teeth as he fries his own. It's four-thirty in the morning, so Adrian knows Lorelei is not pleased.

"Adrian, seriously?"

He steps toward the toaster to remove the bread. "What? You're hungry, right?"

She combs her fingers through her hair, some strands falling in front of her eyes as she yawns. She cuddles up in her robe, rubbing her arms like she's cold. "Not this early in the morning. Why are you up?"

Adrian glances at her slippers that are peeking around the corner of the island. He's always found her morning attire to be adorable. "I've gotta go back to Jeremy's, and Clark and I are both back in the field today. So, I thought I'd throw together some breakfast to make sure we've got enough protein for energy."

Lorelei stares at her stack. "But Adrian, this is too much. Are you kidding me?"

He turns around and places a mound of toast beside her plate also.

"I can't eat all of—" She jumps backward in the stool. "Oh, God. I forgot about your eyes."

Adrian reaches for his plate of eggs and saunters over toward Lorelei, slow and methodically. He widens his eyes, exposing even more redness.

Lorelei grins and covers her face with her hands. "Stop it!" she says. "You're freaking me out."

Adrian slides the plate across the counter toward his seat, generating a screeching sound.

Lorelei moves her hands to her ears, keeping her eyes closed. She peeks from one eye as Adrian starts breathing more loudly and limps as he nears her.

She grabs a forkful of eggs. "I'm ignoring you," she says with a smirk.

He moves closer to her, red eyes glaring, licking his lips.

Lorelei laughs.

Adrian wraps his arms around Lorelei's waist and nestles his mouth into the nape of her neck.

Lorelei screams with every kiss that's tickling her until his kisses become more sensual. She lets out a breath and cocks her neck to the side, allowing him to suck on her skin. She feels the familiar tingling sensation surge through her body as he touches her.

He draws his hands to her arms and rubs them, then rotates the stool as he kisses her jawline. "I'll keep my eyes closed," he whispers as he caresses her face in his hands and kisses her strongly on the lips, just the way she likes it. He lifts her from the stool, her arms around his neck.

"I've gotta open my eyes until we get into bed and then I'll have to *feel* my way around after that," Adrian says.

Lorelei gazes up at his closed eyes and smiles. "I think I'm gonna like this." She rests her head on his shoulder as he carries her.

Adrian opens his eyes. "Wait. All those eggs are gonna get cold."

Lorelei begins kissing Adrian on the neck. "I think they can wait."

He grins and heads down the hallway, shadows whipping back and forth in front of him.

"Jeremy?"

"Hey, Adrian."

"Are you back at the house?"

"Yeah. They suspect me."

"Damn. I'm sorry. No luck finding Wyatt?" Adrian sits up in bed.

"No. He's gone." Jeremy pauses. "I need to face the reality that he's…he's dead," he says, his voice straining.

"Jeremy, you don't know that yet. Keep up the faith. It's too early to think that way. I still believe they're gonna find him."

Jeremy doesn't respond.

"I'm sorry I didn't get over there this morning. I got tied up here."

"That's all right. Cops have been out there since five o'clock this morning. I can't stand the waiting anymore. I feel like I want to pack my bags, get in my truck, and keep driving. I don't want to face this—any of it."

"You can't leave. Besides, when they find Wyatt, he'll want to see you."

"Oh, shut the fuck up, Adrian. Stop with your optimistic, inspirational garbage. Let's face reality here. He's not coming back, and I'm going to jail. End of story."

"You know, you're an asshole sometimes," Adrian replies, frowning. "You're his dad. You can't give up yet."

Lorelei touches Adrian's arm and kisses his shoulder. "He's just upset," she whispers.

Adrian pulls the phone away and takes in a deep breath after Jeremy's chatter stops.

"Look. I'll be there later. We're finding him," Adrian replies and ends the call. He turns to Lorelei, looking downward so his eyes don't cause her to leave. "What the hell is he thinking? He's going to run away? He can't do that. When Wyatt gets back, we'd have to tell him his dad is missing. What the hell? This makes no sense."

"Jeremy's just a basket case right now. Don't pay any attention to what he says."

"I don't know, Lorelei. Something's not adding up. If that were my kid out there, I'd be in the woods, searching. Jeremy hasn't done that yet, not even once. Now, the police suspect that he has a part in this. When I told them there's no way Jeremy had anything to do with this, do you know what they said to me?"

Lorelei shakes her head.

"They said that Jeremy probably abused Wyatt...and Shelly."

Lorelei frowns and says, "I don't believe that he would do that."

"I don't either, but it sounds like Jeremy wants to skip town."

"He's probably just scared," she assures him. "Hopefully, Wyatt just got lost, and they'll find him today." She turns over and swings her legs off the bed. "I'm taking a shower."

Adrian doesn't respond, lost in the thought of Wyatt's disappearance. He thinks back to the first day he went to Jeremy's after he found out that Wyatt was missing. He remembers seeing Jeremy in the garage. Maybe there's a clue he missed. He wasn't thinking of Jeremy as a possible suspect at that time. He replays the night in his mind, visualizing the garage and Jeremy's demeanor. Was he worried for Wyatt…or himself? Jeremy could be strict with Wyatt, but how strict? To the point of abuse?

He gets up from the bed and turns on the television to see if there's an update on the news. He hears the pattering from the shower stop and a screech as the curtain rings move against the rod. His mind wanders to how beautiful Lorelei probably is in that towel right now. He glances up at the dresser mirror. She's not wearing a towel and her loveliness is in full view. The yearning wells up in him again.

She could take another shower.

He gets up from the bed and enters the bathroom.

"Hey, you. You better hurry up and take a shower or you're gonna be late for work," Lorelei says.

Adrian races toward Lorelei and kisses her, pressing up against her to let her know his intentions.

"What's going on with you today?" she asks, smiling between his caresses of her lips.

"I feel so in tune to my senses today. I can't explain it."

"I like it."

"Good. Let's talk about the future when I get home to-night. I think I'm even ready to broach the 'M' word." He suddenly stops kissing her. "Wait. Can you love a guy with red eyes if these are permanent?"

"Adrian, I'd love you with red eyes, green eyes, purple eyes or no eyes. You know that."

Adrian smiles. "Well then, guess we'll be late for work."

Lorelei continues kissing Adrian but soon slows down. "Adrian, we probably shouldn't. I can't be late, and you know you shouldn't be late either. It's your first week. That would probably not go over well."

Adrian sighs and pulls away. "Yeah, you're probably right."

Lorelei quickly dresses and heads toward the bedroom door. "See you later tonight. I'm back at Colt Creek today."

"Sounds good. I'll be going to Jeremy's after work, so I'll be late again."

"Love you. Don't let your eyes get you down."

After Lorelei leaves, Adrian turns on the shower and examines his eyes in the wall mirror above the bathroom sink. Though somewhat lighter, the redness is still revolt-ing, making Adrian flinch.

How am I going to work like this? I'm gonna scare everyone away.

He stares at his eyes, examining whether one side is bet-ter than the other when a shadow creeps into view out of the corner of his eye. He jerks his head to the right, but no one is there. He can feel his pulse rate rise as the shadow appears in his peripheral vision again.

These damn floaters!

He steps away from the mirror.

You've got to ignore them, Adrian.

He takes a shower and slips on his shirt and dress pants. He'll be in the office today, so there's no need for work boots. He turns off the bedroom television and is startled by another shadow slowly moving into his peripheral vision on his right side. He can't help but watch. The hair on his arms stands up. His breathing becomes more rapid, and he's suddenly in tune with all of his senses. Smell, taste, sight, touch—all coalescing into a strange, peculiar cocktail.

He stands still, frozen in fear, yet exuberant by what he's seeing. Something is pulling at him to watch closer. He looks away at first, but soon the figure draws him to watch it in the corner of his eye. The concentration to stay within this thin existence is tiring, as he draws his eyes to the left and watches through his peripheral vision to the right. His eyes tear, causing him to blink, but as long as he keeps his head still, he can see it—a silhouette of a man, blurry at first, but as he waits, the setting becomes clearer.

The smell of organic pine permeates the air, and the taste of blood fills his mouth as he watches the scene unfold before him. A thick forest towers over him, blackness filling the space between the trees. He shudders when a cold breeze whips past his cheek. A couple of birds soar into the thicket, knocking branches around.

He focuses on the scene before him. He can see the back of a beast-like figure in front of the trees with enormous shoulders and muscular arms. Its skin is thick, sunburnt and its head appears shaven. It's hunched over and working at something with its arms, its defined muscles flexing as they move. Adrian tries to see what it's doing, but the width of its shoulders blocks his view. He watches intently until he realizes that the only sound he hears is his own frantic breathing. Adrian stands behind the beast, hands cupped over his face to diminish the sound emanating from his nose. He concentrates on slowing down his breathing so he doesn't expose his presence. He knows he's just trespassed into a scene he's not supposed to see and, at any second, the beast could turn around.

A chain is suddenly thrown over the beast's left shoulder. The beast stands upright, revealing the expanse of its bare shoulders. Adrian lifts his eyes, the beast being a few feet taller than him. He can see the outline of the back of its head, but it's too dark to see any features. Adrian wants to glance away, but he knows he has to keep the scene from ending.

Adrian suddenly finds himself flung face first on the ground behind the beast. He spits out blood and notices his broken lip. He stands up and stumbles, causing him to close his eyes and break the scene before him.

He catches himself on the bedpost, his chest heaving. He scans the room and peripheral vision but the scene is gone. The air smells like Lorelei's perfume. The taste of blood is still present, and he feels a twinge of pain from his lip.

What in the hell just happened?

He takes one step toward the bathroom and his bare foot lands in a small pool of blood.

CHAPTER

8

Adrian closes the door to his office hoping to keep away from his coworkers. The last thing he needs right now is a bunch of gawking scientists spending hours talking about his eyes and giving him advice. He has a professional opinion from the doctor already. The red eyes are broken blood vessels. Probably from stress. The redness will go away. Nothing's wrong.

He presses his finger to his lip to check if it's still bleeding. He gouged it good during his visions earlier, but the bleeding has stopped. The taste of blood was so strong during the vision. It had to be the blood he drooled on the floor, what else could it be? *Thank God it's not coming from my eyes. The doctor better be right.*

Blood red eyes, blood taste, bloody lip, blood pool, bloody foot. He closes his eyes. It's already been a long day.

A light tap on the door jerks his eyes back open.

"Adrian?" The voice is muffled, but he knows it belongs to Fossie.

Crap. I hope she doesn't want me to count pages again.

"Come in," he replies, holding back the annoyance in his voice.

The door pops open and Fossie enters, full of energy about the day ahead. Her gray curly hair flops around while she describes her duties that include copying reports and preparing spreadsheets. And of course, she includes how she needs to keep Clark in line since he forgot to submit field sheets that she has to scan into files, adding stress to her already frantic day. "Oh, yeah, have they found that boy, Wyatt, yet? Clark told me what's been going on. That's why I came to see you," she says, standing in front of his desk.

Adrian answers, "No," but his eyes don't leave the desk.

Fossie studies Adrian. "What, am I so old and crotchety that you can't even look at me?"

God, you sound like Clark.

"You engineer-types need to get better social skills, I swear. Bunch of introverts who hate eye contact. You're just like the rest. I—" There isn't much that can interrupt a sentence by Fossylyn Main midstream, but the sight of Adrian's hideous red eyes and the swollen bottom lip was one for the books. "Holy hell, Adrian. What in the world is going on with you?"

"It's nothing."

"You call that nothing? Your eyes are full of blood and your lip is the size of my thumb. Either your head is starting to explode like one of those astronauts in the Mars movies or you've gotten yourself into some sort of fistfight. Which is it?"

Adrian grins. His lip protrudes more. "Neither."

"What do you mean, neither? Then what in the hell is going on? Is it contagious?" Fossie backs up and sits down in the chair, suspiciously watching his next move.

"No, it's not contagious." Adrian's eyes follow a shadow that streaks across his office and into the corner next to Fossie. "Fuck, not now," Adrian blurts and rubs his eyelids.

"Watch the language, young man."

Adrian rubs his eyes more, trying to extinguish the shadow before it becomes a scene.

"Oh, my God, don't squeeze them! You shouldn't mess with them." Fossie gets up and scurries out of his office. "I'll get you a tissue."

"Fossie, I'm good, really," Adrian replies.

Her eyes squint when she returns and hands him the tissue. "You are one hard man to look at right now."

"It's just broken blood vessels. It'll go away." The shadow is slowly growing into a figure, its shoulders broadening. Adrian gasps, and his heart rate accelerates.

"What on God's green Earth is going on now?"

"Leave," Adrian says.

"Well, you don't have to get all pissy about it. I'm just concerned about you. I mean, you come in here all mysterious and quiet, and then you—"

Chest heaving, Adrian pushes back in his desk chair until it slams against the wall, all of his senses engaged—peppermint candies on Fossie's desk down the hallway, organics on his mud-caked boots, the mustiness of the stack of books on his shelving unit. He hears his rapid breathing, the cyclic clunk of papers being ejected from the copy machine, and the laugh of a co-worker somewhere down the hall. And he tastes blood once again, strong and thick on his tongue. He keeps the figure in the corner of his eye as he motions to Fossie to leave his office, his hand waving her away.

But Fossie doesn't leave, apparently concerned by his behavior, probably assessing him to see if she should call an ambulance or get one of the owners. She follows Adrian's eyes toward the opposite side of the room but sees nothing. "There's nothing there. What the cry firin' hell is up, Adrian?"

Adrian closes his eyes and sighs. "It's just floaters."

"Floaters? You mean the ones the eye doctor sees when he dilates your eyes and shines that God-awful light in them? That makes me bonkers."

Adrian opens his eyes again, the scene unfolding in front of him. Just as before, the creature is hunched over something, surrounded by swaying trees.

"Yes, but these seem different to me. I understand seeing small specks like you're seeing a bug. I've heard of that before. But to see a full scene? Like out of a movie? Is that possible with floaters? I must be going nuts."

Adrian pulls the scene back into his peripheral vision, not waiting for Fossie's response. He can hear her mumbles at first, but then they go away once he's entrenched in the scene again.

It's strange. I can see and even smell. But there's no sound.

The figure's shoulders are moving back and forth, working at something below it, something that doesn't feel right to Adrian. A tingle grows along his neck as he tries to see over the figure's shoulder. Adrian moves closer, rustling through silent leaves as he moves in. He has to see what's going on. The more he does, though, the more the taste of blood coats his mouth. He bends over and gags.

Suddenly, the figure stops and jerks its head to the right, like it's been interrupted and is now listening for something. Though somewhat dark, the face now seems eerily familiar. Adrian moves in a little closer. The figure turns its head to the left, revealing a scar along the jawline—a scar Adrian knows well. As kids, they should have never been playing with that machete.

The scene is suddenly interrupted. "Close your eyes, Adrian! Close them!" Fossie yells.

Adrian snaps out of the scene and flops backward, catching his chair. He stares at Fossie and whispers in shock, "Jeremy."

"What do you mean?"

"I saw him. I just saw him." Adrian closes his eyes and tries to calm his breathing. "I can't believe this." A drop of blood splatters on top of his hand. "Holy hell," he says and searches his desk for a napkin.

Fossie hands him another tissue.

Adrian dabs at his lip, stopping the blood flow. His lip is more swollen. He notices that Fossie looks worried. No, she looks like a wreck, actually. *She must think I'm a freak. Yet, she's sitting here listening. She reminds me of my mom, in a way. Not the harsh side of Fossie, but this soft part of her.*

Adrian doesn't know why, but he feels connected to her somehow.

"Are you okay?" she asks.

"Yeah. I'm fine now." Adrian is solemn.

"What did you see?" she asks, still having a hard time with eye contact.

"Jeremy. I saw Jeremy."

"Who's he?"

"He's Wyatt's dad."

"You know the kid that disappeared then?"

"Yeah. I do."

Why did you tell her? What are you doing?

"I've known him most of my life. We grew up together back in Indiana. We were like brothers, I guess. But he was strange this morning when I spoke with him, saying that he wanted to leave the area." Adrian moves a pencil along the papers on his desk. "And now, I'm seeing him in my visions. It starts off as these dark shadows that lurk around, and if I focus in on them from the corner of my eye, I can see this one scene that never seems to change. It's a figure hunched over something I can't see. A big figure with broad shoulders. At first, I thought it was a creature, but this morning, I saw that it was Jeremy. I know that scar on his face. It was him."

"Does Clark know about this?"

Adrian lowers his eyes. "No, and I need it to stay that way, for now at least. I don't want him to ban me from going to the site yet. I need to know what's going on. Would you do that for me, Fossie? Just for a little while?"

"Sure. Why would I care what that good-for-nothin' man thinks? So, what's the significance?"

"I don't know. The scene is dark, creepy even. I don't know what he's doing. I've been trying to see, but I'm afraid he'll see me."

"Wow. This must have something to do with Wyatt's disappearance, don't you think?" Fossie leans forward. "Maybe you're seeing visions from the crime scene."

"We don't know there was a crime, Fossie. All we know is that Wyatt disappeared. He could have gone off on his own, maybe gotten lost."

Fossie narrows her eyes. "So, you mean to tell me that Jeremy wants to leave the area during his son's investigation, and he has nothing to do with Wyatt's disappearance? If that doesn't spell 'guilty,' I don't know what does. You've got to be seeing visions from the crime. Haven't you heard of those clairvoyant folks who can see a murder afterward? You know, the ones that the police hire to help them because they're stumped on who done it?"

Adrian shakes off Fossie's suggestion. "There's no way Jeremy would hurt Wyatt. He loves his son. He'd do anything for him. I know him."

"Sometimes, Adrian, people change right before your eyes and you don't even know it. I think you're one of those 'sensitives.' You're seeing what happened."

"I find that really hard to believe when I've never had anything like this happen before."

"Well, sometimes things happen for a reason, Adrian."

Adrian doesn't respond. His mind is reeling.

"You could help that boy. Try to see where the scene is unfolding. Maybe go there. Or better yet, tell the police. It would probably help them."

Clark pops his head in. "Hey, Adrian."

Fossie stands. "Think about it," she says and scoots out of Adrian's office.

From the doorway, Clark's holding another work order from the forensics laboratory. "Sounds like the forensics lab identified some interesting results that could be related to Wyatt. They want us to assist with more sampling at the crime scene. I don't think the DNA is back yet, though. Of course, they probably wouldn't tell me anyway." Clark dawdles in the doorway but Adrian doesn't notice. He's too distracted with the events from earlier. "Hey, by the way. I overheard your conversation with Fossie. I'm not sure what happened here this morning, but don't let her get into your head with all her cockamamie stories about people seeing stuff. She reads too much. Ya gotta love her imagination, at least. Clairvoyance, my ass. It's probably all the stress you've been under with your eyes. You don't have to go into the field with me. Might be better to give your eyes a rest."

Adrian doesn't argue.

CHAPTER

9

Adrian pulls his truck into his driveway, wondering if he'll be joined by another shadow or two. He turns off the ignition and gathers his work papers, peering back and forth to each side of the truck. Maybe if he makes a run for it, they won't cut him off as he runs for the front door.

He lifts the handle, gently releasing the door outward, and slides down to the pavement. He scans his surroundings for anything moving, but all is calm. Adrian releases his breath and pushes the truck door shut until the inside light goes out. Glancing behind him, he's relieved that he might get a reprieve from the visions that are plaguing him. It doesn't help that his house is in a remote area. The developer never finished most of the homes in his neighborhood, so they are half-built shells. The place is desolate with no neighbors on his street.

A cool breeze is tickling the back of his neck.

"Well howdy, neighbor," says a voice directly behind him.

Adrian jumps as he turns around, his heart pounding. He sees a man of average height with a denim jacket and an Orlando Magic hat on.

The stranger exhales a laugh as he says, "Sorry, neighbor. Didn't mean to startle ya. I'm out here with my daughter riding our bikes. I didn't realize we had a neighbor at this point. We just moved in a few days back and thought we were alone out here." He smiles wide at Adrian.

After catching his breath, Adrian replies, "You scared me. What are you doing out here in the dark?"

"Sometimes we'll get a ride in before bedtime. You know how it is with kids, right?" A young girl about the age of seven peeks around the neighbor's side. "Oh, this is her, my daughter and magical princess, Taylor." She beams at her dad and shows Adrian her long, sheer veil, which is attached to a golden crown on the top of her head. Her golden locks would definitely pass as royalty.

Adrian grins. "No, I can't say I know what it's like to have kids, actually. It's just my wi…girlfriend and me."

"Almost said wife, huh? Oh, well, in due time, right? I'm Gentry." He extends his hand toward Adrian.

Adrian is thankful that it's too dark for Gentry or Taylor to notice his red eyes. Adrian returns the gesture. "I'm Adrian. My girlfriend is Lorelei. Nice to meet you."

"Same here, buddy. But I should probably get Princess Taylor back to the house. I'll catch up with ya another time. It'll be nice to get in some male conversation for a change. Maybe have a beer, too."

"Sounds good." Adrian opens the front door and once

inside sees that Lorelei is bundled up in the corner of the couch—a coffee mug in one hand and a book in the other. Her glasses are pushed up onto her head, holding back her hair from her eyes, with the exception of a few stragglers. "Hey. How did today go?"

Adrian sets his backpack on a chair next to the door, trying to keep his face out of Lorelei's line of sight. "Some of the test results came back, but I haven't heard much more." He figures no sense in telling Lorelei about a few preliminary hits in the lab work. "Yesterday, it seemed like the forensics team was concentrating on an area about a mile in along the trail and down to the water."

"So, are they thinking he was taken off the bike trail and dragged into the water?"

"I don't know. They haven't said anything to me, but it does look suspicious that way. He rode his bike through there all the time, though. I'm not sure if they can tell if the results are fresh. I don't know enough about it."

"Are you doing okay with this?"

"Yeah." Adrian enters the living room and sits down next to Lorelei who is back to reading a book, so he tries to steal part of her granny square afghan.

"No, no, mister. You have your own over there on the other side of the couch. This is mine."

Adrian ignores her and tugs harder. "But I'm cold, and you're so warm." He presses his cold toes against her calf.

"Adrian!" she yelps and jerks away, pulling on the afghan to bundle up more. She lets go as soon as she sees his face. "Hey, what happened to your lip? Are you okay?"

"Yeah, I'm good. I bit it by accident this morning, and it doesn't seem to want to calm down."

"Dang between your eyes and your lip, it's a good thing

I—"

"You love me?" He grins and wraps his arms around her. "I can keep you warm."

"Well, it *is* very chilly," she replies.

"Just let me warm up my feet, first," he says and immediately presses his cold foot up against her again.

"Adrian! Quit! Your feet are too cold. Besides you're avoiding the subject."

Adrian stops squirming. "What subject?"

"You know. Did you see any shadows today?"

He leans forward, cupping his hands as he rests his arms on his knees. "Yes. But not just shadows. I'm seeing full scenes now." Adrian turns toward Lorelei. "I saw Jeremy."

"What do you mean?"

"He's in my visions now. I was seeing this beast-like figure at first. He has broad shoulders and muscular arms. Then he turned his head, and I saw the machete scar."

Lorelei frowns. "Yeah, I guess it's hard to miss with how jagged it is. I was glad to see that he got over the embarrassment of it and has been shaving more."

"Between the visions and Jeremy leaving town, it's making me wonder. Could he have hurt Wyatt?"

"That's nonsense, and you know it. Jeremy would never do that. He probably wants to leave because he can't handle the enormous stress anymore. As far as your visions, I don't know what to think about them. I thought the shadows were supposed to be floaters."

Adrian shakes his head. "I don't think these are floaters. The visions are too realistic. Things have changed since I've seen the doctor. I think he misdiagnosed this." Adrian leans back. "A lady at work thinks I'm clairvoyant." He studies

Lorelei's expression to see if she seems doubtful, but her expression doesn't change.

"So, she thinks you're seeing the scene of the crime?"

"Yeah, she does."

"What do you think about that?"

"I don't know. It all seems too unbelievable."

"Well, maybe you could just concentrate on trying to find Wyatt. Keep going with the search parties. The police will figure it out. And I'm sure Jeremy will turn up innocent."

Adrian frowns and stares into space for a few seconds when Lorelei flings part of her afghan onto his legs. He smirks. "Oh, so now you're ready to play nice?"

"Maybe," she says and pulls the afghan back off.

Adrian leans in toward Lorelei and pulls her toward him. "I'd kiss you but..."

"I'm good," she replies, squinting at the roundness of his bludgeoned lip.

He then pulls the entire afghan off of her. "This is mine now."

"No, it's not!" Lorelei replies, retrieving her side of it.

She lays her head on his shoulder to snuggle and closes her eyes. "So, are you really doing okay with Wyatt's disappearance? I know this has to be conjuring up some painful memories."

Adrian shakes his head and says, "I'm fine."

Lorelei gazes up at his eyes, despite their redness. "Are you sure you don't want to talk about it? You know, about your brother?"

"Nah. What's there to talk about? He's gone, but I can help find Wyatt."

"This whole situation isn't bothering you? Especially

after what happened to your brother?"

Adrian pauses for a second. He contemplates whether or not to tell Lorelei that it wasn't just his brother who died. He never told her about the rest of the family, fearing she'd think he couldn't help but be messed up after what had happened to them. Who gets over such a thing? "I can't dwell on that. I can only focus on what I can do to help. I'm glad I'm a part of the investigation so I can have the inside scoop on what's going on. Otherwise, I'd probably be going crazy. It keeps me busy and involved."

"How did you say your brother died again?"

Adrian tilts his head back and closes his eyes. "There was an accident. I couldn't save him."

"You never talk about it, Adrian. Why?"

"Because it won't bring him back. What good is it to talk about it? It's better for me to move on."

"Wasn't he the same age as Wyatt?"

"Yes, and it's killing me that Jeremy has to go through this unless of course, he had something to do with it."

"He didn't. You know it."

Adrian pulls at the afghan again. Lorelei giggles.

"Don't sidetrack the conversation, Mister. You need to talk about this stuff. I'm worried about you."

Adrian hugs Lorelei. "I'm glad you care, but I'm fine. I don't need to talk about it. I'd rather forget the bad and move forward with the good. Including you." Adrian laces his fingers through Lorelei's. "You know, I just met our new neighbor before I came in. His name is Gentry. He asked me if I knew about raising kids."

"Uh huh. And what did you say to that?"

"No, of course, but the funny thing is that I almost called you my wife."

Lorelei pauses before saying, "So, what does that mean?"

"Maybe the idea is warming up to me."

A shadow slithers into Adrian's peripheral vision, taking his attention away from the conversation. He jerks his head toward Lorelei so he doesn't see the shadow, but it creeps into view again, and he pushes himself back against the cushion.

"Adrian?" Lorelei asks as she grabs his arm. "What is it?"

Lorelei's voice fades as Adrian is forced into the wooded scene. Once again, the back of a man is facing him, broad and muscular. A wind brushes up against Adrian's cheek, but he hears nothing. Sunlight peeks between swaying branches in an almost rhythmic pattern. He chokes on an iron taste in his mouth that begins at the front of his tongue and makes its way to the back of his throat. Despite the silence, the man once again jerks his head to the right as if he can hear something. Adrian follows his gaze and sees a long path meandering alongside a shoreline. The pungent stench of decaying organics overwhelms his senses. He knows this smell. It's distinctive—a smell that he associates with only one place. He stares down the path again, paying more attention to his surroundings until the realization sets in.

He's in Green Swamp. He'd know it anywhere.

Adrian hears his name being called faintly in the background. He pushes his mind against it. He doesn't want to go back right now. He's gotta see what the man is doing. Could he be leaning over Wyatt? He creeps up to the man's back and ever so carefully peeks over his shoulder, trying not to startle him even with the smallest of breaths. But

Adrian can only see the earthen path. He moves in a little closer, almost to the man's ear, and holds his breath. Inch by inch, he slowly peeks over the beastly shoulder, trying to see what he's doing. And just as he sees sneakers, the man straightens his back and peers down the path to the right again, barely missing Adrian's head. Then the man looks down the path to the left, once again exposing the machete scar. Up close, Adrian can see the familiar jagged line left behind from Jeremy's own doing—not that he meant to. Sometimes he'd get overzealous with his swing. That day the blade came back too high and it planted itself right into his jaw. Adrian winces with the thought.

The man jerks his head forward and leans in again. Adrian quickly moves in too. He's gotta see what's going on. He pushes himself over the man's shoulder when suddenly, Adrian feels a thud against his shoulder blade and he's jerked backward.

"Adrian!" cries Lorelei. "What the hell is going on? Are you with me?"

Adrian squints his eyes with the sudden brightness of his living room.

"Were you in the scene again?"

"Yeah," he replies and holds his hand up to shield his eyes. His chest is heaving, and Lorelei is caressing his shoulders.

"I've never seen you like this. You were non-responsive to me. I almost called an ambulance."

"I'm sorry, Lorelei." Adrian catches his breath. "I almost saw what he was doing and didn't want to snap out of it quite yet."

"The scene? What were you seeing?"

"Jeremy again, leaning over something. I tried to look

over his shoulder to see what was going on, but he jerked up suddenly. I almost freaked, but tried again and never saw because you pulled me back. Why did you do that? You made me miss it when I was so close."

"Oh. I'm sorry. I was just worried. I've never seen you in such a trance before."

"Jesus, Lorelei. I almost had him."

Lorelei slumps on the couch. "Well, I can't handle seeing you like that. You seemed possessed or something. It's scary, okay?"

Adrian can hear the strain in Lorelei's voice like she's about to cry. He softens quickly and hugs her. "Don't worry about it. I saw a sneaker but I couldn't tell if it was Wyatt's."

"Maybe it's better that you don't know."

Adrian pauses to think for a few seconds. "I *do* know. I'd like to help the police. Besides, it seems like Jeremy is involved, so—what?"

"You don't know that. Stop blaming him based on some stupid visions."

"But the scar."

"Fuck the scar. It probably means nothing."

"You don't think I should tell the police?"

"Adrian? Are you kidding me? No. Don't do that. He's your friend." Lorelei gets up off the couch and leaves for the bedroom. "You'd be betraying him for no reason."

He wipes his mouth with the back of his hand, leaving behind a bright red streak. He gags from the taste of blood as it swirls around against his tongue.

This has got to be a sign of something. Maybe Wyatt's bleeding. I've gotta tell the police what's going on.

CHAPTER

10

I t's Friday, and Adrian is up early, preparing for the day, which will include traipsing through the woods looking for Wyatt and checking to see if Jeremy is home. It's been five days since finding out about Wyatt's disappearance. He knows the chances of finding him alive are growing slimmer with each day.

Adrian hesitantly combs his wet hair in the mirror. The last thing he feels like enduring right now is another episode of his visions. His eyes are still red, though blotches of white are starting to show through. He's not sure if this looks better or creepier. Lorelei has already left for her day in the field, so he can't ask her. He bends toward the mirror to get a closer look.

Yep, still creepy. Damn.

His bulging bottom lip isn't helping matters either. Every time he has a vision, he seems to expel blood. It's got to be coming from the lip.

He checks his peripheral vision but all seems clear this morning. No shadows. No exaggerated senses. He knows he's not in the clear yet, though. He can't be.

Adrian decides to report to work first before going to Jeremy's so he can review any laboratory reports that may be in. Luckily, the firm handed him a badge so he can enter the office without the receptionist being around. He heads straight for the fax machine. The darkness of the office is quite in contrast with the oranges and reds of the morning sunrise he can see through the windows. A fax has been sent over regarding the case.

Adrian pops his head up when something catches his attention from the corner of his eye. "Not again," he whispers out loud.

"Ya talkin' about me again?" a voice says from the hallway, sending a surge of fear jolting up Adrian's body.

A man's shadow is standing right outside of Adrian's door.

This can't be another shadow.

"What's the matter?"

Adrian recognizes Clark's voice. "Jesus, Clark. You scared the shit out of me."

"Sorry. What are you doing with those lab reports? I got here early because I wanted to beat you to them. I'm going to recommend to the powers that be that you be removed from this assignment. I don't think it's healthy for you. It's definitely not fair to you."

"Seriously, Clark. I'm fine. I'd rather know what's going on so I feel like I'm helping. What good would it be for me to be kept from it all?

"Adrian, you were talking about having some kind of

visions from this." Clark grabs the results to get a closer look. "I'll give the detective a call. In the meantime, stay out of it, stop waiting for labs, and find another project to work on."

"But, Clark, I—"

"I'm not kidding." Clark doesn't wait for any more protests from Adrian and leaves, holding the latest work orders from the forensics lab.

Adrian leans back in his chair contemplating his next move. Not being out at the site doing sampling is going to be hard for him. He's got to think of a way to convince Clark otherwise.

Fossie flutters by on the way to her desk but stops abruptly when she sees Adrian's office light on. She rushes into his office and lays a bag of groceries on the office chair.

"So..."

"So, what?"

"Any more visions?" she whispers, leaning over his desk.

"Ah. Well, no."

"Nothing more?"

Adrian shakes his head. He hates lying, but the current work situation with Clark will only be fueled more if Fossie blabs about his visions.

"Huh. Well, I still think you should make them known to the police. It might even take them in a different direction."

"I doubt that."

"I really hope a gator didn't get him."

Adrian drops his head into his hands and rubs his eyes.

"Shit. I'm sorry, Adrian. My lack of sensitivity sucks sometimes. Maybe he was just playing in the water and—"

"Forget it, Fossie. I need your help, though. Clark doesn't want me on the case anymore, but I really want to be a part of this. Can you convince him otherwise? I need to stay in touch with the latest. It's the only way."

Fossie stares at Adrian's expression for a minute. "I'll see what I can do. You just tell the police about your visions."

She's down the hallway before he can answer.

A brisk breeze climbs up Adrian's right side, reminding him that January in Florida isn't always as warm as he imagined when he lived in Indiana. He used to envy people who lived in Florida when he'd see the occasional commercial from the sunny beaches. It's a far cry from that today at fifty degrees Fahrenheit. An unusual cold snap came through. With the frequent episodes of rain, Adrian's starting to wish he hadn't talked Fossie into convincing the company's owners that he's pivotal to the forensics project. First off, he's freezing. Second, Clark is pissed. Really pissed. Seethingly pissed. So pissed that Adrian wonders if he's going to get over it. He's been stewing all morning, barely talking to Adrian except for the occasional coordination on sample locations. Luckily, Adrian knows what he's doing now as far as the collection of the samples, since they've been working apart all morning—Adrian collecting water samples along the shoreline, and Clark collecting soil samples along the path. Adrian's convinced there's no coincidence that he's sampling in the cold water while Clark gets to collect them on the warmer path. But he won't complain.

Adrian hands off the samples to the forensic investigator and takes a break once up on the shoreline. He needs to warm up a bit. More importantly, he needs to decide if he'll share his visions with the police. He hasn't seen them around yet, but the area is still taped off. Adrian scans the water, wondering if his visions have been wrong. If Wyatt was dragged in the water by an alligator, he could find—.

Stop. Don't even contemplate it.

More rain stings his face with the incoming wind making his eyes tear.

"Hey, going to get some work done today or what? I want to get going," says Clark, now standing next to him and peering out into the water. He waits for an answer, then sees Adrian's tearing eyes. "Shit, are you kidding me? I told you that you shouldn't be out here."

Adrian frowns, confused over Clark's reaction. His red eyes meet Clark's.

"You just like to torture yourself?" asks Clark.

"What are you talking about?"

"You look upset. You've been crying?"

"Oh! No, no. I'm just freezing. My eyes are tearing up because of the cold wind."

"Uh huh."

"I'm serious, man."

"Yeah." Clark picks up some of the sample bottles next to Adrian. "Maybe next time you could refrain from getting my wife to gang up on me with my boss."

Adrian's mouth drops open. "Your…your wife?"

Clark stands next to Adrian and extends a hand, gesturing to Adrian to take the sample bottles. "Guess no one told you, huh? Come on, let's finish this."

A few minutes after resuming the sampling, Adrian

hears the sound of men's voices coming up the path. He turns around to see if it's the police and bumps into a uniform. The police officer snorts and says, "Watch out where you're going."

"Sorry," Adrian replies, red in the face.

"You still got them there red eyes, huh?" Adrian recognizes that it's the same officer from the other day—Officer Mortensen.

"Yeah, they're starting to get better though."

"Good. They're creepy." The officer turns to the forensics sampler. "Ma'am, a word?"

"Of course," she says. She removes her latex gloves and sloshes through the water in her knee-high rubber boots.

"I heard from my team that you have mapped out the sample results?"

"Yes, yes." The investigator wipes her hands on her pants to dry them and pulls the map out of her clipboard. "Here, let me show you." Adrian sees her point to the various sample results and the police officer nods his head. He then overhears her saying that the location along the trail near him is probably where Wyatt was located last before possibly being dragged into the water.

"Did you take any samples from the edge of the water to that part of the path— you know, up the bank?"

"Yes, we sure did—today. We're also taking more along the trail and along the shoreline."

The officer nods. "Any thoughts on what happened?"

"I can't release that yet," she replies.

Officer Mortensen takes a second look at Adrian. "You're Mr. Corringer's long-time friend, right?"

Wyatt whips his head around to see where Clark is standing. Luckily, he's way down near the shoreline again.

"Yeah, I am."

"Any idea on where he's located right now? I'd like to talk to him."

"I wish I knew. I think he left because he couldn't handle the stress."

"Well, if you talk to him or see him, tell him he needs to get back here or I'm going to put a warrant out."

"I haven't heard from him either. But I'll definitely tell him if I do."

Adrian hears footsteps behind him. Clark strolls up to his side.

"Are you telling the officer about your visions?" Clark asks.

The detective turns toward Adrian with his full attention.

Adrian coughs. He's mortified that Clark brought this up. "I, uh, well, they're nothing."

Detective Mortensen crosses his arms. "Let *me* decide that. What visions?"

Adrian glances over to Clark, then back to the police officer. "I don't know. I sometimes see these scenes with a dude who's back is always to me, so I can't see what he's doing."

"Are you talking about dreams?"

Adrian was about to say, "Yes," but Clark interrupts and says, "No, in broad daylight. They come and go." He turns to Adrian. "Right?"

Adrian lowers his head and nods. *This cop is going to think I'm nuts.*

Officer Mortensen waits for more details, but Adrian remains quiet. He clears his throat, then says, "So, you don't feel like sharing right now?"

This is so embarrassing. Adrian rubs his forehead, then his eyes, followed by his mouth. "Well, I don't know what else to say."

"How about giving me a description of this 'dude,' as you put it."

Adrian stares at the ground for a few seconds and says, "Broad shoulders, muscular, shaved head. He's taller than me. I can only see him from behind."

"And what are the surroundings like?"

"The woods, tall trees swaying."

"What is he doing?"

"I can't see that. I haven't been able to peek over his shoulder long enough yet."

"Peek over his shoulder? Was this a vision or are you saying you were there?"

"I'm saying these are visions. And there's no sound. They started as shadows and now are more like scenes. I went to the eye doctor, and he said they're floaters."

"Is that what's going on with your red eyes?"

"No, that's broken blood vessels. He said it's probably from the stress."

"Yeah, I'm sure." The detective steps in a little closer. "This whole thing must be upsetting you pretty bad, right?"

"Yeah." *Please don't ask me if the visions look like Jeremy. Or if the dude has a scar running down his left jawline. Or if I fucking saw a sneaker. Why am I protecting Jeremy?*

"Anything else?"

"Not really, other than…" Adrian squints as the sun pokes through between the trees. "The path."

"You see the path in the visions?"

Adrian nods.

"What are you, one of those psychics?"

"Not that I know of, but I'm starting to wonder."

"Well, Adrian, is that your name?"

Adrian nods.

"Sounds like you've got nothing, so I guess you're not clairvoyant." The detective turns to walk up to the path. "Unless you can use your powers to find Wyatt's dad. Then maybe I could use that because with him disappearing, well... I'm not sure what to think. What do you think?"

"I have no idea where he could be."

"Well, you keep track of those visions of yours and maybe you'll find out."

Shit, does he know this could be Jeremy?

Stop being paranoid.

"I'm hoping they'll go away with this eye problem. It's probably nothing."

"That or maybe you know more than you're telling me. Could that be possible? This vision stuff is horseshit."

A shadow quickly crawls along the path behind the officer. It's rather small, like a child. Another larger shadow stands over it, reaching for the child.

"Are you listening to me?" the detective asks.

Adrian tries to focus on the detective, but the scene in the background draws his attention away.

"I think he's seeing something right now. Look at him," Clark says.

Both Officer Mortensen and Clark turn toward the path, following Adrian's gaze.

The larger shadow is leaning in toward the smaller one, but Adrian knows that Clark and the officer see nothing.

Adrian's heart starts beating louder. The trees slow down to an infinitesimal sway. He smells the rotten decay of plants so intensely he swears he's stepped in crap.

Sounds grow quieter, almost to a whisper. Wind sweeps past the detective, drawing the faint smell of body odor toward Adrian. And the taste of blood floods Adrian's tongue. He tries hard not to show the officer and Clark that he's seeing another vision, but the two are standing next to him now, grabbing at his arms, steadying him as he loses his balance.

Adrian stares at the path and, once again, sees the figure in the same position as always, except the child's legs are kicking. He's on top of the child, squatting. Adrian feels himself moving forward. He's got to see if this is Wyatt. His heart is racing out of control when he reaches the path.

Once again, the man turns his head to the right, then the left, exposing the deep, mangled scar. Adrian starts to sprint full force so he can knock down the beast before him, but within a second, Adrian is flung onto his back, causing him to close his eyes and break the scene.

"Adrian!" Clark yells. "Can you hear me?"

Adrian gasps, his arms pushing at the hands that are holding him.

"What the hell is wrong with you?" Clark asks.

The detective calls for backup with a knee on Adrian's shoulder.

It registers to Adrian that he's about to be arrested.

"I don't know! It's these eyes. Ever since the floaters came. It makes me go into a trance. I don't know what I'm seeing. I can't hear during it. My sense of smell is exaggerated. I taste blood. But I just saw the shadow of a man hovering over a child right there on the path."

"Yeah, the blood would be because you bit your lip again," Clark says.

Adrian's chest is heaving. His eyes are wild, dilated.

"You gonna stop fighting me now?" the detective asks.

"I didn't know I was," Adrian replies, desperation in his voice. He relaxes his body.

Two other officers run down the path. Officer Mortensen waves at them to go back. "We're good here."

"You sure, Vic?" one of them asks.

"Yeah, just an overly disturbed young man, apparently. He's harmless."

They glance at each other and one says, "We'll hang out just in case."

"You good now?" the detective asks Adrian.

"Yes."

The detective stands and helps Adrian up with one hand. "You had best go back to the eye doctor and get yourself checked out. I don't know what visions you're seeing, but there was nothing going on along the path."

Adrian is too short of breath to answer, but he nods.

"I've got him," says Clark.

"Okay. Finish up and get out of here. He needs some rest."

"You got it," Clark replies.

Once the officers are out of sight, Clark turns to Adrian and says, "Do you even remember what just happened? You seemed to be in a trance."

"Not after he was quizzing me about the details of the scene. A shadow was crawling on the path behind him and —"

"Oh, Adrian. Just quit it. I don't know what kind of shit you're trying to pull, but you almost got yourself arrested. Stop acting like a maniac. Pull yourself together. I'll finish sampling and then we're getting out of here. You are officially off this project—got that?" Clark stands firmly with fierceness in his eyes.

Adrian replies, "I wish you would let me finish."

Clark pushes the bag of sample bottles to Adrian's chest. "Get to work and no more bullshit."

The forensics investigator greets Clark.

As Adrian leaves, he whispers, "I keep seeing Wyatt's dad, Jeremy."

CHAPTER

11

How can you possibly be hungry?" Lorelei asks. "After all that food last night, I think I'm good for a week. Wow."

"Just like to cook, I guess," Adrian says. A piercing whistle screams from the kettle, water spurting out from its tip. Adrian promptly removes it from the burner with a pot-holder and sets a mug next to it. He then places Lorelei's favorite tea bag into the mug and pours steamy water into it.

Lorelei chuckles and says, "Why don't you just get rid of that kettle before it burns one of us. It has to be ancient."

"It's an antique."

"I get that, but it has obviously lost most of its function. It shouldn't spew water like that."

"I can't. It was my mom's."

"Adrian, seriously? We have lots of stuff from your

mom that we use. I'm sure that she'd prefer that we don't end up with third-degree burns."

"If you don't like it, then don't use it. It works just fine."

Lorelei slides out of her stool and goes into the kitchen. "You can be so annoying sometimes."

"Seriously? I just made you all of this breakfast and you tell me this?" He doesn't turn around so he can't see the smirk on Lorelei's face. Adrian flips over several pancakes on the griddle and quickly slides over to the eggs to tend to them before their centers become stiff. He then hands Lorelei the mug without meeting her eyes.

"What, are you cooking for an army?"

Adrian sighs. "Can we just keep things civil today?"

"Civil? I'm just kidding. And what do you mean by 'today?'"

Adrian turns around and is greeted by a sweet kiss from Lorelei. He wraps his arms around her and swoops her up closer to finish. "I thought you were still mad at me from yesterday."

"I'm not mad at you. I'm concerned about you." An egg makes a popping sound. Adrian leaves Lorelei's caress to save it and the others. He gathers the pancakes and brings everything over to the breakfast bar.

"Don't be. Once the floaters go away, everything will be back to normal. The doctor said two weeks, so I've got over a week left."

Lorelei tucks her hair behind her ear. "Fine but maybe you should go back and get your eyes checked out again. It doesn't seem normal that the floaters would be visions."

"Maybe it has nothing to do with the floaters. I keep seeing Jeremy. Something is trying to tell me something."

"Adrian, come on. Listen to what you're saying."

Lorelei leans over and pulls Adrian's arm toward the stools to sit down and eat. "So, we didn't finish another conversation yesterday either."

Adrian knows what she means, but he's not sure about having a wedding talk this early in the morning. Coffee is a must first, and then maybe. Adrian grabs a mug of coffee and sits back down.

"Too early in the morning?"

"Uh, yeah. I think so. I need to wake up before I go committing to anything." He straddles his legs around Lorelei's stool. "So, what's on tap for today? It's Saturday. Maybe we should go kayaking or something."

"You mean, you'd take a break from the hunt for Wyatt?" She pauses, seeming to have a second thought. "Wait. You're changing the subject."

Adrian gives her the crooked smile that she loves.

"I hate you," she says.

He kisses her on the cheek, then the neck. Lorelei's body heaves with every lick near her ear.

"Adrian, you're avoiding the subject again."

"No, I'm not. I just need to wake up." He returns to kissing her, gently sucking her neck with every kiss.

Lorelei gains control of her breathing long enough to say, "I have to work today."

The kissing stops and Adrian drops his head. "You're kidding me, right?"

"I wish I were, but I've got to finish the sampling at Colt Creek today so I can get to another area of it on Monday." Lorelei hugs him. "I'm sorry."

He caresses her again. "You sure you can't stay just for a little while? It's only seven."

"You're very tempting, Adrian, but I have a full day's

worth of work."

Adrian pulls back a strand of hair that's lying across Lorelei's cheek and tucks it behind her ear. He lets her go with a kiss on the cheek.

"I'll make it up to you later," Lorelei says.

Adrian nods and pulls away.

"I love you," she says.

He turns away from her and replies, "I love you, too." Adrian stacks the dishes into the sink and walks to the front door with Lorelei to say goodbye. He watches her walk down the driveway when she's greeted by a man. She drops her field books. Adrian immediately opens the door and rushes out to help her. As he moves closer, he can see that the man is his new neighbor, Gentry.

Gentry squats near Lorelei to grab her field books and hands them to her. "Sorry I startled ya. I didn't mean too. I'm Gentry, Gentry Flanagan, your new neighbor. My wife and I live in the house over on Glidewell Street with our daughter, Taylor. I met your boyfriend last night. Sure is nice to see some faces around here."

Adrian extends his hand to Gentry. "Hey, good morning, Gentry. This is Lorelei. You're out and about awful early in the morning, aren't you?"

"Yeah, well, I've always been an early riser. I like to get a brisk walk in to get it over with before I start my day. Sorry about your notebooks," he replies with a smile.

"Hi, Gentry. Nice to meet you," Lorelei says. "Don't worry about it. They're used to being dropped and thrown around a lot, especially when I'm out in the field."

"In the field? What do you do?"

"I'm a wetland specialist."

"Oh, wow. Very cool. What kind of wetland studies?"

"Mostly the health of the wetlands, so I'm looking for plant species that are usually found in wetlands for the most part."

"Huh. Okay."

"Well, I better get out there." She gives Adrian a kiss on the cheek. "See you later."

"Be safe," Adrian replies as she pulls out of the driveway.

"So, I don't mean to be rude, but what's going on with your eyes?" Gentry asks, glancing at Adrian.

"Somehow, I've managed to break the blood vessels in both eyes. The doctor says it's stress."

"So, you'll recover?"

"Yeah, yeah. They'll be healed in about another week."

"I gotta be honest. They're hard to look at."

Adrian slides on a pair of sunglasses. "This better?"

"Yeah, much better."

"I've been wearing these a lot. Keeps down the gasps from people who don't know me. Hell, even from people who *do* know me."

Gentry grins.

"So, did you stop by for a reason?" asks Adrian.

"Yeah, I did. We're having a housewarming party next weekend and I wanted to invite you and Lorelei."

"Yeah? Well, that sounds great. We'll have to see, though. Lorelei usually works, and I've been tied up with trying to find a missing kid."

"Wow, around here?"

"Yeah. My best friend's son. He lives on the other side of the interstate."

"Jesus. That's terrible. Really sorry to hear that. When did that happen?"

"Last Sunday night. Sounds like he was on his way home from his friend's house when he disappeared, and no one has seen him since."

"Do the police have any clues?"

"Not that they're releasing yet. They took some samples for testing along the bike path and in the water, though, so we might have pinpointed the location."

"We?"

"Yeah, believe it or not, I work for the engineering firm that is collecting the samples. It's been a nightmare."

"Wow. Really sorry. I hope they find him soon."

"Yeah, me too. I feel like he's still alive out there." Adrian stares at the ground.

"Well, if you're free next weekend, we'd love to have you."

"Thanks, that's really nice of you both. Hopefully, it'll work out. I'll let Lorelei know." Adrian pats his front pockets. "If you want to give me your cell number, I can text you." Then his back pockets. "Shit, my phone is in the house. Want to come in for a minute?"

"Yeah, sure. Maybe you could let me know later today. We're taking a head count."

"Gotcha. I think it's on the counter."

Gentry follows Adrian into the house, then the kitchen.

"Damn. What did I do with it?" Adrian's forehead crinkles as he thinks. "Maybe it's in my safe room."

"Safe room?"

"Yeah, it came with the house, but I kind of use it as my man cave. I can block out the world and have lots of food to eat." Adrian laughs.

Adrian leads Gentry down the hall to a door with multiple deadbolts, Gentry following close behind. Inside, there are wall-to-wall shelves filled with canned goods, paper towels, bottled water, batteries, flashlights, radios, clothes, garbage bags, and other various supplies.

Gentry's mouth drops open once he peeks inside. "Holy cow. I guess you weren't kidding!"

Adrian chuckles. "I think we'll be safe during the next hurricane. The whole house could fall around us, and we'll be nice and cozy inside." Adrian starts running his hand along the cushions of a rocker recliner. Along the farthest wall sits a wood block with plywood on top that holds a train set. Not just any train set. Quite an elaborate one.

Gentry strolls over to it. "Wow, this is incredible. It must have taken you forever to put this together."

"I wanted one for years. So, one day I started it, and it's been growing ever since." Adrian walks over to the trainset and moves a lever. The train begins its rounds. Gentry watches it as it chugs by a small town with storefronts, train crossing signals, and some old guy mowing his yard. The little people seem to be waving as the train goes by. Then it makes its ascent to the snow-capped mountain, through a dark tunnel, and over a steel trestle bridge that hovers above a small creek that meanders below. Trees line the rails until it reaches a ski resort with moving ski lift, lighted cabin with snowshoes out front, and the abominable snow-man.

Gentry laughs. "Very cool."

"Like that touch?"

"Yeah, definitely."

The train continues its route, whistling around the various bends and chugging through the neighborhoods as Gentry watches for a few minutes.

"You've got the ultimate man cave here."

"Anytime you want to stop by for a beer, just text me. If only I could find my—" Adrian spies his phone on the end table. "Great, there it is."

"Awesome. I'll take you up on that."

A shadow whips through the door in front of Gentry, startling Adrian. He takes slow breaths, trying to relieve the nervous twitches he feels soaring up his arms. He tries not to look into his peripheral vision, but his curiosity gets the best of him. The shadow of a child is standing in front of the train set. He can only see glimpses of it as the shadow moves in and out of his peripheral vision. Adrian closes his eyes for a couple of seconds, but when he opens them, he continues to see dark movements in the corner of his eye, almost as if it's taunting him, forcing him to see it.

Adrian wipes his brow with the back of his hand. "Wow, it's getting hot in here."

"Are you okay?"

"Yeah, unless I'm coming down with something."

Gentry moves toward the doorway of the safe room. "Well, just in case you are, I think I need more breathing space. Are you sure you're fine, though? You look flushed and your eyes seem to be redder." Gentry cringes once he sees Adrian's eyes.

"My eyes feel worse."

"Maybe it's your blood pressure."

"Maybe. Are you having an inside party? I wouldn't want to scare away your guests if I can't wear sunglasses," Adrian replies with a laugh.

"Have you thought about taking a vacation? Maybe getting away for a while?"

"I wish I could, but I just started a new job, and besides, I've gotta find Wyatt. That's my friend's kid."

Gentry heads out the front door. "I hope you find him."

"I will."

As soon as Gentry exits, Adrian's insides clench with the thought of what he'll find when he turns around. He avoids it by going to the hallway mirror to see the redness of his eyes. Bending forward to get a closer view, he confirms it's worse. The white areas from this morning are mostly gone.

Something moves in the corner of his eye, catching his attention. He concentrates on his peripheral vision and there, in the safe room doorway, he can see the shadow of a child. A chill runs through Adrian. His head feels full. He can hear the wasps building their nest outside the front door, scraping the outer edges of each cup as they huddle. He can hear the click of the tiniest movement from his watch. He can hear blood gushing into his ears. He can feel the trickle of a thick liquid forming on his tongue, then drooling out onto his chin. But despite it all, he can't turn away. He knows what he's about to see, but he still has to watch. Maybe there'll be another clue—something that will take him to Wyatt.

The shadow continues to stand still in Adrian's view. He can feel his eyes straining. His breathing grows more rapid, chest heaving as he tries to keep the shadow in focus. Tears start to fall—the kind that come when eyes are irritated. Slow-moving, full tears. He can hear them move through the pores on his face.

Then, just as fast as it came, the shadow disappears into the safe room. Adrian knows the scene that probably awaits him. He doesn't think he can face it. Not today. In desperation, Adrian closes his eyes, glad for the relief, but his lip is throbbing.

What the hell is going on?

He steps forward slowly at first. Then picking up speed, he runs for the safe room and swings the door shut, locking the shadow away.

CHAPTER

12

Lorelei drops her keys on the table inside the doorway when she arrives home. She notices droplets of blood dotting the floor and hurries across the ceramic tile toward the kitchen. To her right, she sees that the safe room door is open, something that's unusual. Adrian rarely has it unlocked, much less open. It's *his* room, so she doesn't really care, but it intrigues her.

"Adrian?"

He doesn't answer.

She peeks into the room and sees him sitting in the recliner with his eyes shut.

She whispers, "What are you doing?" She scans the room, seeing the sundry of emergency supplies to her left and the train set. She's seen it all before.

"I'm resting my eyes. Why are you whispering?"

"Because it feels like I should with it being so quiet in

here."

"It's exactly what I need right now. Peace."

Lorelei proceeds into the room and places her palm on Adrian's head. "Are you sick?"

Adrian sighs. "I wish."

"Why is there blood on the floor?"

"I don't know."

She gently presses her hand against his cheek and neck to check him for fever. "You don't have a temp. I see you've been cooking again. We're going to have to start a charity home here soon. We'll probably end up there, too, with all the money you're spending. What's up with you?"

"Just thought I'd help out the volunteers at Jeremy's. They're working long hours."

"I see," she replies, a twinge of guilt making her back off. "Well, you could have cleaned up your mess."

Adrian grins. "I know, I'm sorry. I'll get it. I just need to rest my eyes."

"Are they bad again?"

"Yeah."

"Let me see."

"No."

Lorelei moves closer to Adrian's face. "Oh, come on. I've seen worse, I'm sure. You've seen a vision again, haven't you? Your lip is a mess. God, Adrian, what is going on? I'm really getting worried about you."

"Me too," he replies. A tear sprouts from the outside corner of his closed eye and hangs there.

"Let me help you."

"Nah. I'll be fine. I figure if I keep them shut, it'll give them a rest."

"So, did you see a vision again?"

"Yes. This time a child shadow came and visited me."

Lorelei jerks back in surprise. "A shadow of a child? Yikes, that sounds creepy, actually."

"It reminded me of Wyatt—about the same height, thin, bike helmet. I couldn't see any facial features though. Just the silhouette."

Lorelei bends toward Adrian again and puts her head on his shoulder. "Aw, Adrian. I'm so sorry this is happening to you. I think this whole thing is conjuring up some old memories of your brother and manifesting itself as these visions."

"This has nothing to do with Jonathan," Adrian states. "I came to terms with that many years ago. I've told you." Adrian's muscles tense against Lorelei's face.

"I think you need to go to a therapist."

Adrian's body jerks slightly. "I don't need a therapist. I just need these fucking shadows to go away."

"Well, maybe that'd be the only way to get that done."

Adrian sighs. "They are floaters, remember?"

"They're not floaters. You weren't having visions back then, just shadows. Go back to the doctor. I'm sure he'll change his mind," Lorelei says, her voice becoming tense.

"Whatever. I agree that the doctor got the diagnosis wrong and these are probably not floaters. They're visions of some sort. You're never going to believe that I might have some kind of gift, will you? I mean, I'm seeing the crime scene. I was out there again sampling in the wetlands and it happened, right there on the trail. Wyatt and his assailant. Both of them visible behind a police officer's back. He had no clue. How in the hell is he going to solve this case?"

Lorelei lifts her head toward Adrian. "Would you look at me already?"

Adrian shakes his head. "I'm trying to tell you, Lorelei, that I am seeing what happened. And every time I do, I see Jeremy."

Lorelei jumps up and scoffs.

"I see his face, his scar. It's him," Adrian continues.

"Yeah? And what else?"

"The bike path, the trees, the water. I smell the muck."

"This is ridiculous. I hope you haven't told the police about this."

"Not totally. Just that I've been having visions because it happened right in front of them. Even Clark noticed something happening to me. I almost fell over."

"Open your eyes. I want to see them."

"Why? So you can look at me with disgust? Pity?"

"Adrian, I love you. I want to help you. You know that. Just let me."

"I don't need help. I just need to tap into this more. Just a little more and I'll have all the information the police need. I just have to rest my eyes a bit before I try again."

Lorelei cocks her head. "You've been trying to see visions all day?"

"Not all day. Just some of it. I've almost got this solved. You'll see that I'm right."

Lorelei squats next to Adrian and takes his hand. "Let me see. Please, Adrian."

Adrian's eyes flutter slightly.

Lorelei moves in closer. "Please?"

Adrian sighs and gently squeezes Lorelei's hand. "I love you," he says.

"I love you, too. Now, open them."

Adrian turns toward Lorelei and opens his eyes. Eyes filled with dark red blood peer back at her. Dilated pupils pierce through her. The white sclera that was once there has vanished.

Lorelei gasps. Her eyes fill with tears. "Oh, Adrian. We've got to get you to the doctor. Please, let's go now."

"It's late. There won't be anyone open on Saturday anyway."

"I'm talking about an emergency room. Seriously, Adrian. You need to go. I'll drive."

Lorelei stands and tugs at Adrian's arm, but he doesn't budge.

"It'll go away on its own."

"I bet you can't even see."

"I can see. Just forget it for now. I can tackle it on Monday if it's not better. Besides, I want to get over to Jeremy's. I'm hoping the police are still going to continue with the search parties, but the interest seems to be dwindling, even from the neighbors."

Lorelei wraps her fingers through Adrian's and kisses the top of his hand. "Stop worrying about other people. You seriously need to worry about yourself right now. I love you for wanting Wyatt to be safe, but what good will it do if you're in the hospital—or worse? This could be your blood pressure. What if you went blind?"

"Oh, come on, Lorelei. Stop being so dramatic. My blood pressure is fine. Yeah, I'm stressed a little from this whole Wyatt thing, but this is a kid I've known a long time. Of course I'm stressed."

"I know, but you probably need some medication to keep it under control. You probably don't even know your blood pressure is rising."

Adrian pushes the recliner forward and drops Lorelei's hand. "I've got to get ready."

"At least let me drive you. I don't mind. We haven't seen each other much lately."

Adrian concedes and makes his way into the family room and toward the bedroom, holding onto the walls. "This is just temporary. I'll be better when I come back out. Just takes me a minute or two."

Lorelei waits for Adrian at the counter. Noticing the blood on the floor again, she gets up, wets a paper towel under the faucet, and grabs the Lysol.

When Adrian comes out of the bedroom, he finds her on her hands and knees, scrubbing the floor. "Shit, I forgot about that. Probably from my lip earlier." He squats to help her.

She doesn't respond to him or look at him.

"Lorelei?"

"I can't. I just can't." Tears start flowing down her cheeks. "I can't even look at you. I'm so sorry."

Adrian pauses, then cleans up the rest of the floor. "No, I get it. They're gross. I wouldn't want to either."

Lorelei leans her head on his shoulder, wrapping her arms around his waist.

"You still love me anyway?"

"Of course, Adrian. Always and forever. I'm just worried."

"It'll be fine. I promise. Let's get over to Jeremy's."

The drive to Jeremy's is silent with Adrian primarily staring out of the window. His eyes are not sore, surprisingly. Several police cars are parked along the grass in front of Jeremy's as usual. Adrian and Lorelei walk up the driveway. Adrian notices the garage doors are still shut and Jeremy's truck is not there, so he guides Lorelei to the bike trail, wearing his sunglasses. "I'll show you where it happened," he whispers.

The sun has started its descent as it peeks through the branches, casting a yellowish glow to the interior of the woods. Up ahead, it makes the path look almost foggy. "It's right up there," Adrian says. They continue on foot until they see the police officers huddled around something on the ground. "Maybe they found something. That's the exact location. I know it."

"Adrian…" Lorelei says.

"Okay, don't believe me."

"It's Adrian, right?" Officer Mortensen asks. "I met you earlier today?"

"Yeah, with my coworker."

"You're the one with the visions?"

"Yeah."

Lorelei glares at Adrian.

"Well, I gotta admit. We need all the help we can get."

The other officers glance at each other.

"Come on, Vic. Are you kidding me?" one of them says.

"Just humor me. What will it hurt?" Mortensen says to them, then turns to Adrian. "So, check this out. It might be a piece of the reflector from the bike."

One of the police officers throws his hands up in the air and walks away.

Detective Mortensen places the reflector in Adrian's extended palm. Adrian rubs it around in his hand.

"Getting anything?"

"No," Adrian replies.

"Well, we're honestly puzzled by this whole thing. We've searched along the coastline, digging in the sand every so many feet to see if he's buried, but there's nothing. Then we tried digging every few feet up from the bank in areas that were sampled. Nothing. Scuba divers have searched the water and there's nothing. The rain seems to have washed some of the evidence away. The only thing we're going on right now are the remnants of blood on the path, bike marks on the trail, and boot imprints going down to the water. And who knows how long they've been there. Guess we'll have to wait for the DNA results."

"Let me see if I can help." Adrian rushes to the shoreline and studies the open space beyond the trees. The floor of the wetland is completely saturated, so there's no way to say for sure whether Wyatt is at the bottom of it, but Adrian's senses are telling him he's not. The wind kicks up over the water, causing a series of ripples and waves toward Adrian. He can smell the years of rotting leaves and soggy cypress heads that were witness to this crime. They know. But they can't tell. Maybe Adrian can't either.

He scrambles up the embankment, all eyes on him. He suddenly pauses about ten feet from the path. The shadow of the child is back. This time, it's sitting on the ground. Adrian leans forward, unable to move his arms that are now, for some unknown reason, being held back by a police officer. The second shadow proceeds slowly down the path until it's standing over the child. Once again, it squats and turns it's back to Adrian.

Adrian tries to pull away from the police, but their grip is too strong with two of them now holding him back. He can hear Lorelei screaming for him to stop in the background, somewhere behind the sounds of scraping boots along the path and a hoot owl from behind. Adrian glances back at the officer, giving his arms some slack and as soon as they think he's given up, Adrian jerks lose and runs for the shadows. He sees the broad shoulders of a man, arms working at something. Everything slows down, even the songs from the birds that are now drawn-out vowels that make no sense. The man turns his head to the right, then proceeds to turn to the left. Adrian can now see Wyatt's face. It's being taped. Jeremy is taping Wyatt's face.

"You fucking bastard!" Adrian screams, unable to move anymore from the police officers' grasps. He can feel handcuffs wrapping around his hands, the sharp sting of metal cutting into his wrists. The taste of blood has Adrian gagging. "I can see him," he chants, over and over. Adrian feels like he's now mangled between two different senses of reality, no longer sure which he wants to be in. "I need to save him. I have to save him. You don't understand!"

Officer Mortensen grabs Adrian by the shoulder. "Listen to me! You get yourself together or I'm taking you in. Understand? You cannot pull away from the officers."

"But I just saw Wyatt! He's there, right there. Right near your feet. Can't you see him? Can't you fucking see him?" Tears are flowing from Adrian's red eyes as his lip drips with blood.

"No, Adrian. There's no Wyatt." Officer Mortensen backs away from the bike trail.

"Yes, there is! Right there! He's bound with tape. Who does that to a child? Please tell me!" Adrian desperately stares at the police officers surrounding him for answers.

The bewildered officers push Adrian down to his knees to gain better control. The gushing sound of blood pushing up his veins toward his eyes torments Adrian as his senses kick in even further.

"Holy shit! Your eyes are completely black now," one of the officers remarks, squinting.

Wyatt is turned onto his back and rope is wrapped

around his hands. Adrian is completely hysterical. "Please, please, let me go. I need to save Wyatt!"

"What's happening now?" Officer Mortensen asks.

"His hands. His hands are being tied," Adrian sobs. "Now his legs."

"What the hell, Vic?" asks one of the officers. "This guy is a psycho."

"No, wait," says Officer Mortensen. "Let him finish. I want to hear this."

Adrian pulls at the officer's grasp but goes nowhere. "Please. Maybe if I stop the scene, I can break the cycle. Maybe he'll come back."

"No," says Officer Mortensen. "I'm thinking you keep watching and *we* find Wyatt."

Adrian sees Wyatt completely immobilized, twisting his head back and forth, trying to get loose. His eyes and mouth are taped and Adrian can hear the desperate cries from a nine-year-old about to be killed or kidnapped or whatever else, he doesn't know. All he knows is he can no longer watch. So, he closes his eyes, and the scene stops. Adrian drops forward, exhausted from the ordeal, and Lorelei runs to his side.

"Damn it!" yells Detective Mortensen. "Why would you do that? Are you trying to hide the fact you were there?"

Lorelei guffaws. "You think that he's seeing the crime scene?"

"Makes sense doesn't it? Bike tire marks were found here. Adrian must be tapping into something."

"I don't think so," she replies, shaking her head. "Lots of people ride their bikes through here every day."

The police officers that are listening begin laughing.

"There's no way this guy is seeing anything. He's—" one of the officers starts to say.

Adrian's chest is heaving, and blood is now dripping from his eyes. "He needs to go to a hospital. Look at what you did to him!" Lorelei yells.

She pulls out her cell phone and calls 911.

"I can't see, Lorelei. I can't see."

Lorelei cries, her hands trembling as she pulls back his hair. "It'll be okay. I'm getting you help."

"I couldn't save Jonathan either. I tried. I really did. He was strapped into the seat. I couldn't hold on anymore. I failed him, too!"

"Neither of these situations were your fault, Adrian. Believe in that. You're a good soul."

"No, I'm not."

CHAPTER

13

How are you feeling?"

Adrian doesn't answer.

"I know you're awake."

"Mind reader, huh?"

"No, I can just tell. I kind of know you."

"One of the few, Lorelei."

"Can you sit up?"

"Yeah."

Adrian pulls himself up on the bed, and Lorelei props pillows behind his back. Then she removes the night mask from his head. Adrian keeps his eyes closed. "Am I blind?"

"No. The doctors treated you and sent you home, remember? Now, you're on blood pressure meds."

"Oh, yeah. Now I remember."

"Can you see?"

Adrian opens his eyes. He sees distorted colors, some

shifting.

"Not really. I'd have never recognized this as our bedroom."

"Well, the doctors said your sight will be fine soon and that you need to rest. Can you do that?"

"You know I'm not good at that."

"Well, you'll have to if you want to see again. So, lie back and I'll put the eye guard on. A day of rest will probably do you good, and I'm not going anywhere so I can make sure you do. Just relax. I've got it all under control." Lorelei caresses his arm.

Adrian sighs and says, "Fine, boss," with a grin. He soon grows quiet when he thinks of how he was so close to seeing what truly happened to Wyatt. The disappointment shows as he furrows his eyebrows.

"Just relax, Adrian. I can tell by your face that you're thinking too much again."

"I'm so disappointed. I should have continued watching the scene."

"Adrian, you were bleeding from your eyes. No way should you have continued watching."

"I guess."

"Rest." Lorelei gently rubs his arm and exits into the hallway.

A few hours later, Adrian wakes up and glances at the alarm clock to check if he can read.

Shit, it's already three in the afternoon.

He looks around the bedroom, and it's much more vivid than he saw earlier.

My eyesight is back. Thank God.

He doesn't see Lorelei, so he slowly pulls himself out of the bed and uses the toilet.

Lorelei flies in as soon as she hears it flush.

"You're up. Can you see?"

Adrian yawns and says, "Yes."

"Oh, thank you, God!" she replies. "Let me see your eyes."

Adrian opens them slightly. His eyes are more pink than red now.

"Maybe you should lie back down. I'll help you."

"Come on, Lorelei. Quit. I need to get some things done."

"Oh, no, you don't." Lorelei pulls him toward the side of the bed. "Sit. I'll get you some water and then it's back to bed."

"But—"

Lorelei pushes on his shoulders and Adrian sits. "I don't want to hear it. Your eyes are much better. They need more rest and so do you. Lie down."

Adrian slides into the sheets. He really doesn't mind all the fuss, but he feels compelled to get back to the woods. It's such a strong urge because he feels like he might miss the opportunity to find Wyatt if he waits too long to get back there. He regrets closing his eyes on the bike trail, but he didn't want to see the rest of the story in front of everyone. What if he saw Jeremy do something horrible and told the police when his visions were all wrong? He's got to be sure of what he's seeing first. It'll have to make sense.

Adrian pulls out a journal from a pouch hanging from the side of his mattress and begins taking notes on all of the events over the past week. He starts with his new job, finding out about Wyatt that night, sampling, and the approximate time he saw all the shadows. If he remembers right, the shadows started on Monday morning when he was sitting in the reception room at work. The disappearance happened the night before. Could it be that Wyatt has been trying to reach him?

Adrian writes page after page of all the incidences that occurred for the week. There's definitely been a progression. The faint movements in the corner of his eye have now turned into full, life-sized scenes and every time they occur, his senses go wild. It all seems to sync, but he can't figure out why he keeps biting his lip.

He pauses.

It'll be one week tonight.

Curiosity turns to sadness when he thinks about it.

I was supposed to find him. I need to go back to the woods and watch it unfold. He'll just have to hope his eyes don't explode.

Lorelei returns with ice water and a turkey sandwich. "I figured you'd have to be hungry by now."

Adrian smiles at her. "I am. Thanks for taking care of me. I'm sorry I've been freaking you out."

"Well, you stay in bed, and it'll make up for it."

He rolls his eyes and tugs at the sandwich.

"Just eat, and we can talk about it later."

"You're pretty bossy, young lady."

Lorelei smiles and kisses him on the cheek.

"That's my job. Remember that." Lorelei walks toward the bedroom door. "I'm right out here if you need me. I'm reading up on some really informative wetland studies. If you're feeling up to it, I could come in here and read them to you. I know how much you'd love that. It'll help you with your new job."

Adrian pretends to gag on his sandwich. "Yeah, sure. Maybe a little later."

Lorelei laughs. "Uh, huh."

Adrian finishes his lunch, peeking down the hallway occasionally to see if Lorelei is returning. There's no sign of her, so he gets up and quickly pulls on a pair of jeans and a t-shirt, then his jacket. He doesn't particularly want to wear his flip flops in the woods, but oh, well, nothing else is around. He slips them on and bolts out the side door. Once he reaches the truck, he opens the door and hops in.

Now what? She'll follow me as soon as she hears the truck. Maybe I can push it down the street and start it.

He opens the door and sees Lorelei marching toward him from the garage.

"Again? Seriously?" Lorelei's eyes are welling up, but her tone means business. "What, you were going to sneak out on me again?"

Adrian knows the best option is to stay quiet right now.

"Answer me!"

"I...I...I'm sorry."

Lorelei turns to head back toward the house, but Adrian gently grabs her arm. "I'm an idiot, I know, but I can't stay in that bed when I could be in the woods watching the scene right before my eyes and hopefully find Wyatt. I feel like the next time I'm there, I'm going to solve this thing once and for all. Then we can get back to our lives again."

Lorelei listens but doesn't respond.

"Look, I know I'm a jerk sometimes. I need my space. I need my alone time. I don't let you in. I can work on that stuff. But right now, I've gotta get over there. I can solve this...crime...or whatever it is. The scene is going to take me to Wyatt. I'm sure of it."

"But your eyes. Your blood pressure. You need to stay

away from stress."

"Lorelei, time is of the essence here. If my eyes go crazy again, I'll just go back to the emergency room. I'll be fine."

Lorelei frowns. "Or maybe you can just let the police do their jobs. They'll figure it out. Go rest and I'll head out to the grocery store. Soon you'll be waking up to the awesome smell of dinner. You know how good I am at it," Lorelei says with a grin.

"Oh, great. Frozen dinners, then?"

Lorelei slaps him on the arm. "No. You need to have more faith in me. I'm learning this cooking thing."

"Maybe take-out would be better?"

"Adrian!" exclaims Lorelei as she slaps his arm again.

He laughs. "Okay, okay, quit hitting me. I was just kidding."

"Uh, huh. Well, I'm going to prove you wrong."

"You do that," Adrian replies.

Lorelei grabs Adrian's hand. "Please, come inside and rest. You can go back there tomorrow. Just give yourself a day."

Adrian contemplates Lorelei's suggestion for a minute, then reluctantly slides out of the truck and follows her to the house.

Once inside, he removes his jacket and walks to the refrigerator. On the way, he notices the safe room door is open, but no shadows are lurking around in the doorway.

I don't know if I'm happy or sad about that.

He opens his favorite Samichlaus and heads toward the bedroom, slowing down when he notices the open door to the safe room again.

He pauses.

Guess I should lock that.

It's pitch black inside the room. Just for grins, Adrian turns on the light and waits a minute.

No shadows today.

Adrian moves over to the train set. He pushes the lever to "on" and backs up to watch the train make its way around the track. He thinks about how there's something mesmerizing about watching a model train, almost as if one becomes hypnotized by it. Adrian has always found it to be relaxing. He finds his recliner and sits for a while, sipping his beer.

Adrian thinks about how the train should not make him relax. He shouldn't want to be reminded of the accident. That terrible day. He didn't want to go anyway. As a child, his parents would take him on long train rides every year through the Rockies. He hated going—not that he didn't like spending time with his family. They were everything to him. He hated trains. He often wished his parents would just take them to a lodge instead, but they always insisted that their children needed to see the world. Well, a lot of good that did. Adrian has no desire to travel anywhere, much less see the world.

He pulls open the drawer in the side table and feels around until his hand falls upon the top of a box. He slides it forward, carefully grabs it from the drawer, and places it on his lap. Adrian takes another swig from the beer bottle and places it on the table. He holds the box for a while, then opens the lid. Adrian carefully unfolds the tissue paper to reveal its contents as he stands and strolls back to the train set. One by one, Adrian adds them near the tracks, the figurines resembling his family members. He can hardly contain his tears when he gets to Jonathan. His arm twinges in pain as he sets him alongside the others.

Good to see you all together again.

The clank of the front door opening snaps him out of his reminiscing, startling him. He hears Lorelei barrel in toward the kitchen and the rustling of bags. Adrian jerks toward the figures, knocking them over as he tries to wrap them back in the tissue paper. He quickly places them into the box and meanders over to the side table to push them back into the drawer.

"Hey, you're up?" Lorelei has caught him pushing the drawer shut.

He nervously wipes his hands on his pant legs. "Yeah, couldn't sleep, so I came in here to relax."

Lorelei frowns. "You weren't waiting for shadows, were you?"

"No. I had a beer and put the train on."

"Uh, huh."

Adrian notices that he missed removing a figurine on the train set tabletop. His heart rate increases.

"What?" she says.

"Nothing, why?"

"You look nervous all of a sudden. Are you seeing something?"

"No, no." Adrian rushes over to the train set and turns it off. He brushes by Lorelei, knowing she'll follow him out of the room. He locks the door behind her as she leaves. "So, what's the gourmet chef making for dinner?"

"Ha, ha. Very funny. Lasagna."

"Sounds great. When will it be ready? I need to take a walk."

"Oh, come on, Adrian. The last thing you need is a walk. Just sit and relax for a while."

"I think I'd feel better with some fresh air. I'll just go

around the development and come back."

Lorelei stares at Adrian for a few seconds, then turns around to get out the cutting board. "Fine."

"I'll be back."

CHAPTER

14

The offices are dark when Adrian arrives on Monday morning. He's curious if they took more samples along the shoreline yesterday, so he's eager to hear if there's been any news. Because he's seeing Jeremy in his visions, he's more hopeful that Wyatt is still alive. But what would Jeremy be so upset about that would make him tie up Wyatt like that in the middle of the woods? Was Wyatt doing something he wasn't supposed to be doing? It doesn't make sense, really. It's been a week since he found out that Wyatt disappeared. A week. Already. Wherever he is, he's probably lonely, perhaps cold. Unless…Jeremy took him somewhere a few days after the disappearance. But how would he get away with that with the place swarming with cops?

Adrian sits back in his chair.

"So, you beat me to work again," Clark says, post-hole

digger in hand. "You just love to torture yourself, don't you?"

"I guess. Did you sample more yesterday? Any results back?"

"Didn't I mention that you're off this project? You're leaving me no choice but to tell the owners."

"Come on, Clark. You know I can't do that. It would drive me nuts. Just a little information?"

Clark shifts his weight. "Well, I did get a fax this morning with a request to take a few more samples." Clark frowns, straining his eyes to see the fax sheet. "Could they write any smaller?" He pulls the map out a little farther to read it but gets frustrated. "Guess I gotta go get my damn readers."

"You only have five hundred pairs of them. You'd think they wouldn't get lost," Fossie announces from around the corner.

"That's because you keep stealing them from me," Clark calls back. He winks at Adrian and laughs.

Adrian grins. "She's going to kick your ass one of these days," he whispers.

"Hi, Adrian," she says as she trudges down the hallway. "I can hear you both, you know. I'll be right back. I want to hear the latest. Oh, and you're right, Adrian. But I find that nagging him to death is more effective."

"I still can't believe that neither one of you told me you were married. Where's your ring?" Adrian asks Clark.

"I can't wear one of those in the field. It'll get lost or smashed. I'd lose a finger." Clark leans in closer, glancing behind him a few times. "Don't bring it up to her. It's a sore spot."

"Got it."

"Now, quit changing the subject. You're off this project. That's final."

"Off what project? Not the police case, I hope," Fossie says.

Clark rolls his eyes. "It's not your concern."

"Yes, it is. Adrian has already shared his visions with me," Fossie says as she pushes past Clark. "Speaking of which, your eyes look a little better today. Lip too."

"Don't let him fool you," Clark replies. "I heard they took him away by ambulance when he went out there with Lorelei yesterday. His visions got the best of him."

"How did you hear that?" Adrian asks.

"Oh, I have my connections," Clark replies.

"I saw Wyatt on that path. I'd know his face anywhere." Adrian says, standing his ground with Clark. "Just because everyone else couldn't see it, doesn't mean I didn't."

"You'd know Wyatt's face anywhere? How's that? Do you know him?" Clark asks with a stern expression.

Shit.

"You *know* who the police are searching for?" Fossie asks. She glares at Adrian, letting him know to go along with her.

Adrian slumps in his chair, pissed at himself for giving this information away. "Yes. He's my friend's son. Jeremy is my friend."

Clark moves closer to Adrian's desk. "You mean the guy the police says has disappeared? The one at the house?"

"Yes. I've known him a long time. I didn't want to tell you because I knew you'd pull me off the sampling."

"Are you trying to get me fired?" Clark paces. "If the police or owners find out about this, I could lose my job and the samples could be viewed as compromised."

"The police already know. I've been helping with the search parties."

Clark throws his hands up and down. "Unbelievable."

"Wow, that's incredible. So, you saw Wyatt's face?" Fossie asks.

Adrian relaxes and says, "Yes. I saw the silhouette of a child crawling along the path. Then I saw the shadow of a man walk down the path behind him and squat over him."

Fossie covers her mouth with her hand.

"You remember when I told you my visions were always of a broad-shouldered man from behind?"

Fossie nods.

"Well, that's what I was seeing. I just didn't know it. I couldn't figure out what the man was doing, but now I know." Adrian's expression grows solemn. "He was tying up Wyatt, binding his eyes, mouth, hands, and legs."

"Oh, my God," Fossie says, looking as if she can't take any more of the story.

"Wyatt was trying to scream, but it was only in small grunts. No one could hear him, except maybe a hoot owl that lives nearby." Adrian pauses, his eyes dilating. "And once again, I saw the side of the man's face. The scar. It was Jeremy's. I was there when he cut himself when we were young. It was an accident. He was whipping around the machete after his mom told him to be careful. He didn't listen and he almost cut off his face. It sliced him right up through his jaw. I'll never forget it. Blood gushed everywhere. On his shirt. Into his hair. Down his neck. The flap of tissue was hanging outward along his jawline."

Fossie frowns and purses her lips in disgust.

"When I got to him, there was so much blood, he about passed out. I saw his back molars and about lost my lunch.

Needless to say, they stitched him up with what looked like a thousand stitches, and it took him a long time to recover. He laid in bed for a few weeks at first, then watched us play outside from his bedroom window. We were neighbors. I tried to get him to come outside, but his mom was too afraid of something happening to him during the healing process and…" Adrian looks up at Fossie and Clark, both hanging on every word. "Well, anyway, I'd know that scar anywhere. It was Jeremy. No doubt in my mind."

"So, did you tell the police this time?" asked Fossie.

"No."

Fossie scoffs. "Are you kidding me? You could be helping them with the case."

"Fossie, this isn't *Murder She Wrote*. This is real life. You expect him to hang his friend out to dry over some freaky visions he *thinks* he's having?" Clark says.

"I *am* having," Adrian corrects.

"Right. Well, either way, you don't go and tell the police about something that might be wrong about your best friend."

"Have the police sampled for Jeremy's DNA?" asks Fossie, trying to make a point.

"I don't think so, but…" Clark says.

"Maybe you should suggest they do that, Adrian," she continues.

"I don't want to hear any more of this insanity. You guys are both wrong about this," Clark says.

"Wrong, my ass," Fossie replies. "This young man is tapping into some kind of sixth sense. He's sensitive."

"Adrian, come with me." Clark brushes by with Adrian in tow. "We're leaving."

Clark escorts Adrian downstairs and to the parking lot.

They climb into the work van. Clark says, "I'm letting you go with me only because I don't want Fossie filling your mind with more of her mumbo-jumbo talk about seeing things. Now, I'm not saying you're not seeing things. I'm just saying that you should be cautious before you go naming someone who might be innocent. Keep it to yourself, because if you're wrong, how would you feel if Jeremy was convicted? Think about it." Clark glances over to Adrian. "Oh, and let's keep this quiet from the owners. This is probably the last sampling event anyway."

Adrian shakes his head. "I'm hearing you, but he's guilty. I'm not going to say anything just yet though. I want to see where he took Wyatt first—"

"What?"

"The visions. I haven't had any since Saturday. No shadows. No Jeremy. No nothing. Everything is normal right now. I can't believe I want them to come back."

"Don't you remember what happened last time? You're probably better off if they never come back. The police will find Wyatt."

"Why are we going there anyway?"

"They approved more sampling along the bank of the wetland farther down the path and more from the water. Unfortunately, it'll take a while for the DNA samples to come back. I think they're using the organics analyses to see where they want more samples. Not sure. But I already have the containers and paperwork ready, so this shouldn't take too long."

Clark does a double take at Adrian. "Your eyes do look much better today, Adrian. Maybe that has something to do with your visions disappearing. Didn't you mention floaters?"

"Yeah, but that was a separate problem from the broken blood vessels. He said the redness was due to stress."

"Well, you must be healing up with all the good care Lorelei is giving you."

Adrian grins. "Yeah, must be. She made me lasagna last night."

"You're a lucky man, Adrian."

"I just wish she'd knock off the whole marriage pressure thing."

"Ah. She wants a commitment, huh? Something in writing."

"She wants a ring, kids, you know, the whole shebang."

"You don't?"

"Something about it makes me tense, especially the vows. You know, 'til death do us part.' I don't like to think that way."

Clark frowns. "Most people don't even think about it. It just means that you'll stay with each other until the end. Besides, you could write your own vows."

"I don't know. If something happens, I don't think I could take the pain."

"So, you're happy to just live on the outskirts of it without a true commitment from her? Wouldn't that hurt too?"

"No, because she'd stay a pseudo family."

Clark pulls the van up to the garage at Jeremy's house and puts it in park.

"I think it would hurt more than you know."

"It would be worse if she were my wife."

"But you can't live your life like that—waiting for death. You've got a lot of life to live first." Clark looks over to Adrian but he continues to stare out the window. "Ah, well. Look at me acting like I'm your father here. You'll make whatever decision is right for you, I'm sure. Let's go sampling."

Clark and Adrian make their way down to the crime scene and set up the sample locations, aligning them in transects from the path as directed by the forensic investigators. It'll take the bulk of the morning to collect and prepare the samples. The sun is out, warming the cool air. The wind has died down compared to the previous weekend. Adrian is sitting on the ground, preparing the containers with his back to the path. He's a bit apprehensive about falling apart in front of Officer Mortensen again, who's standing behind him.

"No shadows today, Adrian?" the officer asks.

"Not yet, anyway. I'm hoping they'll show up at some point, but there's so much work to do, I can't stand around looking for them."

"I wanted to show you something we found in the woods, just about where you're sitting. See that stake behind you?"

Adrian peeks behind him then turns toward the detective. "Yeah."

"We found a piece of duct tape there."

Clark stops sampling and listens to the conversation, appearing concerned for Adrian.

"Just a small piece, but we're sending it over for a DNA check."

A cold chill climbs up Adrian's back and into his shoulders. His heart jumps. He shakes his head and says, "Well, that makes sense then. Maybe a piece blew away when Wyatt was being...bound."

"We're hoping so. It didn't look weathered. Not much was stuck to it." The officer walks up to the path and stands about twenty feet away from the place where Adrian saw the scene unfold on Saturday. "Perhaps the scene was closer to here."

"Or maybe the tape blew away this far."

"True."

"I saw the scene over there on Saturday," Adrian says, pointing up the path more.

"Are you sure it was there?"

"Yeah. Besides, you found bike tracks near there, right?"

"Yes, but just like the tape, hair and other items can blow around too. And it's rained a lot."

Adrian lowers his eyes. "I guess."

"Well, let me know if you see anything. Keep the visions going as long as possible so you can see where Wyatt was taken. I'd like this to be solved today. Wouldn't that be a good news story if we could bring him home?"

"I'll try."

"I'm sure you will. No pressure," Officer Mortensen says. He leaves to talk with another officer.

Clark plods up to Adrian and says, "No pressure, my ass. Just keep sampling. My vote is for no shadows today."

Adrian and Clark dig up topsoil samples and transfer them into labeled containers for several hours.

"Well, this is taking longer than I thought. Let's take a break for lunch," Clark says.

"I will in a few," Adrian replies. He's already decided that during his lunch he would wait until no one was watching and walk along the water's edge to see if any shadows appear—not to force it but to see if they come on their own. "How do my eyes look?"

"Good, actually. I'm surprised, being they were so bad

on Saturday."

"Yeah," Adrian replies. "I'll be back in a few minutes."

"Adrian…" Clark says in a lower tone. "Don't get us fired here."

"Don't worry."

Clark shakes his head in disagreement, but Adrian rushes off too fast for him to respond.

Adrian slips out of view once he has an opportunity. He doesn't want to compromise the investigation, so he stays away from the marked sampling areas. He jumps when a branch slaps him in the arm as he passes through the thick brush alongside the water. He laughs at his nerves under his breath and continues along the trail. No one is around — finally, some alone time. Adrian comes up to some dense bushes and is forced up to the path. It was that or the water and no way is he traipsing through the gator-infested shore-line. Little stones kick up from his feet as he walks, making a crunching sound. He admires the incredible view. Mossy trees, thick green vegetation and glimmering ripples on the water paint a beautiful portrait before him. He snaps a shot with his phone and views it as he's walking.

He should have watched where he was going.

A tree root catches his foot. He jerks forward and slides on the loose dirt. He extends an arm to the ground and saves himself before he falls. As he brushes himself off, he can hear the sound of metal in the distance — a clanking noise coming closer from down the path. Adrian stops to listen, not wanting the crunching sound from his boots to interfere.

He waits.

He can hear himself breathing and his rapid heart rate pulsing through his neck veins. He can hear the plop from a droplet that hits a leaf along the path. He can hear a bike chain. He sees a boy. He's not paying any attention and pumping the pedals hard. Could it be?

Adrian squints for a better view. As the bike comes closer, Adrian becomes elated. It looks like Wyatt!

It *is* Wyatt!

Adrian extends an arm to wave him down, barely able to contain the excitement of finding him. Finally, Wyatt is home.

But the boy doesn't stop. He speeds by on his blue bike as if he never saw Adrian.

Adrian takes off down the path, calling after him, but the boy keeps going.

Maybe it wasn't Wyatt?

Adrian runs faster to try to catch up to Wyatt, watching him. The last thing he wants to do is let Wyatt out of his sight.

But a movement catches his eye from the woods. A blackness, almost like a moving blob. Then the silhouette of a man jets out of the woods and toward the path.

Adrian frowns.

This scene is similar to my visions.

The boy falls, his bike flipping over and landing near him. Adrian searches for Clark near the water, but Clark has no idea this is going on.

Shit, I've gotta catch up.

Adrian sprints toward Wyatt but then decides he needs to go down near the water since he doesn't want Jeremy to see him. That is, if he can. Adrian catches Clark's eye as he gets closer, but Adrian puts his finger to his mouth and points to the path.

Clark peers in the direction Adrian is pointing but

shakes his head, confused. "Adrian, come on. Maybe we should go," Clark says.

"Shh. They're here," he whispers.

Adrian sneaks up to the path. It's dark, and he can see the bike lying on its side with the light on. Jeremy moves closer to Wyatt, his boots making a crunching sound along the path. He stops between Wyatt and the bike. Wyatt is hurt but manages to sit up. He hears Wyatt call out, "Dad?"

Then Jeremy straddles Wyatt and starts taping him up. Adrian creeps up silently toward Jeremy's back. Once again, Jeremy turns his head to the right and then the left, revealing the same scar. Jeremy's scar. Adrian is still afraid Jeremy will see him so he stays back. Jeremy then ties a rope around Wyatt's wrists. It's so hard for him to watch. He's not sure he can emotionally handle it. But he knows he must. He has to see what happens next.

Jeremy tugs at the rope, as if he's testing its strength.

Adrian can see Wyatt's sneakers, red and scuffed. His small arms are behind his back. His little fingers are clenching onto the rope.

What the hell is he going to do to him? Will it help if I stop the scene? Will it stop him? I can't watch this!

Adrian begins panting as Jeremy lifts Wyatt over his shoulder. He sees Jeremy pick up the bike and plant it on its wheels. Then he sees him trudge toward the shoreline with Wyatt.

"No!" Adrian yells out loud. "No! No! No! Make him stop! I can't watch. I can't!" He falls to the ground, barely able to catch his breath and closes his eyes.

The vision disappears.

"I'm so sorry, Wyatt. I'm so sorry," he says, ashamed. Clark is now by his side with his hand on Adrian's shoulder. "I'm nothing but a coward! I just can't do this," he says to Clark desperately.

Officer Mortensen and his fellow officers are watching from down the path.

Clark yells, "Your eyes!"

CHAPTER

15

The clanking coming from the kitchen is unmistakable. Adrian can tell Lorelei is pissed and she's making it well known. Adrian throws a pillow over his head, but it does little good to block out the racket. He tries to get more comfortable, rolling around in different positions, but his back is aching and his neck is sore. He gives up and opens his eyes.

Oh, yeah, I'm in the safe room.

He sees that the door is ajar, light streaming in from the family room.

Lorelei must have been in here already.

Adrian stretches his back and rotates his neck to loosen up. The recliner was nothing more than a torture chamber on the bones during the night. He sees Lorelei squatting in front of a lower cabinet in the kitchen. She throws a pot onto the floor behind her. Adrian jerks and puts his back out more.

"Lorelei! Quit! I get it already."

She responds with another pot, this time he can hear it slide across the floor and hit another one.

Suddenly, he remembers the day before. *God knows what my eyes look like. I gotta find out.*

Adrian jumps out of the recliner, opens the door, and sprints to the bathroom, eyes half shut.

He flicks on the light, and after adjusting to it, he peers in closely. The thick, dark red areas have returned.

He sighs.

Lorelei is going to kill me.

Adrian takes a deep breath and meanders to the kitchen. He might as well face the wrath now before it festers. He slides into a stool and covers his eyes with his hands. "Good morning, Lorelei."

The rattling stops. Lorelei moans as she pulls herself up. "Oh, so you grace me with your presence now? That was another shit move last night, Adrian."

"I don't know what the hell you're talking about."

"You, disappearing again. I waited up for you until I finally gave up and went to bed. You don't answer your phone or texts. And apparently, I'm not good enough to sleep with now, because I find you all hunched over in a recliner."

"My back and neck are killing me," Adrian replies with a moan.

"Good. I'm glad. Why are you disappearing at night?"

"What do you mean? I'm not disappearing. I'm right here."

"Where have you been going?"

"Same place as always. I go to Jeremy's to find Wyatt.

Is there a crime in that?"

"So, you were out late because you were searching the woods again?"

"Yeah. We finished sampling, headed back to the office to drop off the samples, and then I drove back to Jeremy's. The crowds of neighbors and friends willing to help are dwindling. I can't just leave Wyatt out there without someone searching for him."

Lorelei places raw bacon strips in a pan. She adds pepper and turns the burner on. "You can't possibly keep doing this, Adrian. I hate to say it, but you need to let go."

"Oh, come on, Lorelei. It's only been a week."

Lorelei stops, watching the bacon for a minute and turns toward Adrian. "Wait. You went sampling in the woods?"

Adrian nods, his hands still propping up his head.

"Did you see more visions?" Lorelei steps closer to him.

Adrian doesn't answer.

"Why are you covering your eyes?"

Adrian shrugs his shoulders.

The smell of bacon grease distracts Lorelei, and she returns to the stove to turn off the burner. "I can't believe you," she says with her back to him.

Adrian gets up and approaches her. He gently rubs her arms from behind. "It's just something I have to do."

Lorelei swings around to face him. Adrian stares at the ceramic tiles on the floor. "Let me see."

Adrian throws his head back and meets her gaze. Her eyes narrow, her forehead furrows. "Oh, Adrian, they are worse than ever! Why didn't you go to the hospital?"

She tilts his head back so she can get a better view. They aren't just red. Blood is collecting, causing his eyes to look like they are raised, almost swollen. They have surpassed red eyes. They look grotesque.

Lorelei breaks through Adrian's grasp and storms out of the kitchen. She stops to gather her field supplies near the front door. Adrian follows her and touches her elbow. She pauses, but then she resumes gathering what she needs for the day, including boots, waders, clipboard, and field books. "Hold on, Lorelei."

"I can't watch you do this to yourself. You're obsessed over this because of Jonathan, not so much Wyatt. You're confusing the two." Lorelei slings her backpack over her shoulder. "You're obviously hurting yourself, but you won't stop. You need professional help. I can't do this for you."

"I agree that this is hitting home about Jonathan," Adrian replies, stumbling through Jonathan's name, "but he's not the reason for this. I keep seeing shadows and visions. They're distracting. They come out of nowhere. I wish I could ignore them, but I can't."

Lorelei turns toward the door.

"Lorelei, please. I saw Wyatt yesterday. He was on the path. So was Jeremy. Wyatt was being tied up by him, and his mouth was being taped. I can see the crime scene. I know it sounds bizarre and believe me, I wish this were happening to someone else, but I can't just ignore it, can I?"

Lorelei stays silent.

Adrian grabs her hands. "Please just have patience with me until we find him. I almost saw the whole scene yesterday but then wimped out. I'm afraid to see what he does to Wyatt."

"Yeah and is that when your eyes almost blew out?"

"I wouldn't put it that way."

"Is your life worth risking for Wyatt?"

"It's fine, Lorelei. It'll go away. It looks worse than it is."

Adrian pulls the backpack off and takes the field books out of her hand. "Come on, let's have breakfast together. You still have time, right?"

"Adrian, I—"

"Nonsense. You need breakfast before you go out there. I'll finish cooking. Be right back." Adrian hurries down the hallway to the bedroom.

Once he's gone, Lorelei moseys over to the safe room. The door is open. She quietly enters and flicks on the light. She spies his journal on the end table. She wonders if he's writing again, something he usually does when he's feeling stressed. Normally, she wouldn't intrude, but she's worried about him. She pauses in the doorway, contemplating if she could read his last entry before he returns. The creak of the bedroom door makes her mind up for her, and she turns around and exits.

After breakfast, Lorelei leaves for work and Adrian decides to get ready for his day. Steam rises toward the ceiling as Adrian waits a few more minutes before entering the shower. He leans into the mirror over the sink to see how his eyes are doing. They're still red, but a lot of the clotting has disappeared. He turns his head to the right, then the left to look for any signs of white, but there are none. Adrian sighs and backs away.

Shit, I still look like Satan.

He stares at himself from farther away to see if his eyes are less disgusting but isn't comforted by what he sees in the mirror.

Something moves behind him.

Adrian grabs onto the side of the sink and turns around toward the walk-in closet. No shadows. He turns back toward the mirror and stares into the reflection, staring behind him.

He sees a dark shadow move to the left, then forward.

Adrian's adrenaline kicks up, his breathing accelerates. He can hear the high-pitched screams from the light bulbs above him, and the crunching of the grout between the ceramic tile flooring as he shifts his weight.

When he peers in the mirror again, he sees the back of the broad-shouldered man from the visions.

Adrian turns around to check behind him again but sees nothing in the closet. It's only in the mirror. The man's shoulders are huge, but Jeremy doesn't have huge shoulders. What does this mean?

Jeremy shifts his head to the right, then the left, as usual. The scar is bright red.

No, I'm not doing this right now. You're going to show me on the trail today.

Adrian ignores Jeremy and jumps into the shower. He concentrates on his breathing, slowing it down. The coolness of the water feels good on his shoulders. He leans back to wet his hair, lathers it up and rinses it out.

Adrian happens to look into the bathroom and notices a figure moving. It's distorted by the foggy shower doors. "Lorelei?" Getting no answer, Adrian wipes the fog off one of the shower doors and peers out.

A shadow of a small boy is curled up near the toilet.

Adrian jumps back and winces when he hits his arm on the shower lever.

He searches the bathroom again, but the boy is gone.

This is not happening right now. This needs to happen later.

"Go away!" he yells. He grabs a towel and slowly opens the shower door, his body shaking from the coolness in the bathroom and his nerves. He doesn't see any more shadows, so he jets to the walk-in closet to grab his work clothes. Once dressed, he scurries over to the dresser and notices his polo collar is up on one side and down on the other, his shirt is only halfway tucked into his pants, and his fly is open. Adrian takes a deep breath and fixes his clothing.

Good thing you saw yourself before going to work like this! The shadows are gone. Relax.

Adrian walks down the hallway and into the kitchen. He grabs his keys and lunch and bolts the door after closing it. When he turns around, he sees the shadows are back in full force, swirling around in random directions. Adrian hangs his head for a few seconds, then decides to make a run for it. He dodges the shadows as he races for the truck. They are relentless on his way to work. They taunt him on his way into the office, and up the stairs and down the hall. He pretends everything is normal, smiling at the receptionist when he arrives, all the while wanting to swat at the shadows that are out of control around him. He proceeds straight to his office and shuts the door behind him.

The shadows stop.

He pauses for a few seconds and waits for more to appear but they are gone. He slips out of his jacket and leans on his desk to catch his breath. His heartbeat is out of control. He grasps onto the back of his chair, then sits holding his head in his hands. He's sure he'll be greeted by a headache soon.

A knock on the door breaks his concentration.

"Hey, Adrian. It's me, Fossie."

If I let her in, will the shadows storm in?

"J... just a minute," he replies.

He sits up straight and pats down his hair. He knows he has no choice but to brace himself for whatever comes through the door.

Fossie enters. "Hey, I heard Clark talked with forensics today. He's already gone out to the site."

Adrian relaxes a little. No shadows.

"Yeah? Well, I was delayed at home."

"Everything okay?"

Adrian scans the farthest corner of the room.

Fossie watches him for a few seconds. "You're seeing the shadows again, aren't you?"

Adrian peers down at his desk. "Yeah, really bad today."

"You mean you're seeing lots of them?"

"Yeah, not sure if I'm happy about it or not. I did see a little more of the crime scene yesterday. It's definitely Wyatt and Jeremy. I even saw Wyatt biking down the trail. I do want to face the scene that plays out for me on the trail, but I get to a certain point, and I can't do it. I just can't face what happens to Wyatt. I'm afraid I'm going to see him get hurt. So, I end up closing my eyes to make the visions go away."

"Well, that's understandable. Those guys are almost family to you, right?"

Adrian nods.

"Who'd want to see? I know I wouldn't."

"But, I have to. It could lead us to Wyatt."

"True, but you'll need to be ready. I still think you

should tell the police you're seeing Jeremy. The days keep going by, and they could be tracking him by now."

"They probably already are. One of the officers asked me to tell him to call."

"Have you heard from him?"

"No. I don't want to anyway. I don't know what I'd say at this point."

"Where do you think he went?"

"Maybe his sister's, but I think the police would have found him already if that were the case. I seriously don't know."

The silhouette of a child peeks around Fossie's leg. It's a boy, perhaps ten years old. It's grabbing onto her pants with little fingers. Adrian watches Fossie's expression, but she doesn't seem to notice.

Fossie continues with her advice, but Adrian can't concentrate on the conversation. The boy is squatting. His knees are up to its chest. Adrian can't see his eyes, but he's staring at him. Adrian's heart thumps louder the longer this goes on.

"Are you listening to me?" Fossie finally asks, breaking Adrian's concentration.

"Yeah, of course."

The child starts to creep toward Adrian on all fours.

Fossie searches beside her. "Are you seeing something?"

Adrian pushes his chair back as the child crawls closer.

"Fuck!" he yells, the child now right in front of his desk.

"How many times have I told you about that word, Adrian? I—"

"Oh, God, Fossie! Look right in front of you—in front of my desk. See anything?"

Fossie says she sees nothing unusual.

Adrian's breathing becomes labored. "The…the child is there," Adrian says, pointing forward. "I think it's Wyatt."

Adrian starts to shake. The boy stands still. He's still a black silhouette. The child shakes his head back and forth rapidly.

"Adrian, there's nothing there. Calm down."

"Yes. Yes, there is. It's still there."

The child jumps onto his desk. Adrian jerks backward. "He's coming at me! What the hell?"

Adrian leaps from his chair and stands near the side of the desk. The child turns, too.

"Where is it now?" asks Fossie.

"On the desk! Leave now, Fossie! Now!"

"Don't be silly, Adrian. I'm not going anywhere."

"Fossie, I'm serious. Just go to your desk. I'll leave, and he'll follow me."

"Maybe it really *is* Wyatt, and he's trying to talk to you."

The child turns toward Fossie.

"Fossie, get out! I mean it."

Sherman Graystone pops his head in. "Is there a problem in here? Why am I hearing yelling?"

"No, no, everything's fine," Fossie says. "Adrian was just telling me a story. Sorry if we disturbed you."

Adrian feels sweat beading on his forehead as he watches the child on the desk.

"Adrian? What's going on?" Sherman asks.

The child turns toward the owner, still squatting.

Adrian closes his eyes. "Please make it go away."

The owner frowns.

"It's fine. Adrian's just a little upset today. Nothing to

worry about. Come on, let's go over the report we started to fix yesterday," Fossie says to Sherman.

Adrian opens his eyes. The child is gone. He notices Sherman is still watching him, so he rubs his eyes, pretending to be tired. "Yeah, sorry. I've just been having these horrible headaches." Adrian closes his eyes again.

"Keep your voice down. I could hear you down the hall."

"Got it. Sorry. It won't happen again."

"Make sure it doesn't," Sherman says as he leaves.

Adrian plops into his chair and scans his office.

No shadows.

He calls Clark.

"Yo, what's up."

"Hey, Clark. I heard you're already going to the site. Do I need to come?"

"Yes. They want to collect more samples along the shoreline. Grab a work truck and come out and help me. It'll be at least another day's worth of work. Besides, Officer Mortensen wants to talk with you about yesterday. He's antsy on finding Wyatt, and he seems to think you're the best solution right now."

"Great," Adrian says with a sigh. "No problem. I'll grab a truck and be right out there."

"Good. See you in a few."

Adrian draws in a deep breath.

Maybe this will answer the questions surrounding this mystery, and we can be done with this.

Adrian arrives at Jeremy's and lugs a couple of sample coolers down the path until he reaches Clark. Officer Mortensen and his fellow officers glance back at Adrian for a few seconds, then continue their conversation. Clark has several sample bottles labeled and lined up on top of the cooler.

"Hey," Adrian says as he gently places the coolers next to Clark.

"How's it going?" Clark asks.

Adrian peers back at the investigators. "Hanging in there, I guess."

"Your eyes are still red, I see."

"I think they're going to stay that way until I figure this thing out. So, I guess I better do that soon."

"Officer Mortensen is asking a lot of questions. He can't understand why you stopped yesterday," Clark whispers.

"Guess, I'd be wondering the same thing if I were him. I don't know why myself. Other than maybe I don't really want to see what happens to Wyatt next. God knows what I'll see."

"I get it. You can obviously tell how much this is bothering you."

"Guess I'm not hiding that very well."

"Well, you take the western shoreline, and I'll take the eastern. We'll be sampling until we run out of bottles today."

Adrian nods and grabs a couple of latex gloves.

Clark brushes past Adrian and says, "He's coming." He then follows the forensics investigator to the shoreline with sample bottles in hand. Another investigator stays back with Adrian.

"So, Adrian," Officer Mortensen says as he approaches. "How are you feeling today?"

Adrian raises his eyes. "I've been better."

"Yikes. What in the hell is going on with your eyes? Did the doctor figure it out yet?"

"He says it's stress, and it'll go away on its own."

"Well, that's good, at least. Say, uh, did you have any more visions since yesterday?"

"Not of the scene. Mostly just shadows flying around."

"Yeah? Well, what do you think the chances are of you seeing the scene again today?"

"Probably good. I have to sample though."

"Uh huh. Well, I'd like you to try at some point. Maybe today you can watch it longer."

"It just happens. There's really no trying. But I hope I see more today too. At the same time, I dread it. I'm not sure I really want to see what I'm going to see if that makes sense. It feels bad, dark, evil. I don't know if I could take watching something terrible happen to Wyatt."

"And who would be doing that? Who are you seeing?"

Adrian flinches with the question.

"You know, don't you?"

"I need more time in the scene to tell. I don't want to guess."

The officer studies Adrian's face. "Okay, well later today I want you to meet with one of my officers and describe what you're seeing—every detail—even if you don't see anything new today. Got it?"

"Yes," Adrian replies. "Well, guess I better get to sampling."

"Guess you better."

Adrian walks down to the shoreline, muck squeezing out from below his field boots. Every step causes a sucking sound. At one point, his entire leg sinks into the mud, causing Adrian to heave forward. He quickly grabs onto a tree and pulls himself out, his entire pant leg covered in sediment.

Why am I doing this? And how in the world can Lorelei love this work?

Thinking of her makes him smile. Then frown.

I never asked her where she was working today.

Adrian begins collecting samples. He works swiftly, finishing in less than an hour. He carries them to the cooler where Clark is drinking one of his vitamin waters.

"Good?" Adrian asks.

"Eh."

Adrian grabs a bottle of water and sits on top of another cooler.

"At this rate, we'll be finished before noon."

Something moves near the bottom of Clark's cooler, grabbing Adrian's attention. Adrian tilts his head to see around the cooler better. He can see the shadow of Wyatt once again.

"Clark, shh," Adrian says, then points toward the boy. "I see him. Wyatt is next to you."

Startled, Clark shifts his weight and peers down beside the cooler. "I don't see anything, Adrian."

"I know, but he's there. It's only a shadow, but I know it's him."

"Uh huh," Clark says, studying Adrian's face. "Well, what's he doing?"

"Just sitting there."

Adrian's heart rate speeds up and once again he starts to hear even the smallest of sounds.

Officer Mortensen comes over. "Everything okay?" he asks.

Clark replies, "Well, Adrian says he's seeing Wyatt right here by the cooler."

"He's squatting. Just watching me," Adrian adds.

"No bike? No scene?"

"No. Just a shadow right now. I saw him earlier today in my office too."

Adrian notices another, much larger, shadow walking out of the woods behind Clark on the opposite side of the path. Wyatt watches it for a few seconds, then runs up to the path, falling forward and crawling on all fours. The tall shadow becomes more defined, exposing its facial features.

It's Jeremy.

The shadow of the boy is now crawling down the path with Jeremy heading directly for him. The scene turns darker like it's later in the day. Jeremy straddles his legs around the boy, squats and begins binding him.

Officer Mortensen steps back as Adrian moves toward the path. "Watch the whole thing this time, Adrian."

Adrian sneaks slowly toward Jeremy who glances up and down the path, the familiar deep scar showing once he turns to the left. Adrian doesn't hesitate and moves in closer. He peers over Jeremy's shoulder and can see the side of Wyatt's face, now grimacing as Jeremy ties his hands behind his back.

Jeremy peers up and down the trail again. Adrian is so close, he could grab Wyatt.

Maybe if I grab him, I can break this horrific cycle.

Adrian reaches his hand around Jeremy and stretches it toward Wyatt's shoulder, trying not to touch Jeremy.

But just as he almost grabs him, Jeremy whips his head around and looks directly at Adrian.

Adrian flinches, drawing his hand back. Jeremy continues staring, furrowing his eyebrows as he keeps Adrian in the depths of his dark, ominous eyes.

Adrian jerks backward and hits the ground hard,

breaking the scene before him.

"Holy shit!" he yells, trying to catch his breath as he stares back at an empty path. "He saw me! He fucking saw me!"

CHAPTER

16

Who saw you?" asks Officer Mortensen.

"Jeremy!"

"You saw Jeremy? Is he the man on the trail?"

"Yes! I mean, no! I mean, I don't know," Adrian says, shaking his head.

"You don't know? Which is it?"

"I...I don't know for sure."

"Did you see where Jeremy takes Wyatt?"

"Not today, but yesterday he carried him to the water."

Officer Mortensen leans closer and in a firm voice says, "Adrian, you didn't see any more than that? Which direction did he go in the water?"

"I don't know, but he looked me right in the eye." Adrian shivers as goose bumps cover his arms. "Holy shit, what does that mean?"

Before the officer can answer, Adrian pulls himself up

and paces, thinking of the magnitude of the situation.

Could Jeremy really see me?

Clark steps in and reaches for Adrian's arm. "Hey, let's get back to sampling and get this job done. You can figure it out later. Is that okay with you, detective?"

He nods but doesn't look happy.

Clark guides Adrian over to the shoreline and whispers, "Do you want to go back to the office? Or home, maybe? It's probably best that you're not out here."

"What? Oh, no. I'm good. I just can't believe that the shadow looked back at me. What could that mean? What if he can see me now?"

"I have no idea, Adrian. I think you're getting yourself deeper and deeper into this and pretty soon the police are going to want answers—maybe more than you can give. Finish sampling, and let's get out of here." Clark hands Adrian some gloves. "Oh, and try not to provoke any more shadows. Don't even look up toward the trail if you can help it."

"Believe me, at this point, I don't want to see anymore, but I have no control over it."

"Well, just remember you can leave if it gets bad. I can handle the rest of the sampling."

"Got it."

Adrian follows the forensics investigator to the next sample location. He tries hard not to think about Jeremy, but the importance of this last event is just too significant. He visualizes Jeremy's eyes. They almost seemed like a warning. Perhaps Jeremy was telling him to stay out of this.

He sits down on a cooler to sample and begins the paperwork when a movement out of the corner of his eye taunts Adrian to look up.

I can't do this again.

Adrian glances over to Clark, but his back is to Adrian.

A small red sneaker pushes into Adrian's line of sight. Adrian drops his marker and peers up. There, standing right in front of him is Wyatt. It's not just a shadow this time. Wyatt's hair is tousled, sticking out in all directions. His face and eyelashes are covered in dust, tears streaming down his cheeks. His shirt is torn, Superman's head flapping each time a gentle breeze whips up from the water. His bottom lip is bleeding, and a red tint is covering the inside of his teeth.

The taste of blood fills Adrian's mouth, too. *So, that's why I'm tasting blood.*

Adrian squats. "Wyatt? Are you still alive?"

Wyatt doesn't respond.

"Wyatt, tell me where you are."

But after Adrian blinks, Wyatt disappears. Adrian ignores the investigator who's questioning him about what's going on and searches the area around him, but he can't find Wyatt until he hears muffled screams coming from the trail.

"That son of a bitch!"

Adrian drops the sample bottle and runs up toward the bike trail.

Clark notices and launches after him. "Adrian, don't!"

Adrian hears the stones below Jeremy's boots as they slide in next to Wyatt's face. He hears Jeremy's breathing, fast and steady, determined. He hears the tears stream down through the dust on Wyatt's face, the smallest ebb and flow as they find the path of least resistance.

Adrian marches up behind Jeremy, tensing his arm muscles as he prepares to stop this for once and for all. He can hear the pebbles crunching beneath his own shoes, kicking up dust and sediment as he steps forward along the trail.

He stops a few feet behind Jeremy, who's now staring back at Adrian. Only it's not Jeremy's face he's looking into.

It's his own.

Adrian stands there stunned as he watches himself squatting over Wyatt. He sees his work boots, each cradling the sides of Wyatt's head. He watches himself tape Wyatt's hands, then get up and bind his feet. He feels the sweat gathering on his forehead and the nervousness of not wanting to be caught. Adrian sees the view up and down the pathway, then turns his focus back to Wyatt, where he flips him onto his back. His own hands doing this.

He makes sure Wyatt can still breathe. He feels angry. He tries not to, but he does. He's angry because of the risk that Wyatt takes almost every night, always pushing the time to the limit. Closer and closer to dark. If Jeremy can't keep him safe, then he has no choice but to do it himself. After all, what man doesn't take care of his own child? Jeremy should have taken care of this a long time ago.

He sees the bike light. He sees himself pull out the rope from his own jacket pocket. He sees Wyatt squirming.

He hears himself tell Wyatt that he should be kept safe. He sees himself pick up the bike. He feels Wyatt on his shoulder. But where is he taking him?

A hand clasps onto Adrian's shoulder and shakes him. Adrian snaps out of the scene.

Adrian stumbles backward, feeling shock and awe.

"Hey, are you okay? You'll feel better soon. Just try to relax," Clark says.

Adrian drops to his knees, his throat tightening, and

then he cries in deep, ragged breaths. His chest heaves as he tries to comprehend the abomination of what he just saw. Pulses of disgust and sorrow flow through Adrian's body with an intensity he's never experienced before. He grasps his head between his hands, massaging his temples.

The sounds of footsteps brush their way through the tall weeds and stop next to Adrian. "So, did you see what happened next?" asks Officer Mortensen.

Adrian shakes his head and rocks back and forth as he sits on the bike trail, his arms around his knees.

"What the hell is wrong with you? What did you see?"

I saw me.

Adrian doesn't answer aloud. His head reeling, Adrian continues to rock, emotions flooding his scattered thoughts.

"Jesus, I'm getting sick of this. I'm done," Officer Mortensen announces to Clark and the other officers. "This is getting me nowhere." He stomps off down the path toward Jeremy's house and the other officers follow.

Clark extends his hand to Adrian and helps him stand up. "Whatever you saw, and I know you saw something, remember that this could all just be in your mind. Sometimes our minds play tricks on us so I wouldn't think of it as real. You may just be all caught up and stressed out about this and think you're seeing something that's not the truth. Besides, I don't think your eyes can take anymore. They're deep red again."

Adrian nods and looks away.

"Well, it's almost the end of the day. I can finish up from here. You're always in early, so go home and start fresh tomorrow. Hopefully, you'll get some well-deserved rest and this will all be cleared up once the police figure this out. Sorry I let you come out here today. I shouldn't have, especially knowing the police would be after you for an answer. Plan on working in the office for the rest of the week."

"Yeah, sure. I need to figure some things out," Adrian replies, staring down at the trail.

"I mean it. Go. I got it from here."

Adrian drops off the work truck at the office and drives out in his own truck, not for home—but a place to think.

It was challenging being the eldest of six, especially when most of Adrian's siblings were girls. The incessant chatter and sprawling of doll clothes throughout the house made it hard to take his beastliness seriously. When Adrian was younger, he'd no sooner align his own field of soldiers, armed and ready for war against the enemy, when some frilly, pink Barbie sock would fly into the battlefield completely out of nowhere, ruining the onslaught of blood and guts that was about to ensue. Before the battle could start, he'd have to fling the sock backward, setting off an array of giggles that would drive any boy to the edge of complete madness, but he always chose the high road—something his mom had instilled in him, being he was the oldest. He'd always begin again, seeing himself as one of the protectors of a small town about to be besieged, when sure enough, a sparkly hairclip would catapult through his line of men, taking out their balance and causing every one of them to flop forward as if they had been kicked over by a barrette with ninja powers. Adrian would drop his head in disgust at his men who should be able to fight against this invasion, but alas, there they were, noses to the ground. And of course, the barrage of little giggles didn't help matters.

Thank God Adrian had one hope of sanity—his brother, Jonathan. He was five years younger, but at least they'd be able to confide in each other when Jonathan was old enough. Adrian taught him everything he knew as they grew up, from how to walk with a little strut to how best to part his hair at just the right angle. Jonathan was always at Adrian's heels, listening to and learning from an older brother who loved him dearly. They both knew that someday they'd live up in the tree house their dad would build out back, all the wiser about the goings-on in the neighborhood and able to protect their house and everyone inside from anything, and they meant *anything*, that might be a threat, even a zombie apocalypse. They would be the ultimate heroes with strength and courage that could not be out-beasted, as they put it.

If only that would have been the case.

Instead, Adrian sits in the back of the woods stripped of any strength or dignity. He has no brother to lift him up and no strength to battle the visions in his head. Memories of his childhood have all but left Adrian, shut out by the pain of losing Jonathan at such a young age. There was never a tree house, and Adrian turned into a quiet teenager that wrestled with guilt every day of his life after the accident. He tried to save his brother, but he wasn't strong enough. But what he couldn't accept is that *no one* would have been strong enough. Not The Rock, not Stallone, not even Schwarzenegger. The force against Adrian was extraordinary.

But the little guy was counting on me. He pleaded with me to save him. I'll never forget the look on his face, and his expression once he realized his older brother failed him. I failed him. And now, I've failed Wyatt. What other reason would there be for me seeing my own face on that pathetic beast of a man on the bike trail?

The call of a hoot owl pierces through the trees overhead, a breeze bending their tips, though Adrian can barely see them in the dark. The crickets are loud tonight, almost muffling the sound of the owl. There must be millions, but they are nowhere to be seen. A crescent moon shines in the night sky next to the twinkling of a couple of planets—perhaps Jupiter and Mars. Adrian remembers reading about it on the Internet.

He's doesn't remember how he got there, but he's ended up near the bike path in Green Swamp again. He feels a strong urge to feel closer to Wyatt. Perhaps if he sits here long enough, he'll figure out a way to find him. There are no shadows haunting him tonight, just the darkness between the trees and reflections on the water, in some areas so intertwined it's hard to tell where the base of the tree line begins in the moonlight. The barking of green tree frogs joins in the chorus of crickets and a cool wind blows past Adrian's skin, interrupting his concentration.

Adrian leans forward and covers his ears, trying to block out the distractions. He's determined to sit on the tree stump as long as it takes. Quietly, he waits for the bicycle. Whether the beast shows his face or not, he will watch until the end—whatever it means. He doesn't want it to mean that Wyatt is dragged into the water or eaten alive. He doesn't want it to mean that Wyatt is dead. But this has to stop. No more waiting. No more agony. The mystery will be solved tonight.

Seconds later, Adrian lifts his head up when he hears the clank of a bike chain. His heart rate increases. He hears the sound of tires rustling through the leaves. Adrian waits. The man's head pops up above the brush, then disappears. He sees a small hand grabbing for rocks from his line of sight through the branches. Wyatt has his other hand over his eyes to shield them from the bike light and calls out to his dad. He must be tying Wyatt's legs now, Adrian surmises. The man stands again, glancing up and down the path.

Then he hears the man talk in Adrian's voice.

Adrian stands and sees himself again on the path.

And he feels angry. Very angry.

He sees himself peer down at Wyatt.

Why is this not Jeremy anymore? What is happening?

Then Adrian hears himself say he must keep Wyatt safe.

What does this mean?

Adrian feels a strong flight instinct. He wants to run, get away from this horrific situation. Maybe instead of running toward the scene, he should run away from the scene. Maybe then, this will stop.

But he forces himself to watch.

He sees himself lift Wyatt over his shoulder and pull the bike upright. Then slog into the water with the bike at his side and Wyatt on his shoulder. Adrian follows the vision of himself and sees him lower Wyatt onto a small boat. He places the bike next to him, then grabs the oars and rows away upstream. He can no longer follow.

Adrian is so shocked he falls to his knees in the shallow water, bewildered and disgusted.

What the fuck?

CHAPTER

17

Adrian wakes up to the chugging of his model train rounding a corner toward a little village that leads to the train station. He watches as it makes its way around the table for a few minutes until the reality of what he saw last night hits hard. Adrian leans forward in the recliner, playing the events from the day before over and over in his head, still not sure about the meaning.

Why me and not Jeremy? Clearly, this has to be Jeremy's doing. Wyatt must be trying to show me what happened.

The door to the room opens and Lorelei steps in. "Sleeping here again, I see."

"Sorry."

"Where were you last night?"

"Trying to find Wyatt."

"And did you?"

Adrian closes his eyes. "The scene expanded. He was

dragged into the water, then put on a boat."

Lorelei's eyes widen, and she drops her mouth open. "Holy shit! Did you tell the police?"

"No. They weren't around when the scene played before me. Plus, there was another disturbing scene."

"What's that?"

"I saw Jeremy binding Wyatt, and when I tried to interfere with the scene, he looked straight at me."

"Ew. That's creepy." Lorelei sits in a chair across from Adrian. "What does that mean?"

"I have no idea. That happened yesterday afternoon. The police know about that part."

"Well, what part don't they know about?"

Adrian squirms in his recliner. "While I continued sampling, I saw the scene again." Adrian rubs his eyes with his fingers. "And I no longer saw Jeremy's face."

"Whose face did you see then?"

"Mine," Adrian replies, watching for Lorelei's reaction.

She watches his as well. "What do you mean, you saw your own face?"

"Yeah. I saw my own face. No, let me clarify. I saw myself—my boots straddling his head, my hands binding his wrists and ankles."

Lorelei straightens her back. "What does that mean?"

"I don't know. I saw Wyatt standing right in front of me while I was sampling, his lip bleeding, similar to my lip after the visions. Tears streaming down his face. It's like he's trying to tell me something. And then later…"

"Later?"

"I went back to the crime scene later," he replies. Before Lorelei can respond, he adds, "I had to go back. I know my eyes are a mess, but I figured that if I could solve this, it'd be over. But I only have more questions."

Lorelei shakes her head. "Your eyes do look pretty bad right now."

"I'm sure they do." Adrian closes his eyes, then opens them and stares at Lorelei as he says, "I saw myself again last night, binding Wyatt, picking up his bike and carrying him to the water. But this cannot be. Why I'm seeing myself instead of Jeremy now is messed up."

"Did you ever think that maybe you're worrying yourself over nothing?" Lorelei asks. "I mean, this could all be conjured up in your head."

"I'm more confused now than ever and nowhere closer to finding Wyatt."

"That's why we have the police, Adrian. Let them do their jobs."

"They're counting on me now," he lies, his voice becoming strained.

"Hey, hey," Lorelei replies. "Don't let that get to you. I think you should stay away from there. Just concentrate on your job. You just started it and need to put all of your energy into learning new responsibilities."

"They probably think I'm some kind of weirdo now, too."

Lorelei grins. "Well, you are kind of weird — my kind of weird," she says with a laugh.

"Oh, so you think so, huh?" He widens his eyes so Lorelei can get a good view of the redness.

"Ewww! Quit!"

"I'm going to get you!" Adrian lunges at Lorelei pretending to attack her neck. "You are very tasty, my sweet."

Lorelei screams and pushes Adrian's shoulders back. "That tickles!"

Adrian laughs, then kisses Lorelei gently on the lips. "God, what would I do without you?"

"Oh, you'd survive, I'm sure, especially with all the nagging I do."

"You don't nag." Adrian pauses. "Maybe a little."

Lorelei lightly punches Adrian's arm. "You like it, though." Lorelei pauses. "You know we never had our talk."

"Yeah, right," he says, leaning back in his recliner. "I don't want to go there right now, Lorelei."

"I know," she says. "Maybe after you get past all of this?"

"Honestly, I don't know if I'll ever be ready." Adrian's mood changes, becoming agitated. He rubs his palms on his legs a few times, then gets up and turns off the train.

"Does it have something to do with Jonathan? Are you afraid because you lost Jonathan you'll lose me too?"

Adrian knows the answer but doesn't respond.

"You can't live like that, you know? I really think you need to get the counseling you never had after Jonathan died. You need to move past this. Everything. Wyatt and Jonathan."

Adrian stands and makes his way over to the train set. He leans on the edge of the board that supports the tracks. "That's what I'm trying to tell you. I don't think I'll ever get over it."

Lorelei gets up off her chair and hurries to the doorway in silence, slamming the door shut behind her. Adrian jumps but doesn't turn around to follow Lorelei. Instead, he rushes to the side table, takes out the box of figurines, and places each one at the train station. He then turns the train back on, sits in the recliner, and watches it go round and round along the tracks, the only thing he finds comforting right now.

That evening, Adrian returns home from work instead of going to Jeremy's. He stayed in the office all day, catching up on phone calls and paperwork and avoiding conversations with Fossie, which could lead to telling her more details than she needs to know. Luckily, too, he hasn't been plagued with any shadows today.

As Adrian pulls into the driveway, he sees Gentry's daughter, Taylor, riding her bike down the street. He waits to see if Gentry is with her but doesn't see him.

I wonder if he knows she's out here by herself. Not smart, given the current situation with Wyatt missing. No way would I let my seven-year-old ride around these desolate streets all by herself.

Adrian calls Gentry, but he doesn't answer. He waits in his car, keeping an eye on Taylor until she's out of sight.

What is Gentry thinking?

Adrian waits to see if she'll round the corner again, but she doesn't return. He starts up the engine and drives down the street. This is an isolated area of the neighborhood with no one around. He curses Gentry for allowing her to wander so far away from their house.

As he turns onto the street, he sees Taylor and Gentry in the cul-de-sac. Gentry is fixing Taylor's helmet, which has come loose. Gentry looks up when he hears the truck coming.

Shit, he sees me. Now, I have to explain myself.

He pulls his truck up next to them. "Hey, Gentry. How's it going?"

"Good," Gentry replies, telling Taylor to stay on her bike. "What are you doing down this way?"

"I happened to see Taylor riding by herself over here, so I was just checking to make sure she was okay. I tried to call you. With Wyatt's disappearance, I'm a bit paranoid for other kids, I guess."

"Nice of you to watch out for her, but I've got it under control."

"Yeah, I see that. Sorry to have bothered you."

"No bother, man. Say, when are we going to have that beer? Are you coming over this weekend?"

"I forgot to get with Lorelei about it. I'll text you later tonight."

"Sounds good. Come if you can."

Adrian departs feeling embarrassed but at least he knows Taylor is safe. He doesn't need another child to worry about at this point.

He pulls up to the driveway and sees that Lorelei has arrived.

Shit, can't I ever get any time alone? I don't want to talk about marriage or be around someone who's just going to be mad at me.

He just wants some peace. No pressure, no demands. He wonders why he can't just have his life back. Everything is so fucked up right now. He can't find Wyatt, he can't commit to Lorelei, people at work think he's weird, and he doesn't want to be near anyone. And worst of all, he never knows when the shadows are going to dart out at him and show his own fucking face on them.

Adrian's heart rate accelerates, leaving him trying to

catch his breath.

Okay, just breathe. Relax.

Adrian closes his eyes and tries to think of better times. The best was spending family time on vacations when he was young. There were eight of them including his parents, and his mom and dad would include everyone in the planning each year in advance of the trip. They all had a love for the mountains. Being from Indiana, there were plenty of hills, but not really many mountains, especially ones like the Rockies. Huge and dominating, the Rockies were breathtaking, stunning to him. Adrian always remembered driving up to them—the mountains never seeming to stop growing as the family van grew closer. It was like driving into another realm. Despite the girly stuff, they were all very close. Those times were his best. What he wouldn't give to be back there again.

Adrian's breathing slows as his heart grows calmer. He opens his eyes when he hears sniffles and jerks his head to the right.

Wyatt is sitting next to him. His hands and ankles are bound. Tape is wrapped over his eyes and mouth, fast breathing sounds piercing the air. He's breathing so rapidly, he appears to be convulsing.

Adrian becomes delirious and plunges out of the truck, falling onto the pavement.

I can't watch this. I can't watch this. I can't—

"Adrian? Are you okay?" asks Lorelei. She's standing over him.

"No, I'm not, Lorelei. I'm not okay at all. Are you happy now? Huh?"

Lorelei steps back.

"I've got fucking shadows following me everywhere,

and I can't find Wyatt. No wait, I did find Wyatt. He was just in the front of my car! Yes, that's right! Bound, scared and convulsing. He was right there! Right next to me!"

Lorelei moves closer to Adrian. "Let's go inside before someone sees you. You can go in your safe room, back to the recliner, the train. Whatever. Let's just get you inside."

Adrian pops up onto his feet. "Oh, what, you want to hide the freak? The one who has visions? The one who's losing it?" Adrian grabs his head. "I didn't have visions all day. Why are they back? Why?"

Adrian sees the pain on Lorelei's face. "I don't know. What will help?"

"I need some time alone. I'm feeling claustrophobic." Adrian's breathing becomes rapid again. His chest heaves.

Lorelei moves toward Adrian to grab his arm. He swipes at her to stay away. "I've got to deal with this on my own." He points his finger at her. "You need to stay away from me. I'm no good. I'm broken."

"Adrian, please," Lorelei begs. "Let's go inside and figure this out."

"You go inside. I'm going for a walk to think this through."

"Where are you going?"

"Just...just don't worry about it. I need to get my head straight."

"Adrian, let me help you. Let's—"

"Go inside!" he yells, anger exuding from his eyes and the bend of his lips.

Lorelei turns on her heel, runs to the entryway, and pushes open the front door, slamming it behind her.

Adrian exhales, relief spreading through his inner core.

Then he sprints to his backyard and into the woods.

If there's one place Adrian can feel truly by himself, it's the woods. He walked them as a young boy in Indiana, and he walks them still at the age of twenty-five. It's peaceful and serene, a place where he can block out all the garbage and really get to the problem at hand. He has a few favorite sitting spots in the back of his woods. One, in particular, overlooks the wetlands. White ibis and other birds wade along the shoreline for a bite to eat, along with the occasional squirrel and armadillo. It's nature in its purest form. It clears the head.

Adrian sits on his favorite log, staring ahead. He notices that the sun is about to make its descent. Darkness is on its way. He only has a few more minutes before he'll have to head back to the house. Next time he sees Lorelei, he knows he's going to have to apologize for his actions. He's treated her badly, something she doesn't deserve. He'll make amends, somehow.

But first, he has to figure out his head. He's got to make himself better. Seeing his face in the visions has rattled him. Just the thought is increasing his pulse and the nervous knot that is always sitting at the bottom of his stomach is pushing upward. He wonders if true sensitives get this feeling.

So, where does he go from here? There's not much choice when it comes to the shadows and visions that plague him. They're a definite. Maybe once Wyatt is found, they'll go away. But how can he handle it better in the meantime? What if they never find Wyatt? Will he be plagued forever? They have to go away at some point, right?

Adrian leans forward, arms on his knees, and pulls at a weed. The blade is thick like grass, reminding him of when he was a boy and used to hold one taut between his thumbs, blowing past it and making screeching sounds. Silly times when you made something out of nothing—when you could lie in the grass for hours thinking of all the things you wanted in your life. Adrian's life has turned into one main purpose, though, and when it's disrupted, he feels he must make it right. He wants people to be safe. That's all. No pain and suffering. No loss. Just happy times with the ones you love all around you.

Because loss is deep. It is cold, unwavering. It's the darkness that lurks in every shadow—the ones we rarely pay attention to, but we know they are there.

A blackness that is so disturbing that one has no choice but to hide it in a place unseen.

Adrian's afraid that the shadows are conjuring up his own black hole. One that he keeps hidden to survive. He knows he can't open it. If he does, he may never come back.

The house is dark as Adrian enters through the front door. Lorelei's car is in the driveway. He's happy she's still there, probably looking sweet all snuggled into her pillow. She's always had such an angelic sleeping face.

It's eleven o'clock, still time to prepare a few meals for the rest of the week. He's feeling low so he heads for the kitchen to gain some normalcy. He pulls out a few bottles of marinade and several pounds of chicken. He starts some water for yellow rice. He puts the first bag of broccoli in the microwave and gathers several plastic containers.

Why is it that lids always end up disappearing?

He brings out the aluminum foil.

The smell of the grand meal permeates throughout the house. Soon after, Adrian hears the familiar steps of Lorelei's slippers coming down the hall. He hears the bar stool slide out and the creak as she sits in it.

"Hey," he says.

"Hey. Cooking for an army again?"

"Yeah, well when you grow up in a big family, it's hard to go small."

Adrian opens the first container and fills it. "I'm sorry, Lorelei."

Tears gather in Lorelei's eyes. She stays quiet.

Adrian turns around and sees Lorelei's pain. "I'm hating the misery I'm causing you," he says as he moves toward the bar, his red eyes on her.

She hides her own bloodshot eyes behind her palms, clears her throat and says, "Then don't."

"I'm not trying to. I'm just stuck."

"I hate that this Wyatt thing had to happen for Jeremy and for us. I've never seen such a wild look in your eyes. The obsession you have over this isn't healthy." Lorelei leans closer toward him. "Adrian, don't you see that this whole thing is conjuring up the darkness you try so hard to avoid? And because you don't want to deal with it, you're slipping into it? Please, please see a therapist. If you want, I can make the appointment. We can both go if that helps. The therapist will guide you on how to get past this so you can move on. So, *we* can move on."

Adrian studies Lorelei. "Are you giving me an ultimatum

here?"

"Yes."

Adrian backs up.

"So, if I don't go, we're over?"

"I will not allow you or anyone else to mistreat me the way you did earlier. And if that is how you're going to be from this point forward, whether you mean to or not, then yes, we'll be over. I've known you a long time, Adrian, and I've never seen you like that. You are a loving man. I know, but that loving man is becoming lost to this dark thing I don't want to know."

Lorelei peers down at the counter, as if afraid of his answer at first, but then glares at Adrian with a fierceness he's never seen. He can tell she means business.

"I love you, Adrian. I always have and I always will. You've got to fix this, though."

Adrian nods.

"I'll call the therapist tomorrow then. Goodnight." Lorelei says and returns to the bedroom. No hugs. No kisses. No "everything will be all right." It's real. He just might lose her.

He can't let that happen.

CHAPTER

18

A drian pulls the blanket up to his shoulders after the last head bob finally wakes him up. The recliner is no more comfortable than it was yesterday. He contemplates moving to his bed, but he's not sure Lorelei wants him there and figures it's probably best to give her some space. The digital clock reads 3:45 a.m. It's too early for him to get up, so he closes his eyes and fidgets around into a more comfortable spot. A few minutes pass, but Adrian is still awake.

So, he starts thinking—something he tries to stay away from because it only causes him pain—but there's a mystery to this whole thing with Wyatt. He decides to start piecing everything together from the beginning.

Wyatt goes missing a week ago last Sunday, Adrian starts his new job and finds out about it Monday, the police have been searching since then, samples have been collected, but the DNA results aren't back. There were blood and bike tire marks on the bike trail and boot imprints heading toward the water. Adrian started seeing shadows on Monday, and they've grown into full scenes since then, including the most recent one yesterday where Jeremy not only looks at Adrian, but Adrian turns into the captor. There's been no word from Jeremy since the first few days of the police search and still no Wyatt. Adrian has not only been seeing the crime scene but also visions of Wyatt alone. The scenes started off silent but recently, he's been hearing sounds including yesterday, when Adrian heard Wyatt's sniffles.

So, what, I'll be able to hear the scene now? I'm not sure I want to hear Wyatt's agony. I'm not sure I could bear it.

Adrian's heartbeat increases with the thought of hearing Wyatt's whimpers as he's being bound, but then it heightens when he hears the sound of a sniffle from the other side of the safe room. His thoughts cease as he listens intently.

Another sniffle.

Holy hell! Adrian says to himself as he jumps out of the recliner and flips on the room light.

Sure enough, sitting below the train set is Wyatt, crouching with his eyes and mouth bound.

Adrian hears whimpering.

No, no! I can't do this.

Adrian flings the door open and flies down the hallway to the bedroom, entering quietly so he doesn't disturb Lorelei and enters the master bathroom. He flicks on the light and immediately sees a reflection of Jeremy standing in the closet. Adrian closes his eyes and fumbles his way over to the sink to splash some water on his face. He knows he shouldn't look into the mirror—only bad things are probably standing behind him, but he can't help himself. He has to see what's going on.

He faces the mirror and opens his eyes.

He sees the back of the man he originally thought was a beast. He lets the scene unfold as usual with Adrian standing behind the shoulder of a man that seems to be Jeremy. Adrian moves in to try to help Wyatt and dark eyes pierce into him, only they are not Jeremy's. They are his own.

Adrian watches himself bind Wyatt. He hears Wyatt's muffled screams. He feels the stones beneath his boots and the prickly rope in his hands. He can see up and down the trail.

Then he watches himself carry Wyatt to the water. He sees himself rowing the boat deeper into Green Swamp. With only a hint of light from the moon, he steers the boat to the shoreline, not too far from the crime scene. He lifts Wyatt over his shoulder again and pulls the bike beside him, this time away from the water and to the uplands. He remembers his shoulder aching as he carries him up an embankment and into a pine forest. He sees a chain hanging on the tree ahead.

And he witnesses himself dropping Wyatt into the ground.

"What the hell is happening?" Adrian yells out loud, gasping for air, his eyes deep red again.

Lorelei runs to his side.

Adrian is hysterical, unable to control his breathing or his heart rate. Lorelei tries to comfort him, but he pushes her out of the way and enters the safe room, slamming the door behind him.

He rushes for the recliner and holds onto the arms

while he sits, gripping them tight. It's the one place he feels safe.

After a couple of minutes, his breathing starts to even out, and he calms down. He tries to think about what he just saw, but he can't yet. His mind feels empty, foggy even. He continues sitting in the recliner grasping the arms of the chair like a long-time friend. He feels if he lets go, he'll spiral down into an abyss that he's seen before—one that he never wants to experience again.

But the floodgates have opened and the visions relentlessly plague him, giving him more and more information on the whereabouts and status of Wyatt.

A tear slides down Adrian's cheek after he repeatedly revisits Wyatt's kidnapping. Denial and anger fill his thoughts with every tug of the rope. There's only one explanation for why this is happening. There's no escaping it.

"I did this," he says aloud.

He remembers the anger he felt toward Wyatt and Jeremy, both of them taking risks with Wyatt's safety.

He remembers hearing the hoot owl and watching Wyatt fall on the trail. He had planned on throwing a rock at Wyatt's bike tires, but what great luck for mother nature to take care of things for him.

He remembers his anxiousness with getting Wyatt tied up and out of there before he was caught, and his relief once he placed the lid back on the box in the ground.

Box in the ground? *Where the hell is this*?

You know where, he answers to himself, a chill runs

through his veins that makes his neck twitch. *You know where Wyatt is. Who do you think you're kidding?*

"No!" he yells. "I don't know what you're talking about!"

That's because it was me who was present, not you, the other side of him says with a wicked laugh.

Adrian frowns. *The other side of me? What do you mean? Who are you?*

I'm your dark side. The place you hide things you don't want to see. The place that shelters you from pain. I do your dirty deeds and block them from your memory, because when I'm in charge, you can do nothing about it. You were told about me after the accident—that you had another personality—but you chose to ignore me. I've sheltered you far too long. Now, it's time to let you see.

See what?

You know Wyatt is in the box now, right? How about Jeremy?

"Jeremy? What about him?" Adrian asks.

Think about it. Day three of the investigation. Jeremy disappeared. You know where he is.

Adrian's heart flops as the blanks in time come into focus. He remembers now.

He invited Jeremy over to his house three days after Wyatt went missing. He remembers cooking and still being furious with Jeremy for letting Wyatt ride his bike alone at night. Jeremy went on and on about how he missed Wyatt as Adrian slapped another chicken breast into a plastic container. Jeremy didn't notice Adrian's anger. He was too distraught over his own situation.

Adrian invited Jeremy out to the back deck. The air was cool and still. Adrian pulled out a seat for Jeremy, and they both sat next to their Heinekens. Jeremy continued with his agonizing worry over Wyatt while Adrian quietly listened in disgust to a man who would allow this to happen.

Then, the wind picked up as the one-sided conversation continued, whipping passed their ears now and then. The sky grew darker as the sunset closed in.

"I can't believe those useless police officers haven't found him yet. Maybe we need the FBI," Jeremy said. He took a swig of his beer. "I can't sleep. I can't eat. I'm a mess."

Finally, Adrian piped in. "What would you do differently? Would you have picked up Wyatt instead of allowing him to ride his bike home?"

Jeremy scoffed and said, "Well, no. I mean, we can't protect our kids every minute of the day or they wouldn't be independent."

Adrian nodded, his jawline firm. "Just terrible what happened."

"Yeah, terrible isn't even the word for it. Heart-wrenching maybe. I don't know. I'm about to go out of my mind worrying."

"Well, maybe you should go away for a while," Adrian replied, clenching his fingers around the arm of his chair.

"Go away? Now? Are you crazy? The police would hunt me down in a minute and besides, I couldn't do that. What if Wyatt came home?"

"Maybe somewhere no one could find you. Maybe you need a break."

"Fucking-A, I need a break. I'm going to lose it. If only I had a chance to see him again." Jeremy lowered his head and wiped his eyebrow. "I mean it, man. I'm going to be a lunatic by the time this is over."

Adrian's lips jerked.

"Hey, did you hear that?" Jeremy asked.

"Hear what?"

"Sounded like kids yelling."

Adrian tilted his head. "Nope."

"There it is again." Jeremy got up. "You don't hear it? It's like a scream."

The wind kicked up again. Adrian listened. "Oh, yeah, I do hear something." Adrian rose and threw his beer into the trash. "It sounds like those stupid kids trespassing on my property again. They've been trying to build a tree house in the back of the woods for months. I'm going to have to go chase them out. Wanna join me?"

Jeremy listened again and heard another yell. "Huh, really? How do you chase them out?"

"I go down there with a ladder. Sometimes, I surprise them when I pop my head into their partially built tree house. They get so busy talking, they don't always hear me coming up. Their faces always look stunned when I tell them to get out. Guess I'm too nice because they always come back."

Jeremy chuckled. He drank from his beer bottle and placed it back on the table. "Sure. Why not? It'll keep me busy."

"Great. Help me get the ladder. It's pretty long."

Adrian and Jeremy pulled the ladder off the side of the shed. "Okay, you should probably go backward since I know where I'm going. I'll guide you."

"Oh, great. Don't let me step in a hole."

Adrian laughed under his breath. "I won't."

After a while, Jeremy no longer sees the house. Another scream pierced the woods. "Sounds like they're having a good time back there," he said.

"Sounds like it all right. Just keep going straight back. We should see them soon."

Adrian pushed Jeremy along as they moved farther back into the woods. He saw a shimmer from the setting sun bounce off something in the distance, letting him know he was on the right path. "Just a little longer."

"Damn, I keep getting slapped by all these branches on the ground. Makes me think they're snakes trying to bite me."

"Do you want to rest?"

"Nah, I'm good. How much farther?"

Adrian looked beyond Jeremy. "About a hundred more feet or so."

Jeremy glanced behind his feet and continued walking backward. Adrian lined him up with the chain hanging from the tree.

"The screams are getting closer." Jeremy frowned. "But it only seems like one."

"Hmm...maybe you're right. Maybe there's only one. That'd be good."

A scream emanated from the ground and Jeremy looked down. He frowned. "That sounded like it was from below, not above."

Adrian peered down, too. "The sound is probably just bouncing off the ground." He looked up into the trees behind Jeremy. "I think I see them. Move! Quick!" he yelled, jerking Jeremy backward with the ladder and watching as his best friend dropped into the ground. He quickly slid the steel trap door over the opening and locked it. Then he scanned the area around him, grabbed the ladder, and walked back toward the house.

On the way, he muttered, "Now, maybe you'll learn to

properly take care of your son."

He walked up to the house and stopped to listen. Adrian heard no more screaming. "Good. Now that I have a father *and* a son, it's on to finding some girls." He then threw away Jeremy's beer and phone.

At least I won't need to worry about him calling anyone.

Adrian shuts off this memory. He can take no more. His heart is pounding and he can feel fluttering in his chest. He sits in his recliner, staring into space.

Could this be real? he asks himself.

He feels numb, devoid of empathy or sympathy or sorrow or any emotion, really. It's almost as if he's left his body.

It's better not to feel right now.

Suddenly, weight begins pressing on his insides. When his self-loathing returns, his disgust with his actions are relentless. He shakes uncontrollably. The pressure that Adrian now feels is unbearable.

It's he who is the beast.

It's he who is the unforgivable one.

This beast is not the one he wanted to be as a child, the one who watched over the house with his little brother. This beast is wretched, disgusting, despicable. Loathsome.

I can't be this person.

But there's only one way to find out.

Adrian pulls himself up from the chair and opens the door to the safe room. He enters the kitchen and pauses.

Is this why I've been cooking so much? To feed prisoners?

He shakes his head, not wanting to know the answer, and steps out onto the back porch. He notices that the empty Heinekens are still in the trashcan.

It can't be.

Adrian marches straight through his backyard and into the woods. He stops for a second to look back at the shed. The ladder is hanging on the sidewall. Then he proceeds, his feet taking him exactly where he needs to go.

Lorelei tip-toes out of the bedroom and into the hallway as soon as she hears the screeching from the sliding glass doors opening. She enters the dining room and peers out of the window in time to see Adrian walk into the woods. It's daybreak. The door to the safe room is open, so she quickly enters to see if she can find a clue as to what is going on with Adrian. Everything is pretty much the same as usual: the walls stacked with emergency supplies, the train set, the recliner, and the end table. Lorelei bolts for the end table and finds Adrian's diary. She swore she'd never read it, but with everything that has been going on, she feels she has no choice. She runs her hands across the velvety front, then opens it, flipping the pages until she can see the last entry. All it describes is the events from Wyatt's kidnapping—a summary of events she already knew.

Crap.

Lorelei quickly returns the diary back into the drawer when she sees the corner of a box. She removes it from the drawer and unwraps its contents. Several figurines fly out of the tissue paper and fall onto the floor. Lorelei fumbles with the rest, trying not to drop them too. She swears under her breath and picks up the rest of the figurines, holding them all in her hands. She counts two adults and six children. Puzzled, she stares at them, wondering why they're hidden away in the drawer. She's never seen them before.

The doorbell rings, startling Lorelei. She hastily wraps the figurines back in the tissue paper, slides them into the box and drawer, and rushes to the front door.

It's Gentry.

"Oh, hey, Lorelei. I was hoping to catch one of you home tonight. How are you?"

"Doing well, Gentry. And yourself?"

"Good. Say, I was wondering if Adrian had a chance to talk with you about coming over this weekend. We're having a housewarming party."

Lorelei frowns, trying to remember a conversation about this with Adrian.

"Well," Gentry says, "with the Wyatt situation and all, I'm sure it hasn't been the foremost thing on Adrian's mind," Gentry says.

"Yeah, he probably forgot to tell me. Count on us there, though. I'm sure he'd like to hang out."

"Sounds great! Tell him I said thank you again for watching out for Taylor the other evening too. It's good to have caring neighbors. It's not like there are many in the neighborhood." Gentry laughs as he backs away from the door.

"Thanks, Gentry. I'll be sure to tell him."

Lorelei closes the door and heads straight for the bedroom before Adrian returns.

CHAPTER

19

The early morning dew glistens along the branches of the oaks as the sun rises in the east. Adrian moves quickly through the woods, noticing a puff of smoke when he exhales. He carefully steps around moss-covered limbs that have broken loose and fallen to the ground through the years. There's no path from the back-yard to follow, but he knows the way. He doesn't always take the same route. Why would he? It's better that the ground look disheveled, kept to its natural state. Pine needles coat the area beneath the trees, almost appearing to be a sea of hay. The birds are chattering throughout his hike, seemingly unafraid of the stranger in the woods.

Straight ahead, Adrian can see the chain hanging loosely from a nail in a tree. His heart rate jumps immediately and he stops, afraid of what he will see as he moves closer.

But he proceeds.

He has to.

He aligns himself with the chain and peers down at the ground. There should be a trap door, one that flips over once it's pulled up along its hinges. One that's metal with a locked latch. One that is well camouflaged under the offerings from the trees. He hears the leaves and needles crunching under his feet until his foot hits solid metal.

He gently clears the debris from the door with his hand. He tugs on the lock, half expecting it to drop open. Seeing that it doesn't, he twists the dial back and forth to the right combination. The lock slides open with a click.

Adrian grabs the handle and slowly pulls up, revealing the area beneath it, just enough to peek through.

He sees a soft glow from a light, then a pair of eyes staring back at him from several feet below, startling Adrian. The door slips out of his hands and slams back down to the ground.

Adrian can hear the faint sound of a small boy's voice say, "No! No! Please don't go! Please!"

Then the voice from a man says, "Adrian? Is that you? Come on, man, let us out of here!"

Adrian sits on the door, his mind reeling as he comes to terms with having two kidnapped people below him.

Who does this? What kind of wretched soul does this to good souls?

The other side of you, he answers to himself. *When I take over.*

He bends his head down and covers his mouth with his hand. A slew of emotions surges through his body at once, the worst being self-loathing.

I hate you, he says to himself. *You are a monster. Let them out. You deserve jail time. You deserve everything coming to you, you rotten scum of the earth.*

"Please! Please! Help us!" the young boy repeats over and over again.

Adrian listens to the boy's voice and sighs.

It's Wyatt. It's confirmed. I've really done this horrible crime. I snatched my friend's son and dropped him into this box. This box. This box on my property. Adrian's hands begin to shake.

I've been hidden away too long, Adrian. I couldn't let you see. I've been helping you get your family back.

Yelling, promises, and pleas ensue from below, but Adrian concentrates on remembering the box through his cloudy mind.

What is this place? he asks himself.

You know. It's the place you turned into a mini-apartment. Only there are no windows and the only escape to the outside world is kept locked, he answers.

I did this?

Well, I did actually. What, you don't remember fixin' up the old place down there? It's got beds, supplies, running water, lights and even a toilet! Who wouldn't want to live down in that creepy box in the ground?

Memories flood into Adrian's consciousness. He remembers the day he found the box. There was no mention of it from the previous owners. He just happened to be taking a walk through the woods when he crossed over the door and found out it was an empty box a little bigger than a train car. The previous owners seemed to use it as a safe room of some sort. So, naturally, Adrian started to think of it in that way, too, and eventually stocked it with all the necessities he might need during a tornado. And as the months passed, his ideas grew more and more grand, thinking how it would be nice to have a bathroom and storage shelves. He even hooked up an overhead shower and drain, though he'd have to bathe in front of anyone else that might be in the small space with him. But he considered it a small price to pay for safety during emergency events. Who else would be in there besides Lorelei anyway? Not that she knows about the box.

Adrian rubs his eyes with his fingers, then the back of his neck. A second wave of memories flashes before him. He remembers missing his family, especially Jonathan. How he wished they were still with him. How he wished he could go back in time and be with his best friend, the brother who'd always been by his side. A wave of pain shoots up Adrian's face and spreads out along his forehead. He's blocked out the memory of his brother's death for so long, he hasn't been able to face the grief even to this day. It cuts too deep.

And then I came soon after the accident. You've tried to fight me all these years, but here I am.

Another scream for help breaks through his thoughts. Adrian stands and steps to the side of the door.

What are you gonna do, Adrian?

I don't know.

Yes, you do.

Adrian opens the sliding glass door and steps into the dining room. It's eight in the morning, so he picks up his cell to let work know he's going to be late. He calls out to Lorelei as he hurries down the hallway and into the bedroom, but she's already left for work. He goes into the bathroom to face himself in the mirror.

Hopefully, she's at Colt Creek again this morning. We wouldn't want her finding some unexpected friends in the ground, now, would we?

Colt Creek is way on the other side of Green Swamp, so they should be good.

I need to go back there and let them out.

No, you don't. It's time for the family to be back together.

The family can never be back together, you know that. I need to let these people go.

They'll be safer in there. You won't have to worry about them anymore.

I need to let them go.

No.

I need to.

No.

I need to let Jeremy and Wyatt go back to their normal lives.

Hell, no! Are you not hearing me? You won't have to worry about Wyatt traipsing around some swamp by himself. He's still with his father. That should count for something.

That's not good enough.

It'll have to be. You did this just as much as I did, so don't look at me that way.

Adrian shifts his eyes from the mirror.

How in the world can you live with yourself?

The same as you. Don't kid yourself into thinking you are different from me. We are one and the same. Only you think you have a conscience now.

The scene plays out again in the mirror and the beast tapes Wyatt's mouth as he speaks to Adrian. Adrian peers back at himself, then to the beast.

"I hate you!" Adrian says. "You are the epitome of everything I hate in myself," he continues.

That's unfortunate, Adrian, because you are starting to lose yourself to the darkest side of you.

Adrian turns away from the mirror and heads toward the dining room, only he doesn't go out the sliding glass doors to free Wyatt and Jeremy. He opens the door to the safe room and locks himself inside. He reaches over from his recliner to the side table drawer and finds the box of figurines. He opens it and immediately notices that the figurines are not in the same order as he left them. They are shoved into the tissue paper, not neatly wound in order of youngest to oldest. Even worse, his sister, Amy Lynn, is missing.

He searches around the end table and on the floor for Amy, his heart rate increasing with every second she's lost. He gets on all fours and sees her arm from behind the leg of the recliner. Relief flows from his stomach into his chest when he finds her intact.

"There you are," he says, smiling at first, then growing concern. "Lorelei must have been snooping around in here."

You're going to have to deal with that, you know.

Adrian walks over to the train set, placing each figurine at the train station. Then he turns on the train, losing himself in the circular track and feeling as if he, too, is there, watching through the eyes of his figurine. He would love nothing more than to stand there again with his family. He can't help but feel connected to them through this display. The train. The tracks. The mountains. The river. The trestle bridge. They are all intricately connected to Adrian and his family in a way he will never forget. He usually focuses on the good years, ones in which they traveled together without tragedy. But on that cool summer day ten years ago, Adrian's life changed forever, and with it, Adrian changed too.

CHAPTER

20

TEN YEARS AGO

Adrian presses his forehead against the cold window to see the trestle bridge as it comes into view. A maze of crosshatched steel rises from the valley floor to hold the rails in place. Patches of snow dot the mountainous terrain ahead, and the morning mist is steaming upward over portions of the tracks. Rusted tracks. All he can think about is whether or not the bridge will hold up against decades of train crossings.

Even at the age of fifteen, Adrian senses the inherent risk. He worries the wear from pounding, churning wheels have stressed the railheads to the point of fatigue which could cause them to fail. And if they fail, especially so high up, the train could fall. Adrian jerks his head to extinguish the thought. He turns his attention to the inside of the train car and listens to the excited discussions by his beloved parents and five brothers and sisters. The tangy smell of cheese crackers and gummy bears lingers in the air. He smiles when he remembers why he's here. This is supposed to be a fun family vacation. He can't let his fear ruin it.

He takes a deep breath and exhales slowly.

Jonathan presses his cheek against Adrian's arm. "It looks cold out there, Adrian. I'm glad we're here in this nice, warm train," he says with the hint of a southern accent.

"Yeah, me too."

Jonathan studies his older brother's expression for a minute. "Are you worried again, Adrian?"

Adrian scoffs. "Of course not. We'll be off this train soon enough, and we're going to play football just like I promised. We'll beat all those girls, too." He kicks the seat in front of him.

"Oh, you think so," a voice squeaks from seven-year-old Amy, who's sitting in front of them. "You two *wish* you could beat us girls. There are more of us than you, you know. Four against two. We're going to beat you!" She peeks one eye between the seats until a quick jerk from the train bounces her back into her seat.

"Yeah! We're going to beat you guys!" a chorus of girls replies from ahead, followed by chatter, the sound of which reminds Adrian of his neighbor's small dogs back in Indiana whose incessant yipping wakes him up way too early on Saturday mornings. Adrian listens to the excited discussions over dolls, crayons, music, and boys over the rumbling of the train tracks—a mixture of interests for girls, ages two to fourteen. He knows he probably has no chance against their sheer numbers, especially being that Jonathan is only nine years old. *The girls will be disorganized though*, he thinks. *Perhaps that would be their demise.*

"Okay, girls," Adrian's mother warns after catching the eye of an annoyed older lady. "Keep it down. We'll be there before you know it. Remember—inside voices."

Adrian glances at his dad who has his headphones on, so he decides to put his on, too. He pulls them out of his pocket, fumbling with the cords until he finally gets them untangled and places them over his ears. He attaches the other end to his mp3 player and whips through his library until he finds some distracting music. He rests his head back, happy to escape the cabin noise. That is, until he peers out of the window and sees that the train is seconds away from crossing the trestle bridge.

He immediately sits upright, paying attention to every shake and rattle from the train. His senses sharpen as he watches the engine move along the tracks, followed by car after car. Cars with people in them. Cars with loved ones in them.

Thick trees suddenly hug the tracks and block his view. He turns to Jonathan who's sleeping despite his bobbing head. He can hear the train clanking louder as his car nears the bridge. He pulls off his headphones. This is the worst part for him. He's been through this before.

He closes his eyes and tries to calm his pounding heart. He knows he's just being silly, but he can't control his reactions. Fear has taken over.

Jonathan tugs on Adrian's sleeve and places his hand on his forearm. The distraction pulls Adrian out of his delusions about falling and saving his family. He opens his eyes and sees that the sunshine is lighting up the cabin. The wheels strain against the transition between land tracks and bridge tracks, and the trees suddenly give way to a vast openness. A clear blue April sky and a plunging mountainside draw Adrian's attention and, as always, he feels like he's being pulled over the edge. He clasps his fingers around the arms of the seat to hold on in case he falls, barely able to catch his breath.

"It'll be okay," Jonathan whispers.

Adrian clears his voice and replies, "Yeah, of course. It'll just be a few minutes." He plops his head back onto the headrest and closes his eyes.

"Adrian, don't you want to see outside? Look how small the stream is below."

Adrian reluctantly tries to enjoy the view. He focuses on the pure expanse of the valley at first with steep mountain faces and clustered evergreens adorning each side. The view is stunning to him at first but quickly turns to dread when he sees the stream. "That's no stream, Jon. That's a raging river. It just appears like it's small from way up here."

"Why are you so nervous, Adrian? Do you think we'll fall?"

Adrian hesitates with his answer. He contemplates whether to be truthful, as his mother has always taught him or to lie so that Jonathan won't be tormented by the same fear of heights. Instead of replying, Adrian peers out of the window toward the front of the train—to the engine, hoping it would be nearing the other side and he would hear the change in the clanking when he's once again on safe, solid land. His hopes are thwarted though when he sees the engine pulling the train is only nearing the middle of the valley. *Soon*, he tells himself.

Jonathan pats his arm. Adrian grins at Jonathan's consoling gesture but returns to watch the train chug onward.

He hums the rhythmic sound as each wheel passes through the attached rails along with the squeaking of metal-against-metal which resonates within the cabin—all normal sounds from a train taking its routine route through the majestic Rocky Mountains.

Adrian's pulse slows. He feels comforted that half of the bridge is now behind him. *We're almost there,* he says to himself and readjusts in his seat to relax his tense neck.

He turns to Jonathan and smiles.

Suddenly, they both lurch forward, their seatbelts the only thing keeping them in their seats. Loud skidding sounds groan through the cabin from the wheels that are having difficulty gripping the tracks. Jonathan covers his ears and screams Adrian's name.

Adrian peers outside and sees that the engine has made it onto land, but several cars ahead of them are dangling along the side of the trestle bridge, pulling other cars down with them. He instinctively presses his right foot down in front of him, as if he has the brake, and grabs for Jonathan's hand. He yells to his mom, but she can't hear him through the loud racket. His dad's headphones are now dangling around his chest. None of his family members know what's about to happen. Their window blinds are closed.

Adrian screams at them. He warns them that the train is falling off the tracks ahead, to make sure their seatbelts are on, to hold onto each other, all of which cannot be heard. Finally, Amy opens her window blind with shaking arms caused by the erratic train movements. Adrian waves his hands at his mom and points for her to look outside.

The realization of what is about to occur floods onto her face and panic sets in as she unbuckles herself to help protect her "babies." Dad follows out of reaction at first until he, too, realizes the train is falling. As soon as he releases his buckle, though, he is thrown forward into the seat in front of him, unable to control his limbs that are being tossed around. Adrian watches in horror as his train car is pulled off the tracks and shifted onto its side, revealing the depths of the gorge below through the windows as it hangs from the bridge. His mother falls onto the window in front of him, followed by his dad, who flies sideways and ends up just above Adrian's head. Adrian flings his right arm across Jonathan and holds onto the armrest to shield him.

Then, the front part of the cabin twists until the seats are upside down, separating itself from the back part of the cabin which remains sideways. He sees his sisters hanging from their seats, screaming in terror. Adrian tries to think quickly. He is, after all, one of the school's strongest engineering candidates, so he has been told. He certainly can think of something to do. He's the oldest. He has to keep his family safe.

Adrian grasps onto Jonathan, as he peers through the window that's holding his dad. He reaches for his dad's leg with his left arm and cries for his mom whom he cannot reach. The train car groans and drops a few more inches, pulling it further apart. Adrian can see the valley below through a crack between the two windows, separating his mom from his dad. A gust of cold wind engulfs the cars, pushing them back and forth. A car located two ahead screeches downward as it hits the sides of the bridge, muffling the screams from inside and causing the car in front of them to slide headfirst toward the valley below. Adrian's train car is pulled apart even further.

There are only seconds. No time for his dad or mom to react. No time for Adrian to engineer a happy ending. No time for Adrian to grab onto his dad before he falls straight down toward the river after part of the cabin pulls off, or his mom who slides along the interior of the windows until she, too, falls. No time for Adrian to save his sisters, whose seats break off from the floor seconds later and crash through the windows, the force of which causes the entire front of the train car to catapult toward the river. He sees their desperate faces as their bodies tumble and limbs flail as they drop.

Adrian clutches onto Jonathan as they both hang sideways, strapped into their seats. Adrian screams in agony as the trauma of losing his family sinks in. His mind becomes clouded, dazed.

After a few seconds, Adrian notices the chaos has grown silent. He hears the wind whipping past his ears. He shivers in the cold air. All he can see is a color palette of blues, whites, and greens as he stares into the valley below. His breathing is erratic as he tries to comprehend what just happened and what he needs to do next. Adrian turns and sees that the back of the train car is still attached to the tracks, despite hanging sideways. He's surrounded by wires and steel rods sticking out around them. Strong winds push at them from the west, gripping and pulling at their seats as it goes by.

Adrian sees Jonathan pushing his feet against his seat to escape backward. "Jonathan! No!" Adrian screams. "Don't wiggle too much!"

But fear has taken over. Jonathan pushes harder against the bottom of the seat to climb out. Adrian grabs at him, but Jonathan wiggles out of his seatbelt. The train car lunges downward a few inches. Jonathan falls out of his seat, but luckily the seatbelt entangles his foot, holding him. Adrian grabs onto Jonathan's leg, then his arm. He knows he's strong enough to hold him. He can save him. Jonathan peers up at Adrian, looking relieved.

Adrian pulls up on Jonathan's leg, but the force involved with hanging from the train quickly causes Adrian's arm to fatigue. He tries to pull him up again, when Jonathan's seat detaches from the floor, slides past Adrian, and falls, jerking Jonathan's leg from Adrian's grip. Adrian desperately grabs onto Jonathan's arm with both hands, preventing him from falling. He can see the seat dangling below, Jonathan's leg still entangled in the seatbelt.

Wind pushes up against Jonathan, causing him to swing and slip out of Adrian's left hand.

Adrian yells in agony, holding Jonathan with his right hand. He grabs at Jonathan's arm again with his free hand, but can't reach it. Jonathan begins spinning in the wind.

With a loud pop, Adrian's right arm pulls out of its socket.

Adrian screams, "No!" but there's nothing he can do. He watches the terror in his brother's eyes as the weight of the seat wins against Adrian's weakened arm. Their hands slide quickly past each other, and Jonathan's body jerks out of control as he falls. Adrian yells for him until he can no longer see him. Tears blur his vision as he sobs for Jonathan and the rest of his lost family.

Bewildered, Adrian stares into the valley floor below, then at himself as he hangs sideways, his seatbelt still holding him in place. He suddenly feels alone. He has no one left. How could he truly live a full life again? Could he go on?

He decides he can't.

Adrian thrashes and jumps in his own seat to make the

car fall, frantically pressing the button holding his seatbelt, but it won't budge. He cries in frustration, slamming his fists against the armrests until he gives up and stares at the river that probably now holds his family in its rushing current—his dead family.

He hopes he'll soon join them.

The wait is agonizing, but he soon feels an enormous force around him, as his seatbelt breaks loose.

CHAPTER

21

Adrian awakens on the floor of the safe room. He can hear the train rounding the tracks. His right arm aches. It's been weak since the accident.

The clock on the end table reads two in the afternoon. He's missed most of his workday, but he doesn't care right now. An enormous feeling of guilt and rage has built up for so many years and is taking over. Flashes of the tragedy continually rewind in his mind along with all the should-haves. Why didn't he warn his parents about the aging track? He saw a news report about it years before. He should have told them about it. Why didn't he pretend he was sick since he had the premonition something bad would happen? He should have faked a bad cold. Perhaps that would have delayed the trip a day or two and they could have caught a different train in another town. Why wasn't he strong enough to hold Jonathan? He should have worked out more, should have had stronger shoulders.

He peers down at the ten-year-old newspaper article he's holding in his hands and reads it once again:

BREAKING NEWS: BOY, 15, ONLY SURVIVOR of a family of eight following train wreck at Corning Pass, Colorado. The accident occurred late Monday morning as a passenger train was crossing a 325-foot-high trestle bridge in the Rockies. Reports indicate several train cars fell into the valley below. Adrian Webster, his parents, and five brothers and sisters were traveling on a family vacation when the accident occurred. Witnesses reported that the fifteen-year-old made every attempt to save his family including the youngest brother, Jonathan. Investigators are still recovering the bodies of the family and other passengers. The deceased Webster family members were residents of Floyd County, Indiana and included father, Parker James (age 35); mother, Corrine Kay (age 36); Gracie Ann (age 14); Michelle Jane (age 12); Jonathan Roy (age 9); Amy Lynn (age 7); and Reagan Marie (age 2). Funeral arrangements are pending.

Adrian pulls himself up and turns off the train.

I am broken.

Yes, you are.

He closes his eyes.

I have to get my family back.

Yes, you do.

Jeremy can be the dad and Wyatt can be Jonathan. I need to find Jeremy a wife. A good one, just like my mom. And Wyatt, I mean Jonathan, will have sisters. Four of them. They can be chatty down there in the box. I insulated it well. No one will hear them, right?

Absolutely.

And then I can visit them every day. Bring them food and water. Medicine. Books. Games. Even the newspaper so they can keep up with the times. I'll build a mesh screen so I can let the sunlight in every day for a couple of hours just like a skylight. They'd appreciate the feeling of being outside, and I wouldn't want them to get eaten alive by bugs.

And you know how to cook for a large family.

Yes! I'll take fresh food to them every day. It'll be so great to talk to my family again and hear them laugh and play. I miss them so much. It'll be like old times.

Then, go make it happen.

Adrian grabs a couple of blankets and pillows and jogs out to the woods with a smile on his face and excitement he hasn't felt in a long time.

"Adrian?" Lorelei says as she places grocery bags onto the counter. "I have some heavy groceries I need you to bring inside."

She pauses to hear him respond. "Adrian?"

Still no response.

"Great," she says with a smirk. She returns to her car and struggles with the pack of bottled water as she starts to lift it into her arms.

"Lorelei! Wait!"

Lorelei sees a truck pull up. Gentry jumps out and approaches her. His expression is serious, not the normal good-ole-boy smile he usually wears. "Hey Lorelei, have you seen my daughter, Taylor?"

"No, I just got home. Why?"

"We were out riding bikes together and she rode off ahead of me. I wasn't sure which street she went down and we got separated. I went back home to grab my truck to search for her, but I can't find her. She likes coming down this way, so I thought maybe you might've seen her."

"No, as I said, I just pulled in and have been taking the groceries inside. I didn't see her riding by or anything. Did you look down the street in the cul-de-sac?"

"Yeah, there's no sign of her. I'm getting really worried because it's already five, and it'll be dark soon. I can't imagine where she went." Gentry paces in front of his truck for a few seconds. "Wait, is Adrian home? Can you ask if he saw her?"

"I just yelled for him inside, but he didn't answer me. Let me check if he's asleep or something. Come on in."

Gentry shakes his head. "I can't. I have to keep searching. Can you ask him and give me a call as soon as you can?"

"Sure, Gentry. No problem. I'm sure she's just gotten herself turned around somewhere and will be back home soon. Is your wife there? If not, I can go wait for Taylor at your house, if you'd like."

"No, no. My wife is there. If you see or hear anything let me know."

"I will. Let me know when you find her."

"Sounds good." Gentry pulls out his business card with his cell phone number and hands it to Lorelei. His face is flushed and his hands are shaking. "Please let me know what Adrian says."

Lorelei nods and replies, "I promise."

Gentry takes off, and Lorelei runs into the house with the last of the grocery bags.

"Adrian, are you here?" She drops the bags on the counter and listens for a second. She races to the bedroom but doesn't find him, then runs to the dining room. "Adrian, where are you?" She notices the door to the safe room is ajar, sprints over to it, and peeks inside, but Adrian is not there either.

Where are you? Your truck is outside.

She makes her way over to the refrigerator to see if he left a message on the small whiteboard, but it's empty. Then she peers outside through the glass doors.

Maybe he went for a walk in the woods again.

Lorelei slides the glass door open and yells for him. Getting no response, she picks up her cell and texts him.

Still no response.

She goes back to the front yard and combs the nearby streets to help Gentry, but there's no sign of Taylor. Most of the houses in the neighborhood are half built and vacant, so there's no one around to help with the search.

Lorelei calls Gentry. "Hey, it's Lorelei. Any luck?"

"No. I've called the police. This is bad. I know it. She has never ridden off before."

"I'm sure they'll find her. I haven't been able to ask Adrian yet, but I will as soon as I see him. Let me know if I can do anything else."

"I will. Thanks, Lorelei."

Lorelei returns to the house. Adrian is still nowhere to be found. She goes down the hallway, but there's something about the safe room that draws her in. She flicks on the light and stares at the end table.

"Looking for something?"

Lorelei jumps, covering her chest with her hand.

Adrian laughs. Lorelei sees him standing near the train-set. His jeans have blotches of dirt at the knees and his hair is greasy. It's apparent to Lorelei that he hasn't showered.

"You scared me! What are you doing over there in the dark?"

"I was just turning everything off to come out and see you."

"I've been searching everywhere for you. I saw your truck here, but couldn't find you to ask about Taylor."

"Taylor?"

"Yes, she's missing and Gentry was here asking if we've seen her. He's been looking everywhere."

"Well, how did he lose her?"

"He said he was riding his bike with her, and she rode off out of his sight. He hasn't seen her since."

Adrian shakes his head. "Well, that doesn't surprise me."

"Why? He said she hasn't done that before."

"Oh, really? Well, I saw her do it a few days ago."

Lorelei raises an eyebrow. "Really?"

"Yeah. I was coming down the street after work, and I saw her riding all by herself. So, I backed out and followed her because I saw her turn into the cul-de-sac. When I got there, Gentry was talking with her. But still, she was out of his sight, and he didn't seem too concerned about it."

"So, you didn't see her tonight then?"

Adrian ignores her question and pulls his cell out of his pocket. "I'm calling the police."

"You don't need to, Gentry already did."

"Oh, damn, Lorelei. Sorry I didn't see your text."

"Where were you anyway?"

"I went for a walk in the woods and then came back to the safe room."

"How come you're not over at Jeremy's place?"

Adrian leaves the safe room. Lorelei follows.

"Because I…I didn't go to work today."

"What?"

"Did you call in?"

"Yeah. I didn't want to go over to Jeremy's though in case Clark was sampling. It'd be kind of weird, being I told them I'd be late."

Lorelei frowns. "Thought you said you called out all day."

"I called in, but told them I'd be late, but then I fell asleep and ended up sleeping until mid-afternoon. I figured at that point, I might as well just take the day. They won't care."

"But Adrian, you just started this job."

"I know." Adrian looks up at her.

Lorelei pauses. "Hey, I just noticed something. Your eyes," she says.

"Bad, I know."

"No, they are completely healed up. Wow!"

Lorelei moves closer to examine his eyes and smiles. "I'm so glad to see them normal again."

"You're kidding."

"No, go look for yourself," she says. "In the meantime, I'm going to unpack my work gear."

Adrian enters the bedroom, then the bathroom. He turns on the light and peers at his eyes in the mirror. Sure enough, the whites of his eyes are clear from any redness.

See, family life is good for you.

Adrian closes his eyes for a second and sighs. He then returns to Lorelei who's tying her sneaker laces near the front door.

"Well, I would have never believed it."

Lorelei stands up. "The doctor did say about two weeks for your eyes to heal though, right? So, maybe it was just that you needed time."

Adrian snorts and says, "I guess so. I'm glad you remembered that because I didn't. Feels like it's been forever."

"I also haven't forgotten our talk last night too. I didn't get a chance to call a therapist today, but I will tomorrow."

"Great," Adrian replies unenthusiastically.

You can't let her do that.

"Well, anyway, do you want to call Gentry to get the status and see if he needs us? Otherwise, I'm going out to search for her. I can't believe I'm having to deal with another missing child," Adrian says.

Lorelei grabs his hand. "Don't let this get to you. I'm sure she just got turned around somehow."

"Yeah," he replies.

"This is why I think it's important for you to go to the therapist. I'm afraid you're going to get lost in all of this."

"I told you already, Lorelei. I'm broken."

"No, you're not. Stop thinking that way."

Adrian stares at the floor. "You know, I just noticed that all of the shadows and scenes have disappeared." He glances around the room. "I haven't seen any at all today."

"Really?"

"Yeah. It's kind of a freeing feeling. I never knew when they would dart out. Maybe I should call Clark to see if they found Wyatt today."

"Huh, might be a good idea. In the meantime, I'm calling Gentry to let him know you didn't see Taylor and to get an update."

Adrian nods and watches Lorelei as she leaves for the back porch to talk to Gentry. Then, he hurries to the safe room and closes the door. He sits on the recliner and holds onto the arms of the chair. Sweat begins collecting along his neckline.

Don't lose it now, Adrian. You can't let her see.

I know.

Adrian closes his eyes and tries concentrating on the good times.

I thought you were excited about getting your family back.

Adrian's opens his eyes. His chest is heaving. *I am.*

Then, what's the problem?

I had a terrible thought.

Oh?

I'm not sure I could live with it, though.

What's that?

Adrian frowns.

Lorelei wants to be a wife and I can't give that to her.

Uh huh.

And I can't have her calling therapists and watching me. But I can't lose her either.

What are you saying, Adrian?

Fuck. Adrian looks up at the ceiling. *God help me.*

Would she be a good wife?

Adrian drops his head. *Yes.*

Jeremy needs a wife.

I know, but I don't know if I could give her up.

You wouldn't be giving her up. You'd have her for a long time. Plus, she'd always be safe, not running around in those wetlands all the time. You wouldn't have to deal with her suspicions either. Nice and clean. You get a life with your family and no one is the wiser since she doesn't keep in touch with her family.

Adrian falls deep into his thoughts. He imagines life without Lorelei in the house. *It would be so lonely, though.*

Who else do you know that would make a good wife for Jeremy?

No one.

Right. And it solves all of the problems. She'd take good care of everyone.

CHAPTER

22

Adrian holds onto the arms of the chair as tightly as he did the day of the train accident. Then, he gets up and turns on the train, listening to it round the track. After a few minutes, he returns to the recliner. He pulls the box out of the drawer and gazes at the figurine that represents his mother, thinking how much he has missed her. Her smile. Her country breakfasts. Her love for his dad.

The door opens to the safe room and Lorelei enters. She glances toward the train set then at the figurines in Adrian's trembling hand.

"You've seen these before, right?" Adrian asks with half a smile.

"Adrian, I'm—"

"No need to apologize. Please don't, actually."

Lorelei's shoulders relax a little. "Why do you have them?" she asks, pointing to his hand.

"They represent my family. There were eight of us at one point."

"Eight?" Lorelei asks, sounding surprised. "But you've never talked about them, only Jonathan. Why not?"

Adrian watches the train. "Because of the accident. I can barely think about that day."

"Maybe you should tell me about it."

Adrian nods. "Maybe I should." He leans forward, his hands clasped together with his arms on his knees. He can't look at her.

"Ten years ago, we all went on our family vacation train ride in the Rockies. We used to go every year. Little did we know this would be the last time."

"Was there a train crash?" Lorelei's eyes grow concerned.

Adrian lowers his head. "I never really liked going, but I especially didn't like trestle bridges. They are so high and who knew if anyone routinely checked them."

Lorelei sits down in a chair near Adrian and caresses his arm. "Maybe if you tell me it'll make you feel better to get it out."

Adrian glances down at her hand. "I saw the trestle bridge coming up and I felt sick to my stomach, but I didn't want to say anything to Jonathan. I wanted to be the strong older brother. I felt it was my duty. We were all in the same train car with rows of plush individual seats, and Jonathan was sitting next to me." Adrian's voice cracks.

Lorelei wraps her arms tighter around his arm.

"I kept telling myself that I was just being paranoid. That we'd be fine. But I was wrong. We weren't fine." Adrian takes a minute to gather himself. "I saw it happening, and I couldn't do anything." He looks back at Lorelei with tear-filled eyes. "I couldn't stop it." He wipes his eyes with the palm of his hand. "I saw the engine reach the other side. It made land. But then I saw that a couple of the cars behind it began to sag off the side of the trestle bridge." He begins to sob and shake his head. "It happened so fast."

Lorelei pulls her head up to look at Adrian.

"Before I could warn my family, our train car fell off the side, too, and all of my family fell out of it and down into the river."

Lorelei grasps her face into her hands. "Oh, no! Oh, my God!"

"All except Jonathan. He was still hanging so I grabbed him with my hand." Adrian stares at his hand, reliving the feeling of Jonathan's touch. "I thought for sure I could save him. But I was too weak. My shoulder popped and—" Adrian closes his eyes. "And he fell too."

"Oh, my God, Adrian. I'm so sorry!" She sobs with him.

"I lost them all that day. All at the same time. Not just Jonathan." After a couple of minutes, Adrian adds, "And I wanted to fall, too. How was I supposed to live without my family?"

"How did you survive?"

"My seat held. We were the last train car to hang from the edge of the bridge. The force was too much on our train car which ended up ripping it in half. The front end fell to the valley below with my family. The back end stayed attached to the car behind it. Some people saw what was happening and saved me, I guess. I don't know how. I blacked out."

Lorelei hugs Adrian for a few minutes. "So, that's why you have the train set and figurines."

"Yeah, for whatever reason, it has been my only

comfort—to hear the train wind around the tracks, go over the trestle bridge, and make it to the other side every time." He looks down at his hands, still holding the figurines. "Sometimes I'll put them near the train station to remind me. I don't want to ever forget."

He pulls out of Lorelei's arms, walks over to the train set, and places each figurine at the train station.

She glances up at him then back down to her hands. "I'm just dumbfounded. I don't know how you've been living with this all these years. I don't know what to say other than that I love you and am here for you."

Adrian glares back at her, his sorrow rapidly switching to anger. "Are you? You want to ship me off to some therapist and leave me. Isn't that what you said last night?"

Lorelei peers back up at him. "I didn't mean—"

"Yeah, well enough about that. We need to find Taylor. What did Gentry say?"

"They haven't found Taylor yet."

"Have they looked in the woods yet?"

"I...I don't think so. Adrian, don't you think you should stay here? I'm afraid that if you find Taylor harmed—"

"What, I won't be able to handle it? That your psycho boyfriend will lose it? I won't because she's not hurt. I know it."

"Well, you don't know for sure and with the trauma from your family, I don't think it'd be good for you."

Adrian sighs. "I'm fine. It's just hard to go through the memory of it." He grabs a flashlight and leaves the safe room. "Are you coming?"

Lorelei watches him for a few seconds, then follows him to the front door and puts on her work boots. "Shouldn't we coordinate with the police?"

"Not from what I saw with Wyatt. It'll take hours for them to get organized. Besides, it won't hurt to search on our own."

Lorelei nods. "Right."

They walk swiftly through the backyard. "Oh, wait. I forgot my cell," Lorelei says.

Adrian replies, "We don't have time to go back. We're good. I've got mine."

"But what if we get separated?"

"We won't. Just stay right behind me. Besides we're not even going to be that far away from the house. Come on."

Lorelei glances back at the house, then follows Adrian into the woods.

The farther they walk, the less Lorelei can see in front of her. She's worked in the wetlands many times but always closer to the water where the reflection of the moonlight would oftentimes provide enough light to see a few feet ahead. Tonight, the light from the moon is only coming through the trees occasionally. She stumbles over large logs and brush, staying as close to Adrian as possible. She notices Adrian is walking effortlessly.

"Don't you think we should be searching in some kind of pattern?"

Without hesitation, he says, "Yeah, I'm just getting us to the back of the woods so we can plan. There's a huge drop-off where the uplands transition to wetlands, but no worries, I know exactly where that is because it opens up wide."

"Okay, makes sense," she replies.

A wind climbs up Lorelei's back, giving her a chill as it makes its way through her hair. She pulls her hood over her head and zips her jacket up to her neck when she hears a faint yell from ahead, almost as if it's coming in and out with the breeze. "Did you hear that?"

Adrian stops. "Hear what?"

"I thought I heard someone."

"You did?" Adrian waits. Then he hears it too. A very faint voice. "Oh, my God, maybe that's her!"

Adrian grabs Lorelei's hand and races toward the sound.

Lorelei pulls back on Adrian's grip. "Wait, I heard it again. It sounds like someone is crying."

"That's got to be her," Adrian replies.

They move through the woods quickly, snapping twigs and limbs as they make their way through the thick brush. The cries are getting closer and Adrian is acting upbeat, excited, even laughing.

Lorelei tries to see his face, but it's too dark.

"Adrian, why are you laughing?"

He stops and faces her. "Because the whole time everyone was looking for Taylor, she was right in our backyard."

"I don't think that's very funny, Adrian."

"Of course, you wouldn't."

Adrian's demeanor turns to anger. "You never think anything is funny. You're always so serious all the time. Lighten up." He continues walking briskly.

"What's the matter with you?" Lorelei asks from behind.

Adrian drops his head and sighs. "There's nothing wrong. Let's just go find her."

"Adrian?"

Adrian broadens his shoulders. "What?" he yells, but not in his normal voice. In a deep growl that Lorelei has never heard before.

"Adrian?"

He turns around on his heel and charges toward Lorelei. Through the dim light, she can see his face. His eyes look enraged, piercing.

Lorelei turns and runs away from him.

In a deep whispering voice, Adrian says, "Don't run. Don't you want to find Taylor?"

But Lorelei ignores him. She runs as fast as she can toward the house.

Adrian follows her but paces himself. He knows she'll run out of steam. She's not a runner or an athlete of any kind. He's not either, so he has to make sure he keeps up his strength.

The moonlight shines through just enough for Adrian to see that Lorelei is bending over, grasping her side. She's already turned to the east, too. He knows she'll never find the house in that direction.

Maybe you can get her to go south again in the direction of the box.

Adrian moves quickly and quietly around her, not wanting to spook her yet. He snaps a few branches so she'll know where he is and runs toward her.

Lorelei peers back at him and screams, turning to the south. The woods are better lit now with the moonlight showing through the clouds, and Adrian can see her every move. He sees a shimmer ahead of her from the chain hanging on the tree. She's headed straight for the box.

Are you sure about this, Adrian? There's no going back. She will be with Jeremy, and you know that times of crises often bring people together. The months and years will go by. He will comfort her. You will lose her to him. Be sure. Decide now!

"Lorelei, no! Stop! It's a trap!"

Lorelei stops. "What trap?" She turns around in every direction, her eyes wild and fierce. She hears yelling in the distance. "How do you know about a trap, Adrian?" she calls back to him.

She tilts her head, listening for the voices. As she runs closer to them, she can hear: *Help us! Help us! Down here!*

"Because it's mine. It's my trap. I just...I just want to keep everyone safe and I really, really need my family back." Adrian's voice returns to normal.

Adrian takes a step toward her. Lorelei is too quick for him to catch her, and she runs for the screams.

"I'm coming!" she yells. "I'm going to help you!"

"Nooooo!" Adrian yells, running toward her.

The clouds begin covering the moon again. It's hard for Lorelei to see ahead. She doesn't notice the pile of ground cover removed from the trap door or the black hole ahead. She doesn't realize that the screams are echoing off the trees, deflecting the location of their true origin. It doesn't register to her that the screams she's hearing may not be Taylor's. Fear has her running without thinking.

She notices a chain hanging from a tree ahead of her and hears the yelling coming from below. She slows down as she gets closer and sees a dark opening in the ground. Just as she's about to squat down, Adrian reaches her and grabs her arm, holding onto her with a tight grip, but Lorelei's footing slips and she plunges into the hole. She frantically grabs onto Adrian's arm, but the force is enormous on his weak shoulder. She can see that he's trying to pull her up, but his shoulder pops out of its socket, forcing him to let go. Lorelei slams her head onto the edge of the opening, then disappears into the box below. Adrian screams in agony, partly from the pain in his shoulder and partly from the sorrow of letting her go.

Despite the surface being soft, Lorelei slams onto a mattress hard enough to expunge the breath from her lungs and it feels like the weight of ten million bricks is on her chest. Lorelei sits up, gasping for air, but all that is coming out are short, tiny breaths with a squeaking sound. She panics and reaches her arms around in the dark to hold onto something and stand up, hoping her breathing will kick in again. Lorelei scans the area around her but doesn't see anyone. She raises her eyes and sees the night sky. She tries to cry Adrian's name, but there's not enough air in her lungs to make a sound. She continues gasping, each breath easing up on the tightness in her chest. Her fingers find the edge of the walls, but the surface is smooth with nothing to hold onto. She peers up again, trying to speak, but all she can do is whisper. A second later, the door to the box closes with a thud and she can hear the rattle of what she surmises is a lock snapping shut. Then she hears the sound of dirt and branches dropped on top of the door above.

Lorelei crouches and shakes, bewildered. She gasps, now taking in more air when she feels a gash on the back of her head and smells blood on her fingertips. A twinge of pain begins gnawing at her. Breathing still labored, Lorelei pays attention to her body to see if anything is broken, but she feels okay otherwise.

A light suddenly flicks on and illuminates her surroundings. "Lorelei?"

Lorelei whips her head around to see who's calling her name, increasing the pain from the back of her head.

She focuses in.

There, standing in front of her is Jeremy with Taylor and Wyatt by his side.

CHAPTER

23

Adrian slams the sliding glass door shut when he arrives home. He can feel his pulse racing through his neck. He's not sure what to do now—now, that he has no one.

He paces back and forth in the safe room, turns on the train, then paces again.

I should let her out. I think she hit her head on the way down.

You can't do that. She knows about the others now.

I don't care.

You will when you're sitting in jail and have no one. Don't you want your family back?

Yes.

Adrian sits down on the recliner and holds its arms, clenching his fingers like he's about to fall out of a train car.

Well, then you're getting closer to restoring that family you wanted back. Who else is better to play wife and mom than

Lorelei?

But Lorelei is mine, not his.

Not anymore. You think she'll just go on in life with you and forget this whole thing? Not tell the police what's going on? Go about her day knowing that there are people in a box in the back of the woods, including children?

What do I do?

You do what you set out to do. Don't deviate now. That would be stupid.

Adrian closes his eyes and concentrates on his breathing. He feels like he's going to explode.

She still loves me.

Oh, of course, she does. No woman minds being locked in an underground box where her boyfriend has hidden three people.

Adrian snorts. *Maybe I can get her to forgive me or understand, at least.*

You keep telling yourself that. My bet is that she'll try to use that to get you to let her free and first chance she gets, she's off to the police station, or maybe a local psychiatrist to get you locked away in a loony bin. You are a people hoarder with a split personality, after all.

Adrian gets up and walks to the train set, collecting the figurines in his hand. He then turns back to the end table and shoves them in the drawer. *Guess I don't need these anymore.*

Nope, you've got the real thing now or at least a good start on it.

Adrian's mood quickly calms, and he smiles.

"I do, don't I?" he whispers aloud in a deep raspy tone.

The doorbell rings. Adrian jerks his head toward the doorway and proceeds to the front door to look through the peephole. *Shit, it's Gentry.* He glances at his watch. It's nine in the evening. *Kind of late, isn't it?*

He shakes out his hands to gather himself, then opens the door.

"Hey, man. I'm so sorry to hear about Taylor."

A couple of police officers are walking up the driveway toward the front door.

Gentry's face is flushed, and his voice shakes as he says, "Yeah. You warned me this could happen. I messed up big time, and now my little girl is gone." Gentry weeps.

"Do you want to come in for a while?"

"No, no. I need to keep looking. Will you help me?"

"Yes, yes, of course. What am I thinking?"

Gentry peers into Adrian's home. "Is Lorelei able to help too?"

"Um, not right now. She searched earlier though. Didn't she call you?"

"Yeah, yeah, she did."

"Let me get my jacket."

"Mr. Webster, is it?" one of the police officers asks abruptly before Adrian steps away.

"Yes, Adrian Webster."

"Hey, aren't you the same guy that's been searching and sampling at the Corringer's crime scene?"

Adrian peers in closer at the officer's face. It's Mortensen.

"Oh, hey, yeah that's me."

"Huh, that's a bit of a coincidence, isn't it?"

"I guess."

"Do you mind if we come in and talk for a few minutes? We need a statement."

"Statement of what?"

"Just routine information gathering."

"Oh, sure."

Adrian opens the door for the officers and they both enter. His heart rate increases, but he tries not to show his nervousness by remaining calm outwardly. He hopes he can keep himself together long enough for a few questions, then they should be on their way.

"Guess I might as well come in too, then," Gentry says.

Adrian extends a hand to greet Gentry, then turns to the officers.

"Have a seat, officers. Can I get you a drink?"

"Nah, we're good," Detective Mortensen replies as he glances around the house.

"You, Gentry?" Adrian asks.

"No, but thanks." Gentry doesn't sit. He stands and paces in the living room while the officers begin their questions.

"So, did you see Gentry's daughter, Taylor, tonight?" the detective asks.

"No."

"When did you last see her?"

Cool and calm, Adrian answers, "I think it was last night when she was out riding with Gentry."

"Want to tell us about that?"

"Ah, sure. Well, I came home and noticed she was riding down the street. I didn't see Gentry around, so I drove my truck her way just to make sure she wasn't alone and then I saw Gentry in the cul-de-sac."

"But you didn't see her riding her bike alone this way tonight?"

"No, no."

"So, you've been home all night?"

"Yeah, I've been here all day, actually. I didn't go to

work today."

"Sick or somethin'? Your eyes seem better."

"Not getting a lot of sleep. Been working long hours."

"What company do you work for again?"

"The Graystone Group. An engineering firm."

"Oh, so, you're really an engineer then?"

"Yeah."

"Well, that's a good profession. Surprised they'd have you sampling."

Adrian nods. "I guess."

"Do you mind if we look around a bit?"

Adrian's eyebrows raise in surprise. "Oh, sure, go ahead."

"Ah, you don't have to do that, officers. I can vouch for him. He's a caring man. He wouldn't hurt anyone," Gentry says.

Mortensen smiles and says, "This is just protocol. You know, we're just checking every avenue."

"It's okay, Gentry," Adrian replies. "Search all you like."

Mortensen starts for the hallway but then pauses. "Oh, wait. Uh, don't you have a wife or something?"

"I have a girlfriend. I'm not married."

"And, where is she? I'd like to ask her some questions, too."

"Well, she's not here right now. Do you want me to have her call you?"

Officer Mortensen watches Adrian's eyes. He pulls out a card from his pocket and says, "Yes, if you don't mind."

"Not a problem."

"Good," he replies with half a smile. As he moves closer to the safe room, the officer becomes curious. "Hey, what's that sound? Is that a train set?"

"Yeah, it's running. Go ahead and check it out."

Mortensen walks up to the tracks and watches the train make its rounds. "I've always loved train sets. Reminds me of when I was a kid and went to Bear Mountain in New York. They had a huge display there many moons ago. Ever been?"

"Ah, no, can't say I have," Adrian replies.

"Haven't been back in a long time. Not sure if they still have it." The detective becomes sidetracked with all the emergency supplies. "Say, ah, you into emergency supplies or somethin'?"

Adrian glances at the full shelves. "Guess you could say that. The house came with this safe room, so I just went with it. Figured it'd be useful if we get any hurricanes."

"Uh huh." The detective looks at the supplies again. "So, why the train set?"

"Just a hobby. This is my man cave, of sorts."

The detective scoffs. "You're one lucky dude. There's no way my wife would let me have a room like this."

"All clear, Vic," the other officer says as he sticks his head in the room.

"Well good. See, that wasn't too painful, right?"

Adrian nods.

"I gotta admit, though. There's something odd about a man who would have a train set hidden away in his man cave. I mean, most collectors like to show their work. You know, shelving near the top of the walls, or maybe in the living room."

Adrian pretends to be puzzled. "Well, not sure why. I like it out of the way."

The detective watches Adrian's eyes again. "And it's

also kind of strange you'd be involved in two missing children cases, don't you think?"

"I don't know what you mean. This is a small town."

"Right. Well, you have a good night then. Remember to tell your girlfriend to call me. What's her name?"

"Lorelei," Adrian says as he shows the officers out.

"Lorelei. I like that name. It'll be easy for me to remember." The officer glances over to Gentry who's pacing and wringing his hands. "Say, ah, maybe it would be better for you to keep him occupied until we get a search party together. Can you do that?"

"Yeah, of course."

"He looks kinda rough."

"Wouldn't *you* be?" Adrian keeps his gaze.

"Yeah, I'm sure I would."

He closes the door as the officers exit and his eyes in relief.

Gentry stops pacing and says, "You okay, man?"

"Yeah. I just can't imagine your pain right now. Sounds like we can't do anything yet. They have to organize a search party. Do you want me to walk you to your house? Or do you want to hang out here for a while?"

"I…I don't really know what I want."

"Okay, well we can stay here for a while and then I can take you home. Sound good?"

You need to get to the woods and make sure the police don't find them.

If I go out there right now, they'll sure as hell suspect me. Did you not see the way that detective was staring at me?

They'll surely search the woods. The box is sealed, so they shouldn't hear any yells, but if they step on the trap door, it's over. You're going to have to be careful when you go out to feed them tomorrow.

I'm not an idiot. You don't think I know that?

Adrian can feel his face flush.

"Hey man, I know you're going through a lot with Wyatt and all. I'll just go and update you tomorrow. Hopefully, they'll find her and this will all be over."

"I'm sorry, man. Guess this is hitting home for me."

"No Wyatt yet, either?"

"No."

"You know what I'm afraid of?"

Adrian darts his eyes away from Gentry.

"It's the same person who took Wyatt."

"Don't even say that. I'm sure she'll be home tonight."

Gentry's eyes look heavy, bags forming below them.

"I'm sorry, man. I've gotta go. Tell Lorelei I stopped by."

"I will."

Adrian watches Gentry as he leaves the house, then he storms into the safe room.

You can't worry about that.

Did you see his face? I didn't think about how this would hurt Gentry.

You can't. Besides, you need to start thinking about the next sister for your family.

How can I think of that already?

You can, and you will.

CHAPTER

24

Adrian arrives to work at seven in the morning, hoping to make up a little for being out yesterday. He flicks on the light to his office and sits in his chair. More engineering reports are stacked in his inbox, along with a sticky note from Fossie wishing him well. Chatter emanates down the hallway. Adrian can tell it's Fossie and Clark. As usual, Clark sticks his head in the doorway.

"Back at it, huh?"

"Sorry about yesterday. I wasn't feeling well."

"So, I heard. You didn't miss much."

"Did you sample more?"

"No. I think they were expecting the DNA samples to come back soon."

Adrian's arm flinches. "Wow, already?"

"Yeah, I was surprised, too. It can take a couple of months. Maybe they rushed them because a missing boy is involved. The only reason I know anything is because they asked if I could be available for further sampling upstream if needed. Sounds like they are still short-staffed as far as samplers. I told them I would, of course."

"More work. That'd be great."

"I'm still waiting for a callback, though. So, we'll see."

"Yeah, hope it leads to something."

"No word on the boy, huh?"

"No."

"How are the visions?"

"They're gone for now. Maybe I just needed more sleep."

"Could be. Your eyes look better too."

Adrian nods, his leg shaking. He's anxious for Clark to leave.

"Okay, let me know if you hear anything more."

"Yep." Clark takes off down the hallway.

How could they be getting sampling hits upstream? Wyatt didn't fall out of the boat or anything. Maybe some of his hair flew out of the boat? And why is this happening? Wetland water is usually stagnant.

It's been raining so much, maybe the water is flowing downstream faster than normal.

Adrian boots up his laptop and finds a map of the area, zooming in on Jeremy's house, then on the trail and wetlands. He follows the shoreline to the west and notices that it eventually ends up behind his property.

Holy shit! If they keep sampling, they're going to eventually find out that the origin of this evidence is my property.

Adrian takes a closer look at his property and the proximity of the shoreline. He locates the approximate location of the box.

It is upgradient of the wetlands, of course. I guess it's possible that rain could be carrying anything that dropped off Wyatt as I carried him to the box, but it just seems like that would take a lot of time to reach the water. The sheet flow might be carrying it, but what are the chances?

He reviews the map again, following the terrain from the box to the wetlands, then lowers his head.

I'm an idiot. It's probably from the sewer discharge pipe, which is connected to the toilet in the box. The discharge from the sewer pipe must be leaking into the wetlands. Maybe urine and feces are moving east toward the bike trail with the torrential rains. I can't believe how fast this has happened. I need to get this rectified. And quickly.

What am I going to do now?

Fossie steps into Adrian's office. "Hey, feeling better?"

"Yes, thanks."

"Any more visions? Did you see Wyatt in your visions again?"

"No, actually. I'm all cleared up." He points to his eyes.

"Holy cow, that was quick! And your lip too. I wonder why the visions stopped. Wyatt hasn't been found yet, right?"

"Right. Well, sounds like the DNA results might be in, so, hopefully, they will help."

"Did you tell the police about Jeremy being the captor in your visions?"

"Yeah," he lies. "That's why they're searching his house."

"Oh, good. I think that's for the best. That way you should be kept out of it, being he is your friend and all." Fossie pauses. "So, the visions just vanished, huh? Shadows too?"

"Yeah, they didn't bother me at all yesterday. I'm glad they're gone. They were driving me crazy."

Okay, that might be a little white lie. No way am I telling her I saw myself.

"I still say you must have some kind of clairvoyant skills."

Adrian grins and raises his shoulders. "Who would have guessed?"

"Sampling again today?"

"No, doesn't sound like it'll be needed."

"Maybe you should just take it easy today anyway since you were sick yesterday."

"Well, we'll see what Clark wants to do."

"That old coot pissed me off this morning, so I'm not talking to him. Don't send him my way for anything."

"Got it," Adrian replies. He holds himself back from laughing outwardly.

"Oh, you…you think it's funny, don't you? He has got to be the most stubborn, ridiculous man I've ever met."

Adrian puts his hand up. "Okay, okay. I don't want any more details."

Fossie huffs and exits from his office.

Adrian collapses back into his seat.

Just concentrate on the new family.

I can't wait to see them all together once again.

Later that night, Adrian arrives home exuberant that he'll need to cook dinner for his family. He stops in the safe room first and turns on the train to relax for a bit. The train rounds a corner and begins its travel over the trestle bridge for the millionth time since Adrian set up the tracks. He wonders how many times it'll take before it fails. It may be similar to the number of times the train crossed the trestle bridge out West before his family dropped over a thousand feet to their deaths in some river.

So, are you excited? Adrian asks himself.

Adrian's hand flinches. *Yes,* he answers.

Are you worried about Lorelei?

Of course. She hit her head on the way down. Hopefully, she's not hurt. Jeremy used to be a paramedic, though, so I'm sure he'll give her first aid.

Adrian sets up four family members at the train station. Mom, Dad, Jonathan, and Amy.

So nice to see Amy back.

Yes, I've missed her.

Who's coming back next?

Guess it'll have to be a surprise.

I like surprises. We need to celebrate after each one comes home.

Adrian feels more energized than he has in a long time. The thought of taking care of his family by bringing food and supplies to help them survive invigorates him. He reaches for a grocery bag and fills it with dinner and a few odds-and-ends including his flashlight in case it's dark on the way back.

It's time.

There's a gentle breeze frolicking through the tips of the trees like the mild lapping of waves on a quiet shoreline. The temperature is cool, almost brisk, and the sky is a wash of yellows, oranges, and blues. The sun has descended and nightfall has arrived. The faint smell of cedar lingers in the air from the wetlands beyond Adrian's property.

I should probably go down to the wetlands and see if the pipe is sticking out and leaking sewer debris. Maybe the shoreline eroded around it. It's getting dark, though, so that's probably a better task for tomorrow.

He sneaks up to the trap door and lies down, resting his head near the opening to hear how his new family is getting along. Hearing nothing, he gently removes the lock and slowly pushes the latch up. His heart rate is increasing. He's not sure why the thought of seeing his new family settling in together makes him almost weep. As softly as he can, he lifts up on the door just enough to see through a crack and sticks a piece of nearby wood within it to hold the door open. Light fans out in front of him. He can barely stand the anticipation as he adjusts the angle of his cell phone camera to peek in on them.

A soft, warm glow greets him as he focuses in on his family. He's been waiting so long for this reunion of sorts and he feels nostalgic when he thinks about how safe and happy they will be.

But it soon fades when he sees them.

They're barely interacting with each other. Dad is helping Jonathan with reading, but they both look sad. Amy is drawing a picture of her other family at the desk. Mom is sleeping in her bed, but her face is almost as white as the bandages wrapped around her head. Dad pauses for a minute to check on her, taking her temperature and checking her forehead before resuming his time with Jonathan. But Dad is not caressing Mom in her time of need.

But they will soon care for each other. These things take time. In a few months, maybe weeks, they'll all be surrounded by new faces and family bonds in a place where they won't have to worry about the flu or thieves or tele-marketers or train accidents.

Lorelei doesn't look well.

No, she doesn't. It seems Jeremy is doing the best he can though.

Yes.

You don't seem happy.

Well, they're not really a family yet.

These things take time. They will be. Perhaps another family member will help.

Yes. I think someone new would help.

You'll have to work on it tomorrow.

Adrian smiles. *This is going to work.*

He watches their expressions as he lifts the lid and lets it squeak so they'll know he's there.

They all peer up at him. He smiles at them warmly.

"Get that smile off your face, Adrian," Jeremy says. "Don't you see what you're doing to us?"

"You just need more time," Adrian responds in a deep whisper. He drops the bag and four containers bounce off the mattress and onto the floor. "That's dinner."

Jeremy moves closer. "Adrian, stop doing this. Let us out."

"No, I can't do that."

"Sure, you can. You have the ladder."

Adrian smiles. "I do, but it's not here. Are you taking care of Mom?"

"Mom?"

"Lorelei."

"Yes, but she's really sick. If we don't get her to the hospital, she could die."

"You won't let her die. Here." In drops a pill bottle of

penicillin. "I had them left over from another illness. They should work."

"Adrian, she probably needs debridement of the wound."

"You can do that."

"She needs to see a doctor. They may want to do a head scan. Don't you care anymore?"

Adrian becomes furious. His breathing is raspy. "Of course, I care! Why do you think I'm doing this in the first place?"

"Okay, man, just relax. At least take Lorelei out of here."

Adrian backs away from the opening and says, "No! She's pivotal. Here are some more supplies." Numerous items fly onto the mattress including toilet paper, granola bars, and bandages.

"I thought you loved Lorelei. I thought you two would be together forever. How can you do this to her?"

Lorelei starts to say something, but she can barely move her head.

"She's better off with someone who can give her what she needs. That's not me."

"What are you talking about?"

"She knows. Ask her."

Jeremy glances over to Lorelei but her eyes are closed.

"Adrian!" Jeremy yells.

"Sweet dreams, everyone."

"Adrian!"

Adrian lets the door slam shut, locks it, and adds more debris on top of the door to disguise it.

He stops abruptly and hits the ground when he hears a whistle nearby. He's not sure which direction it came from, but he's not going to waste any time guessing. He needs to get out of the woods.

Adrian turns off his flashlight and crawls away from the box, scanning the area in all directions for any signs of someone hanging around. He hears another whistling sound coming from straight ahead, then the voices of men. His heart leaps with anxiety. He sees heads moving around in the distance. There must be at least ten of them, he surmises, but it's hard to tell in the dark.

Adrian stands up behind a tree and peeks around the side. The men are huddled together, so he starts moving in a large circle around them, hoping to keep hidden from their view and get back to the house. As he rounds them, he notices that some of them are police officers. He halts.

Wait, are these the search and rescue volunteers for Taylor? I can't let them find the box.

He watches them for a minute while he contemplates his next move.

It'd probably look better if I come from my yard rather than the woods to meet up with them. If I walk up to them from this angle, they'll probably question why I was in the woods in the first place.

Adrian ducks down low and crawls toward the edge of his backyard. He's careful not to make any noise that would draw attention to him. He steps onto his lawn, but quickly backs up when he sees two officers walk across his backyard toward the road. Once they're out of view, Adrian reaches the boundary of the woods and crawls toward a thick tree trunk. He stands behind it and gathers himself, then walks toward the group from his yard. He waves at them with the flashlight aimed toward his face so they can see him.

"Hey, saw you from my window over there," Adrian says as he points to his house. "What's going on?"

"Oh, hey! You must be the property owner. We knocked on your door but didn't get an answer. We're searching for Taylor, you know, Gentry's daughter?" one of the searchers says.

"Yeah, he was over last night. Still no word from her, huh?"

"No."

"Well, I'll save you some time. My girlfriend and I already searched through the woods behind our yard. There was no sign of her this evening. We searched a wide area in both directions. I was just about to go over Gentry's house to see what I could do. Sorry, I didn't hear you knock."

"Oh, that's okay." The man peers at the rest of his group. "Well, maybe we should head over to the other side of the roadway then. We can cross this parcel off the list, it sounds like."

"Are you working with the police?"

"Yeah, they gave us this map."

"Huh, I see. Well, I'll catch up with Gentry and see where he wants me to go next. Good luck. I hope you find her."

They all head out of the woods and toward the roadway. Adrian runs back into the house, barely able to catch his breath.

This is crazy.

He sprints to his front door and sees that the group is walking away.

They are going to find them. I know it! What do I do?
Quit freaking out.
I'm so screwed. Adrian grabs the back of his neck with

his hands.

Relax.

They're going to tell the police that I told them we searched out back already and had them scratch it off the list. That detective from last night seemed suspicious of me.

That was just routine. Keep the box well covered in case they do happen to go by it, but I doubt they'd do that. There's a lot of area for them to cover. Gentry trusts you, so he probably won't question it either.

That's sick. He trusts me. I stole his daughter and he trusts me.

Adrian paces the floor.

Get yourself together!

Adrian stops pacing and starts taking deep breaths until he finally gains control. Then, he takes out his cell and calls Gentry.

"Hey, man. It's Adrian. I just saw one of the search teams. No sign of Taylor, huh?"

"No," Gentry replies. He clears his throat.

"Man, I'm sorry. I thought for sure you found her last night. What can we do to help?"

"Well, the police have already put together the search teams in the area, so if you see another team you could always join in or maybe search on your own in another area. I don't know at this point. My mind's a fog."

"Okay, hang in there. Lorelei and I will search out back again just in case. I'll need to get over to look for Wyatt too, but I'll help search in this area later. Let me know if I can do anything else."

"I appreciate it. I've gotta run."

Gentry hangs up before Adrian can respond.

Adrian enters the safe room. He tries not to be bothered

by the emptiness in the house. He tries not to dwell on the fact that he will be alone in his bed tonight, no softness or warmth lying next to him. He tries not to think about how he will explain Lorelei's whereabouts in time, her car parked in the driveway. He tries not to focus on whether her parents will come looking for her, estranged and all. And he tries hard, very hard, not to let the bad thoughts in, the ones that want to rise up in him and cause his head to explode.

CHAPTER

25

Adrian peeks out of his front window. There are numerous vehicles parked along his street. He watches the families gather, mostly adults, but a few appear to be middle-school aged. It's still dark, so some of them are carrying flashlights and bundled up in hats and jackets. He decides he should get dressed and join them to make sure they stay away from his backwoods. He grabs his flashlight, exits his house through the front door, and jogs down his driveway. There's no more parking left along the street and most cars are heading one street over from him. The early morning chill bites into him and soon his cheeks are cold. He walks down the street and sees a large crowd gathered in the cul-de-sac with a few policemen. Light is streaming out in several directions from the flashlights. Adrian turns his off and slows his pace.

You're not really out here to look for Taylor, are you?

Shut up.

Adrian pauses near a house that's under construction and proceeds to the open doorway. He wants to watch for now.

Yeah, and what are you watching for? What are you really wanting, Adrian?

He scrunches his forehead to make the thoughts go away, but they are relentless.

Look. Look over there. What do you see? Is there anyone who might fit?

Adrian closes his eyes. *No, I can't.*

This is perfect timing. Search them. Who reminds you of her?

Which her?

You pick. There are several of your sisters left to choose from.

Mumbled voices carry through the neighborhood and bounce off the interior shell of cement block and wood frame. The smell of wood excites Adrian's senses. He's always loved it. Wind circulates through the windows and exits out the doorway, causing the rustling of palms outside.

You're losing precious time. Pick one!

Adrian rubs his eyes, then studies the activities down the street. He has a clear view from the doorway.

Find a weak one or a vulnerable lamb left behind. Hunt it!

I can't.

Now!

Adrian watches the crowd. There are numerous teenagers in the mix. His eyes dart around, stopping on each one. It's difficult to see their faces, but he can make out silhouettes and see their body movements. Occasionally, flashlights illuminate their faces so he can see them. Most of the parents and other family members are hovered around them, along with other siblings or friends. There doesn't seem to be an angle.

Keep watching. Look along the outskirts. Who's left behind?

No one. They're all with the flock.

It won't stay that way, I promise you.

"I'll catch up with you!" a voice yells, sounding close to the house.

Adrian can hear footsteps passing by. He peeks out around the front door. It's a young girl, perhaps middle-school aged.

Perfect! See I told you! Which one is she?

She kind of looks like Michelle.

Well, then. Pretend you're searching for Taylor.

Adrian takes off behind the houses toward his own. He runs quickly to get ahead of her so he can pretend to be leaving his house. She has to be going back to one of the vehicles to get something she forgot.

Adrian flies up to his back door and turns the knob. It's locked.

Shit. Okay, just get to the front quickly.

He scrambles past the side of his home and into the front flower garden and once again down the driveway. He pretends to be reading his cell phone.

He glances up and sees the young girl. She stops when she sees him. Adrian senses her apprehension.

Don't lose your chance, Adrian.

She looks down the street, then back at Adrian.

"Oh, hey! Are you part of the search party?"

She nods.

"Do you know where everyone is meeting?"

The young girl barely makes eye contact and says, "Yeah, in the cul-de-sac."

Adrian studies her. She's got to be eleven or twelve. Her hair is long, slightly auburn in the street light behind her.

"Do you want me to wait for you and walk you back?"

"No. I'm good."

Adrian sees that the girl grabs her keys between her fingers, leaving the tips protruding probably just in case she's looking at a creep. Her mom has obviously warned her about strange men.

She continues walking but moves up to the sidewalk on the other side of the cars to be farther away from Adrian.

"Crap, I forgot something," Adrian says aloud and runs back to his house. He opens the front door and walks in, turning to his left to watch her from the front window.

The young girl opens a car door and grabs something from inside. Adrian can see the light from a cell phone. She closes the door and the car beeps when she locks it. Adrian knows he's got to get to her soon or she might start talking on the phone.

He quickly grabs his flashlight and exits his house, walking swiftly down his driveway again. "Oh, hey. It's you again," he says with a smile.

The young girl doesn't acknowledge him.

"Oh, sorry."

She sticks to the sidewalk and Adrian stays on the road.

"So, how do you know Taylor? Is she your friend? I know her from the neighborhood. Her dad comes over with her all the time. You know Gentry, right?"

She starts walking slower. "Yeah, they've been friends of the family for a long time."

"Yeah? Wow. They're a nice family. I'm sure Taylor is around somewhere. Probably just got lost. Are you with your parents?"

She nods.

"Hey, it looks like they've already left for the woods. I know where they're going, so I'm going to cross over this way. You can go with me if you want to meet up with your family. It's up to you."

The young girl hesitates as she stares down the road. "My dad will be looking for me, so I better stick to the main road."

Oh, shit. What am I thinking? I didn't open the trap door. This is not doable.

"Sure, no problem. Maybe I'll see you at the search party then."

Adrian turns around and heads for his backyard, figuring he'd wait a few minutes, then go inside his house through the front door. He sits on his back stoop to think. *That could have been bad. I can't just spontaneously find kids to drop in the box. I've got to plan it better. Fuck, what am I saying. I'm the most deplorable, sick fucktard I've ever known. I'm the worst human being alive. I don't know how I can go on like this.*

"Hello?"

Adrian jerks his head around, and there standing several feet away, is the young girl. His heart leaps.

"Holy crap. You scared me."

The girl giggles. "Sorry. Aren't you going to meet up with the search party?"

"Yeah was just sitting here for a minute to see if I can hear them. How about you?"

She pushes her hair away from her face just like Michelle used to do, first tucking it behind her ear and then bending sideways and jerking her head so her hair swings behind her back.

"I couldn't find them. Can you take me to them?"

Adrian's leg starts to shake. *You've got to be kidding me. Do it.*

I can't. Look at her.

She looks just like Michelle.

Does she? I can't see her in the dark.

Her hair does, at least. This could be number five. Figure out a way.

Adrian sighs.

"Oh, I'm sorry. I didn't mean to bother you," she says.

"Oh, no. I was just thinking that maybe it'd be better if you stay here on the stoop while I search for them. I don't want you to get lost with it being so dark. It might take me about fifteen minutes to get back here though. Would that be all right?" *Please say no.*

"Okay. I can do that."

Adrian gets up from the stoop and starts walking toward the woods. "By the way, what's your name in case I find them."

"Nadine."

"And how old are you?"

"Twelve."

Energy sears through Adrian's body.

Damn, I'm good.

"I'll be right back."

Adrian darts through the woods faster than he's ever done before. He dodges trees and fallen limbs, escapes from a long vine that ensnares his feet, and jumps over tree stumps. That is until he almost reaches the trap door. He slows down when he sees the chain shimmering in the moonlight and steps carefully, avoiding any twigs or leaves that could let his family know he's arrived back home. He crawls around to the door, then gently lifts the lock and twists the dial until it releases. He removes the lock in silence, then carefully lifts the lid to avoid sound, holding it up for a minute to check to make sure they're still sleeping.

He peeks in with one eye. A soft glow emanates from within acting like a night light. He can see them all nestled in the blankets and pillows, motionless. A serene scene. It takes his breath away.

Get going!

He snaps himself out of it and lifts the lid over to expose the box below and slowly places it on the ground. Then he exits as stealth-like as he came, increasing his speed at a safe distance from them. His chest feels warm with excitement as he thinks about adding another member to his family. It's unbelievable to him that he may have another sister soon.

Adrian dodges the same trees and limbs as before and bursts out into the open yard, his heart pounding now. He goes to the back of the house, his pace slowing once he sees that the young girl is gone. He turns around to see if she's waiting somewhere else, but he doesn't see her. He covers his forehead with his hands, clenching his temples. A deep disappointment begins creeping into his core.

Oh, no! She must have gone with her father.

Good for her.

"Hi!" she says from the side of the house.

Adrian jumps. "Oh! You scared me again, young lady! I thought maybe you found your dad and left."

"Did you find them?"

"No, but I did hear some noise down near the wetlands area. I can take you there if you want. I understand though if you'd rather just wait for your dad in the car or something."

The night sky has started to lift, revealing the features

of Nadine's face. *It really is Michelle. She found me.*

"I'll go," she says.

"It's this way then, Michelle."

"It's Nadine."

"Oh, yeah. Sorry. You actually remind me of my little sister."

Shut up! Don't tell her stuff like that.

"Oh, okay," Nadine replies.

Adrian leads Nadine into the woods, being careful to avoid any vegetation that would slap her in the face or prick her skin. Adrian keeps her talking to distract her until they reach the area near the box. The long chain shimmers in the morning sun.

"Let's be quiet as we walk now. We're getting closer to the wetlands, and I want to listen for them. Try not to step on any twigs or anything."

She nods with a smile.

Adrian gulps, thinking how sweet she is.

God, why can't I stop this? Her life is about to change forever.

Maybe her life is miserable now and a new one would be better for her.

I doubt that. She doesn't look abused. Her hair is healthy, and she's average weight and height.

Her hair swings back and forth, peaking out behind her back as she tip-toes through the woods.

I truly hate myself for this.

Oh, stop. You're being an idiot. This young girl was handed to you. It's meant to be. She'll be fine and the family will be better for it. Just concentrate on getting her in the box.

Adrian closes his eyes in disgust, then proceeds toward the chain.

"Let's go this way. We need to watch out for bats,

though. Look up at the treetops through here." Adrian jerks his head upward, drawing her to do the same. Then puts his finger to his mouth for her to keep quiet.

Adrian guides her toward the box, walking slightly behind her. He pulls the cell phone from her back pocket as she pushes through the brush. He waves her on and points to the trees above her. "It's okay, Michelle," he whispers.

She glares over to Adrian and stops walking. "It's Nadine. Stop calling me that."

"I'm sorry about that. But it truly will be fine, Michelle," Adrian replies with a raspier voice.

Nadine frowns at him.

"Watch out for the bats! Run!" he yells.

CHAPTER

26

Adrian stares at Michelle for a few minutes as the train rounds the track. *Why is Michelle here?*

Don't act like you don't remember, Adrian. You should be celebrating anyway. You're up to five family members now.

Adrian steps away from the train set, somewhat stunned. *Why do I always block out these things afterward?*

Oh, come on. Seriously? You're going to have everything you've always wanted—since the accident, at least.

I'm a monster.

For what? Providing safety to a family you love?

Safety? Lorelei is hurt. She probably needs to go to a hospital. And what about the emotional toll this is taking on all of them? Three are kids.

Adrian paces the floor a few times, then sits in his recliner.

They'll be fine in time. Who's next?

I can't do this anymore.

Gracie? Oh, I know, how about Reagan? At two, she'll keep them busy, for sure. Don't forget to send down diapers.

Adrian holds onto the arms of his recliner, trying to fight back the memories of the accident. His eyes dilate as he remembers his sisters screaming while they tried to grab onto something, anything, before they plunged into the valley. But luck was not on their side that day. He would never forget watching their small bodies accelerating downward with wild eyes and thrashing limbs.

I said I can't do this anymore.

Don't be ridiculous. Of course, you can, and you will. Trust me. The momentum has started, and there's no way you'll be able to stop. Just watch. In a few days, they'll all be having a good time with each other, just like a true family. And the more family members that can join them, the better. You're halfway there.

Adrian gets up and turns off the train set.

I'm done. No more.

He goes to the kitchen to throw together some breakfast, knowing he'd better leave for the woods soon before another search party ends up at his front door. Obviously, they haven't found Taylor, and soon they'll wonder what happened to Nadine.

Why did I do that? So young, so innocent.

You're killing me. You suddenly care?

Adrian sighs and pulls out some eggs from the refrigerator. He grabs a package of bagels and starts toasting them, including one for himself.

You're in a perfect position here. Maybe there's another one you can adopt into the family from the search party.

No. It's too soon. It's already bad enough there are two missing from the neighborhood now. Michelle—I mean Nadine—

doesn't live in the development, but people will know she was in the search party. It's only a matter of time.

Not if you keep your mouth shut. What are you going to do to get more? Go to the mall? It's not like you live in a busy metropolis in this neighborhood.

I'll figure it out. Wait. No, I won't. I told you. No more.

So, you'll be happy with a family of five, not including you.

Yeah.

That's not big enough. You may as well have had your own kids. I'm telling you, get the two-year-old in there. They'll have a harder time trying to escape because they'll have to keep up with her. She'll have to stay with at least one of them all the time, too.

Adrian's hands start to shake as soon as he hears the word "escape."

They cannot leave.

Exactly. You are bound by this now, but isn't it worth it? I'm just trying to help make sure they'll have extra baggage in case they get any ideas. Oh, and you had better watch yourself when you open that trap door. In time, they'll try to overpower you and escape. Be ready for it. Be quiet when you go there, lift the lid in silence, slide the food and supplies in, and leave quickly. It'll be harder to do while you coax another kid to fall in and have to leave the trap door open, but just make it quick.

Adrian begins filling the containers with breakfast, stopping to make a point.

Oh, and that's another thing. If I do that to a two-year-old, she could easily be killed. I don't want her to be hurt.

Well, I don't know. They land on a mattress, don't they?

Yeah, but it's a long way down, especially for the size of them.

Maybe tie them to a rope?

Adrian snaps a container shut with a smirk on his face.

Oh, yeah, and give Jeremy a chance to grab the rope and pull me in? No way.

Maybe you could hold onto their arms as far as possible to cut off some of the fall. Tie yourself to a tree or something.

Adrian scratches the back of his head and stretches his neck.

I don't know. Sounds risky. Besides, I'm done.

Uh huh, if you say so. Have fun with half of your family then. It could be so much better.

Shut up. Just shut the fuck up!

The doorbell rings, interrupting his thoughts. Adrian circles around, trying to figure out if he can hide the containers, but he knows it'd take too much time.

He messes up his hair and acts tired as he strolls up to the door.

It's Officer Mortensen.

Shit. What does he want?

Adrian opens the door in his boxers and bare feet. He squints his eyes, pretending to be blinded by the sun.

"Good morning, Adrian."

"Mornin'."

"Well, Adrian, I got to thinkin' last night—this mind of mine can be such a curse. It never shuts off. Can I come in and talk to you for a few?"

"I guess, but I was in the middle of cooking some eggs for the search parties. I wanted to join them soon."

"It won't take but a minute. Ya mind?"

"Sure."

The officer enters the living room.

"Holy cow, that smells good."

"Do you want some? I've got eggs and bagels. I just need to finish packing them so they don't get cold."

"Nah, I'm good, but I can talk to you while you prepare

the meals."

Officer Mortensen follows Adrian into the kitchen area and sits down at the bar. Adrian returns to doling out the portions.

"Really nice of you to do that."

"Yeah, well, I've always liked to cook, and I feel like I'm helping this way."

"Never heard from your girlfriend." The officer surveys the place from his seat.

"Oh, Lorelei? Yeah. She's not usually here on Saturday mornings. She leaves early to study wetlands even on the weekends."

"Oh, really? She's a scientist?"

"Yeah, she is."

"So, what's your specialty at the company you work for?"

"Me? Oh, I'm just a beginning engineer. I just started there about two weeks ago. I have zero specialties at this point."

"Uh huh. Paying your dues, huh? How come you haven't been out sampling lately?"

"Well, actually, my coworkers have been worried about me having those visions. Lorelei, too. So, I'm taking a break from it. And as you can see, my eyes have been happy about it. I'm still concerned about Wyatt though, and now the girl in my neighborhood."

"You mean Taylor Flanagan?"

"Yes. Any word yet?"

"No, there hasn't been. Don't you think it's kind of funny that there are two disappearances that have popped up in locations near you?"

Adrian turns around and studies the detective's

expression. "What are you saying?"

"Well, I just find it funny. Kind of a coincidence." Adrian can tell the detective is watching his body language and eye movements.

"You're kidding me, right? I've been busting my ass to help and you suspect *me* now? I already told you that I saw Jeremy squatting over Wyatt in the visions. Maybe I can help with Taylor, too."

"Problem is, Adrian, no one has seen or heard from Jeremy in over a week. Where do you suppose he disappeared to?"

"How do I know?"

"Shouldn't you? He's your best friend."

Adrian piles the containers on top of each other and carries them over to the bar. "Not anymore."

"Oh? Why not?"

"Because anyone who would hurt their own child should be locked away forever. He sickens me."

"Uh, huh. Then, if he did this terrible thing to Wyatt, which by the way, we don't even know what happened to Wyatt, then why is there another child missing? That was Jeremy, too?"

"How do I know?" Adrian says, raising his shoulders.

Keep your cool. He's just testing you.

"Sorry, guess I'm on edge this morning. I'm worried about both of them now. Believe me, I'd rather not be involved in any disappearances."

"Uh, huh. Well, I also find it funny that you don't have any more visions suddenly. What changed? We didn't find Wyatt, and you'd think your eyes would be redder with all the stress of a second disappearance."

Adrian closes his eyes for a second. "I have no idea. I

can go visit the doctor, but this is about the time he said it would go away. He told me to give it two weeks so it may have just happened naturally. I can get a copy of my medical record if you want."

The detective stands. "No, that won't be necessary for now. Need some help with those containers?"

"No, I've got them. I'm going to call Gentry to see where he wants them."

"You have a good day then."

Adrian extends his hand. "Let me know if you need anything else."

The detective shakes Adrian's hand. "Which wetland is Lorelei studying anyway?"

"Oh, which one? Umm... I'm trying to remember. I think she said Colt Creek. It's on the other side of Green Swamp."

"But isn't her vehicle in the driveway?"

Adrian thinks quickly. "Yeah, that's hers. She took a student in the field with her. He picked her up. I couldn't be happier. I don't like it when she works in the wetlands by herself. It's not safe."

The detective nods. "I agree with that. It's probably better to have a partner in crime, so to say."

Adrian smiles. "Funny one."

The detective leaves and Adrian moves toward the living room slowly until Mortensen is out of sight, then runs to the safe room and shuts the door. He bends over the arm of the recliner, like he's about to puke, then sits down. *Fuck, fuck, fuck. He knows. He knows!*

Nah. If he did, he would have brought you down to the station for questioning. Haven't you watched any crime shows?

He suspects me.

Then another thought hits him.

Or, if I can help it, he'll blame Lorelei. It wouldn't do any harm to frame her. He'll never find her anyway.

CHAPTER

27

You were stupid for going there this morning. The police are combing the neighborhood, and there you go, leading them right to the box. Are you insane? You need to be concentrating on finding your next sister so she can be part of the family.

Adrian grabs his head into his shaking hands.

If I take another one, they are going to know it's me. I need to slow down. God, what am I doing?

You're almost there, Adrian. Did you see your family together? They were bonding. You must be excited.

A warmth wells up in Adrian's chest similar to the one he would get during his childhood. He always felt safe when the family was together. His parents always made sure they had fun. They worked hard, too, with the endless cooking, cleaning, and laundry with so many people around, but Adrian didn't mind it. In fact, he kind of liked it. It felt good to be part of a busy household. It was almost like a community.

Adrian hears a car door slam shut near the front of his house.

More people, Adrian. More opportunities. Go join the search parties. It'll come across good for you, and you can also assess all the two-year-old Reagans out there.

No. I can't do that.

Oh, here we go again. Are you going to do this every time? Because it's getting old. Get the hell out there and find more family members. If you lose this opportunity, you're going to regret it. Hell, get one, or two, or all three. Just stop wasting time.

Adrian heads toward the front window to assess the crowds. He doesn't see many people, but the number of cars parked along the street has increased. He exits out the back door and into the woods. Half-built houses and vacant lots are lined up beyond Adrian's house, so he knows he won't be seen by anyone peeking out of their windows. Besides, this will give him an opportunity to assess whether anyone is running around in the woods. As he makes his way to the back end of the cul-de-sac, he can see people gathering in groups on the street. He turns around to scan the woods.

This might be another good location to find a family member and have a straight shot back to the box. It could work.

He turns back around and about leaps out of his shoes. Gentry is standing on the roadway right in front of him.

"Hey, Gentry," Adrian says with a wave.

"What are ya doin' back there? Aren't you going to join the search party?"

"Yeah. Guess I was hoping that I'd find Taylor if I walked through my backyard and the woods. No such luck."

Adrian meets up with Gentry. The sun is at its highest peak and cascading warmth to anyone the rays meet. "At least it warmed up a little bit."

As Adrian gets closer, he can see that Gentry has large purple circles around his eyes and his mouth is drawn downward at the sides. He's a concerned dad who's losing hope.

"Come with me. I want to introduce you to my wife, Audrey. We won't be having the house-warming party this weekend, of course, but at least you can meet her."

Adrian's gut cringes and a nervous tension builds in his neck. He can feel his head jerk. Dread fills his every step and his pace slows as Gentry grabs his wife's hand and pulls her toward Adrian. Gentry picks up his stride. "This is Adrian. He lives in our neighborhood. He's the one I've been telling you about. Adrian, this is Audrey."

"Thank you for coming to search for Taylor. I truly appreciate it. Gentry speaks so highly of you and your wife. I hear you've been searching since you found out—not only for Taylor but also the little boy. He's your friend's son, right?"

I suck. I'm the lowest lowlife that ever existed.

"I'm so sorry, Audrey. I truly am."

Audrey's eyes begin to fill with tears.

"And yes, I've been looking for my friend's son as well. I'm sure we'll find them. Maybe they're playing together." Adrian tries to break a smile, but his response was idiotic, so he ends up showing his awkwardness instead with half a smile and talking to her feet.

Audrey glances at Gentry. "Well, I'm sure you've been missing sleep, too. Is your wife here?"

"Oh, Lorelei? No, she's at work as usual."

"And she's not his wife. She's his girlfriend, but I'm sure there will be wedding bells soon. They're the perfect couple," Gentry adds.

Adrian shifts his weight. "Not sure about that wedding stuff, but she is amazing."

"Aww. It's a beautiful thing, Adrian. You two will figure it out. Joining in the next search party?" Gentry asks.

"Sure am. Where are they going next?"

Gentry points to the same area of the woods Adrian just came from.

Adrian cringes. "Oh, really? Huh, I'm kind of surprised being that it's already been checked."

"They won't be searching the woods too much, mostly the wetlands beyond it."

"Ohh, okay, I see. Makes sense." Adrian visualizes how far away the search party will be from the box. He's going to have to get on the outer edge of the search party to control the situation, but it should be doable.

Just going to have to hope there are no strays scattered around that I'll have to herd in. As long as they stay in the wetlands, they shouldn't stumble across the box.

Don't forget to find a young family member. Who would be a good candidate?

Not now.

Yes, now. Start looking.

There aren't any. The only kids I see are in their teens.

Well, you may have to make do.

Adrian closes his eyes for a second and takes a deep breath to calm his nerves.

"We'll see you over there," Gentry says as he escorts his wife to the edge of the woods. The crowd follows them, walking by Adrian as he searches for sister options.

As the crowd parts, he locks eyes with Officer Mortensen who's standing with his arms crossed just beyond the cul-de-sac.

Please stop me. Can't you see I didn't bring the food? Adrian thinks as he keeps the detective's gaze. *Please stop the monster I've become.*

Adrian waves, but the officer doesn't return his gesture. So, Adrian turns around and follows the crowd.

Fossie is more than a little perturbed at Clark for convincing her to drive all the way from Altamonte Springs to Davenport. Clark insisted that he had to check on laboratory results that could just as easily have been be checked on Monday. The weekends are sacred to her, especially Saturday, because this is the day that she runs most of her errands and gets her laundry done. Now, with this rather lengthy detour to the office, her day is shot, which will mean less relaxation on Sunday.

"I told you, you didn't have to come. Stop driving like a maniac," Clarks says with one hand on the dashboard.

"What, and have you guilting me all weekend about not going? No."

Clark rolls his eyes. "Me? Guilt? You wrote the textbook on that word."

Fossie takes a turn too fast as punishment for his remark.

"Seriously? You're the most difficult woman I have ever met. Pull over and let me out before you kill me."

"Don't tempt me."

"Which? Pulling over or killing me?"

Fossie contemplates both but remains silent.

"What, you didn't have to have the last word?"

Fossie slows down somewhat. Her rage becoming less intense.

Clark relaxes. "You really need to control your temper, Fossie. I'm not getting any younger, you know."

"Oh, how I know."

Clark glares at her. "What does that mean?"

"Nothing."

"What, I don't have my boyish good looks anymore? My muscular stature? My dance moves?"

Fossie laughs under her breath. "The only dance moves you have are the jiggles around the middle."

"Hey now, be nice. I've still got it."

"Uh, huh," Fossie says with a grin. "The only thing you've got going on right now is the God-blessed odor of rotten fish combined with Old Spice aftershave. Why do you always try to cover up your stank with that stuff? It doesn't work," Fossie continues, her nose scrunched up.

"Why, Fossie, if I didn't know better, I'd say you have a crush on me."

"I did at one time. Now, forget it. You and your old field clothing can go live somewhere else. I'm sick of it."

"Okay, okay. I'll wash them tonight—unless *you* want to," he replies looking out the window at the office building with a grin.

"What? No way. Those things could stand on their own. Why don't you just get new ones."

"Because I love to drive you crazy, Fossylyn."

Fossie jerks the car to a stop. "Don't call me that."

"I'll be right back," Clark says as he exits the car and

shuts the door, then whispers, "Fossil," with a grin until he notices she can probably see him in the reflection of the office windows.

That woman.

Clark climbs the stairs up to the third floor and heads straight for the fax machine. There are no further requests for sampling, so Clark exits the office and climbs into the passenger seat.

"Well, that was quick. No more sampling?" Fossie asks.

"No," Clark says, frowning.

"What?"

"I don't know. They had us sample in the water, but I just wonder if we should have sampled more along the waterway. I wish I knew where the sampling hits were located, but they're keeping us in the dark."

"Well, I'm sure the confidentiality of the case is important."

"Yeah, I guess. The whole thing is just bugging me. For some reason, I want to take a ride upstream in the kayak and see what's up there. I already know that downstream is the interstate and then more Green Swamp beyond it. But upstream, I'm not sure. Of course, if there were sampling hits upstream it would mean... he's..." Clark stops midsentence. He can't even say the thought aloud.

"He's buried there?" Fossie has no problem.

"Jesus, Fossie. Could you be a little more sensitive?"

"Sorry, but what other explanation is there?"

Clark shakes his head in protest. "I don't know. Something is telling me to kayak up that way."

"I'm coming with you."

"What?"

"I'm coming with you."

"Fossie, I don't think you'd like this kind of thing. I have to take the kayak off the roof and you'll probably get wet and—"

"I insist. You don't have Adrian to help you these days. There's no reason why I couldn't. Let's go get it done."

"But your laundry."

"It can wait. I've always loved crime novels. This will be right up my alley."

"You'll smell like fish when you're done," he warns.

"Well, then we can smell alike. This will be exciting."

"Yeah. Exciting."

The pair drive to a nearby apartment complex and park in the back; this way they'll be far enough away from the crime scene not to interfere or be stopped.

Clark pulls the kayak off of their truck and drags it into the water. He hands Fossie a life vest, then loads a couple of sample bottles.

"What are you doing?"

"Just in case. Here's a paddle."

"For me? I have to paddle?"

"Yes, if you want to go, you have to paddle."

Fossie responds, but Clark can't hear her since he has already whipped the kayak around so she's facing forward and away from him. Then he climbs in and pushes off. Fossie helps with the paddling, but she splashes the water so much that Clark tells her to stop. He wants only limited disturbance of the water once he rounds the corner.

"Sounds like there are quite a few people up there at the shoreline," Fossie yells, some alarm in her voice. "There are a few officers there. I wonder if they found Wyatt."

"Crap, those are the same officers from Wyatt's investigation and they've seen us."

Officer Mortensen's phone rings as he watches Fossie and Clark paddle toward the shoreline. He wonders what they're doing there. He gestures for them to come ashore. He's got his expensive sneakers on, so he doesn't want to get them wet. He figures it's better for *them* to get their feet wet, rather than him. He pushes his thumb across the screen to answer the phone.

"Vic, you there?" one of his officers asks.

"Hey, what's up? Are you still up near Adrian's house?"

"Yeah. We've got a situation, and I think you need to come up here."

"Well, I'm kind of tied up at the moment. Is it urgent?"

"Yeah. I've got a couple of parents who say that their child is missing."

Officer Mortensen has several furrows on his forehead that grow especially pronounced when he can't figure something out. He turns to look down to the wetland edge where Gentry and Audrey are standing, not expecting to see the couple *he's* helping.

"What do you mean? They're standing along the shoreline near me."

Mortensen sees Adrian sliding down the embankment.

"Uh, well, I've got a couple here, too."

Clark and Fossie exit the boat.

Officer Mortensen's voice becomes more strained. "I have the parents here. I don't know who you have." He can hear a muffled conversation on the other end. "Hello?"

"Yeah, boss. I'm here. Just talking with them. They've

lost their little girl."

"What the hell? Does this child have two parents? I'm confused."

More mumbled conversation.

"They say they want to file a missing children's report."

"Ask them how old their child is."

"She's twelve. A girl by the name of Nadine."

"What?" Officer Mortensen replies with a groan. "*Another* kidnapping? Holy hell! What's going on?"

"I don't know."

"Well, I'm about to find out. Keep the parents there until I'm finished here."

"They said fine."

"No, it's not a question. Make sure they do."

"Got it."

Officer Mortensen returns his attention to the pair of kayakers and struts down to the shoreline.

"Hey, don't I know you? Aren't you one of the samplers from the Corringer investigation?"

"Yeah, we've met. I'm Clark, and this is my wife, Fossie."

"So, what brings you out here on a Saturday afternoon?"

"Just trying to help."

Fossie remains quiet.

"Yeah? Where's the forensics team? They're not working with you?"

"No, I didn't think they needed to since we aren't taking any samples. I was just curious about what was upstream."

"Look, I've got enough people around here to keep track of and we've just found out there's another kid missing. So, go back from where you came from and stay out of the way."

Clark and Fossie's mouths drop open.

"Holy cow," Clark says.

"I mean it. No private investigating. Work only with the forensics team or sign up for a search party. The sign-in is in the cul-de-sac near Adrian's house. Understand?"

"Adrian's house?"

"Yes, don't you know where he lives?"

"No, actually."

Right up there beyond the embankment.

Clark sees Adrian standing in front of the embankment, then turn around to climb back up it. Clark looks over at Fossie and says, "Adrian."

Fossie shakes her head and glares back at him.

Clark turns his attention back to Mortensen. "Officer, you do understand that this property is not far from the crime scene, right? If girls are missing here, the two cases could be related."

"What do you mean the two scenes are close by?"

"Like, around the corner is Colin's apartment complex and just beyond it is the crime scene."

"Huh." Mortensen pauses to think. "Thanks for that info. Now go."

Clark pushes off and begins paddling downstream.

Mortensen turns around and sees Adrian climbing back up the embankment.

"Hey, Adrian!"

Adrian stops at the top of the embankment abruptly and turns around.

"Wait up!"

Officer Mortensen climbs the embankment, carefully

stepping in dry areas so he won't wreck his sneaks. Once he catches up with him, he asks, "So, what are you doing out here all by yourself?"

"Searching. You?" Mortensen continues walking with Adrian toward the house.

"Why aren't you with the others?"

"Well, I live right here, so I thought I'd search while everyone else is answering questions and catch up later.

"We now have three missing kids, apparently. Three kids. All near you. Kinda weird, don't you think? What do you think is the common denominator here?"

Adrian shakes his head. "I'm not sure what you mean. I live here. I work with Clark. We're working on Wyatt's disappearance. What do you mean three missing?" Adrian starts to move away from the box and toward the path out of the woods.

"Wyatt and now two girls."

"*Two* girls?"

"Yeah. You know about Taylor, right? Well, it seems there's another—a twelve-year-old named Nadine."

Adrian stops to look at Officer Mortensen and frowns. "What the hell is going on? Is this all related?"

"Not sure yet, but I'm going to find out, Adrian."

"I have no idea either."

"You wouldn't be hiding something, would you?"

"Like what?"

"Oh, I don't know. I'm just asking."

"I don't know what other information I can give you."

Officer Mortensen leans over and whispers into Adrian's ear. "Just keep in mind that I'm watching."

Adrian scoffs and leaves.

CHAPTER

28

Adrian was unable to get food to his family the night before with all the commotion nearby. He hopes they're not too hungry. He fills another five containers with breakfast and peeks out the back window. Seeing no sign of anyone around, he sneaks out the back door and quietly enters the woods. He's careful not to step on anything that would make noise. It's amazing how good he's gotten at this in such a short amount of time.

He runs toward the back of the woods to the underground storage box. Excitement fills his veins as he gets closer since he figures he'll observe his family this time if he has a chance. Being the eldest child in his family, he remembers watching his siblings play. He used to think they were silly sometimes—that they needed to take things more seriously, but looking back, he knows they were right. He should have stayed a child as long as he could. He should have enjoyed the small moments. And that's exactly what he wants to do this morning: get a glimpse of how they are getting along and watch them play, at least the kids, anyway.

Adrian quietly rounds the trap door and silently lifts it open, not wanting to disturb the family in case they're still sleeping. He peeks through the opening and, in the dim of a night light, he sees the mattress directly below. He put it there so their fall would be cushioned. No one is on it. Adrian feels elated that Michelle has joined the family. How well this has all worked out!

A dim light provides a view of the room. It's a storage container, so it's about the size of a mobile home. Adrian sees five of the seven mattresses on the floor. The other two are waiting for the rest of the family. When he first put them in there, he was concerned they'd be able to stack them and escape, but he tried that out first and he still couldn't reach the ceiling. The container is deep. It must have been specially made by the previous owners.

Adrian shifts his focus. There, lying peacefully snuggled into their beds, is his family. There's no ruckus. There's no fighting. There's no squabbling over who goes first. There's no parental involvement. Just a peaceful slumber. Adrian was hoping to watch them interact, but somehow this is even sweeter to him. They're all sleeping in their beds, just like the old days when they would pretend they were camping in their living room, all lined up on the floor.

He watches them for a few minutes, then tries to lower the food containers as far as he can without waking anyone, but they dislodge and fall onto the mattress with a bang. Startled, Adrian jumps up and reaches for the trap door. He pulls it over to lock it when he sees a movement within the box. He peers in closer before shutting the door and there, right below him, is Jonathan. He's soon joined by Michelle and Amy. All of them say nothing. They are just looking up and staring at him with sad expressions.

Adrian is taken aback by the scene. Here they are, watching him all together. He sees Wyatt raise his hand and wave, and the girls join in and wave also.

They are saying, "Hi."

Adrian waves back. He can't help but smile at them and pauses before shutting the door all the way.

Get ahold of yourself, Adrian. It's too soon. Something's not adding up.

Adrian's mood quickly changes, and he jerks his head toward the room again.

They are all standing there so innocently. He sees Jonathan smiling back.

Don't trust them yet. Just get out of here.

Wyatt asks, "Why have you locked us down here, Adrian?"

"I'm protecting you," Adrian answers, a rasp to his voice again.

"From what?"

"From this terrible world. You're better off down there, trust me. It's no good out here. You will all be together and protected. Nothing will happen to you. You will all grow up in a happy home with loving parents. You'll help them, right Jonathan?"

Wyatt jumps a little when he hears Adrian call him Jonathan. "I guess, but I need help down here with all these girls. You know how crazy they can be."

The two girls look over at Wyatt, both of them appearing perturbed by his insult.

"Just go along with it right now," he says to them under his breath.

"I'm sure you can handle it just fine, Jonathan. I have faith in you."

"When are you going to join us, Adrian?" Wyatt asks.

"Oh, I don't know. After a while, I'll probably visit. I want you to get used to things first. It's great in there, isn't it?"

"Yeah, you've thought of everything." Wyatt picks up the food containers. "Smells delicious."

Adrian smiles. "Sausage and gravy today."

"Thank you, Adrian," Wyatt says. "I have a bag of old containers. Do you want them?"

Lorelei stirs, distracting Adrian for a second.

"It's probably too far for you to throw them. I'll get them another time." Besides, you'll wake up your parents.

He nudges the girls. "Thanks," they add.

Adrian suddenly hears some voices in the distance. He surmises it's the search party. "I've got to go."

"Don't go!" Wyatt yells. "Play with us."

"I can't, Jonathan."

"Please?"

"No. Quit your whining. Just play with the girls."

Wyatt stomps his foot and crosses his arms. "They stink."

Adrian inspects the woods around him.

"You'll just have to get used to it. I'll be back." Adrian quickly secures the lock and covers the door with sticks and leaves before running off toward his house. The sky is lighter, making it easier for his footing. He races across the woods as gently as a deer until he reaches his lawn and changes to a more normal gait. He picks up some hoses and empty flowerpots in his yard and stacks them under the porch stairs, as if he's cleaning up his yard before he goes inside, just in case someone is watching. He pushes the back door open and nonchalantly enters his home.

I made it.

Good. Now go out there and get some more family. There's plenty for the pickin's.

Wow, did you see them? My family is adjusting well.

I wouldn't put too much stock in that. They might be tricking you. It's too soon.

I don't know. They seemed sincere. They're just kids.

Yeah, I guess. Get the last two and then you can concentrate on taking care of them. Hopefully, the search teams will bring lots of young ones today. It's Sunday, so maybe they'll come after church.

I doubt it. Why would they bring their kids to a search party?

Well, if nothing else, get ready for a barrage of questions from the police. I'm sure they'll be sniffing around here today, especially since they heard about Nadine missing. You need to focus on pinning this on someone to distract them. Maybe Clark?

Nah. I think it'd be better if it were Lorelei. She won't be back, so it'll be an unsolved case if she's even noticed. I can use it as an excuse as to why she didn't return home. Clark would be more difficult.

Guess that's true. Makes sense. At least you know the family is fed for now. You need to concentrate on your story about Lorelei and a way to keep the police and searchers away from that box.

Well, it's soundproof and camouflaged. I'm not sure how much more I can do.

The police might bring the dogs. You need to figure that out.

I'll research it. Maybe I can distract them somehow.

After.

Adrian closes his eyes.

I'm not sure how I can pull this off in broad daylight.

They wouldn't be expecting it.

True.

Adrian watches for the police out his front window but doesn't see anyone yet.

Boy, they seem late this morning, especially after finding out another girl is missing.

There's not one car on the road?

No.

That's weird. It's almost seven in the morning. I wonder what they're up to. Maybe you should call Gentry. Besides, you'll still want to act concerned about Taylor, right?

Right. If no one shows up by eight, I'll call him. It's too early now.

The doorbell rings. Adrian sees Gentry's forehead through the door window.

Jesus. He's here. What's he reading my mind now?

Be cool.

Adrian opens the door. "Hey, man, I was just going to call you. I don't see the search parties yet."

Gentry enters, slumping slightly. "They haven't found her yet."

"I figured as much since you didn't call me."

"She's got to be dead. Maybe I should get used to that idea."

Maybe he should.

Stop.

"Don't think that way. They're going to find her."

"I don't think so. We've searched everywhere. We might have a serial killer on our hands with all the recent disappearances."

Adrian lowers his eyes. "Don't say that. I don't know what's going on, but you shouldn't give up. It's only been a few days."

"She's gone. I can feel it."

"What's the count up to? Three?"

"Yeah, Wyatt, Taylor, and Nadine. So weird."

"So, what's up today?"

"Oh, they're down near the water. They went in through the back way with some small boats and kayaks or at least that was the plan last night."

"That explains it. I was wondering why no one was here."

Shit.

I know.

"So, no more search crews over this way today?" Adrian asks Gentry.

"Doubt it. They've moved over to the wetlands."

"Maybe I'll get my kayak out then."

"I'm headed down to the wetlands soon. The wife wanted to sleep in a little today. It's really been hard on her, of course." Gentry's eyes turn glossy.

"I'm really sorry, man. I hope they find her soon. I'm going to head over to Wyatt's side of the swamp today, too, and see if they're still searching over there. They may have changed search locations also, I don't know."

"Maybe it's all pointing to the wetlands. Maybe this asshole, low-life is hiding them there… or—"

Gentry jerks his head and turns toward the door. Then, he stops. "Oh, hey. Haven't seen Lorelei around."

"Yeah, sorry. She's been on a major project and leaving before I even get up. Hopefully, she'll finish today."

"Oh, okay. Her car is here, though."

"Yeah, she's been riding with a student. Haven't met him yet, but he's supposed to be some stellar Ph.D. student she met through the university."

"Gotcha."

Yikes, that's fitting. Gotcha!

Shut up.

"Well, hopefully, I'll see you later today, Adrian."

"And hopefully, they'll find them all safe."

Yeah, like you want them to find the box underground.

"Take care, Gentry."

"Thanks, Adrian."

Adrian returns to his safe room. He slumps into his recliner and holds onto its arms.

I can't do this.

Oh, here we go again. You've already done it. You can't go back now. Finish it. Don't you dare act like this in front of the police.

Adrian takes a deep breath. *I know you're right, but I'm breaking that man's heart. What kind of person does that to his neighbor?*

One that just wants his family back. Gentry can have another kid. You need your family. Look at you. You're a mess. Remember the elation you were feeling ten minutes ago when you came back. Remember seeing them together. You loved that.

I did.

Okay, then.

So, there's another complication.

What?

They're down near the water, not up this way today. How am I supposed to find more family members?

Well, that's actually better as far as keeping them away from the box, but yeah, you're right. It makes it more complicated, but you can do it. Just think positively.

Right. Maybe I'll get lucky and there will be some wanderers who leave their parent's sight for a couple of minutes.

That's it. You better get down there.

Adrian jumps up, invigorated from his talk, trying to stay focused on more family time. He knows he's probably just a few hours away from seeing another member of the family.

He runs out back and enters the woods, this time staying clear of the door to the box. He tramps down to the water, having to slide down the embankment and slosh through wet plants. He stops for a few seconds to remember the day he brought Wyatt home. He remembers that Wyatt was scared, trying to get the tape off. How Wyatt had no clue that he was going to drop into the box. He knows he probably scared Wyatt, but convinces himself that, in the end, Wyatt will be grateful. Adrian grins, then continues into the wetlands where he sees about a dozen people gathering near the shoreline. He sees a boy around ten-years-old, then another boy about the same age, but no girls. There are a couple of kayaks in the water that are being paddled by some adults.

This isn't looking good. *Even if there were girls, how would I get one up the embankment without anyone seeing?* Adrian can feel his nerves through the tensing muscles in his neck. When he brought Wyatt home it was dark, and there was no one around. Adrian catches sight of Mortensen, standing with a clipboard in one hand, talking with two other officers. Adrian sees Mortensen look at him and wave him over.

As Adrian moves in closer, he sees there are several empty boats lined up, oars in their holders.

"So, what do you think, Adrian?"

"About what?"

"There are three kids missing now."

Adrian rounds Mortensen and says, "Yeah, you told me that already."

Mortensen turns around to watch Adrian's expression.

Adrian peers up at Mortensen. He doesn't allow his face to show his fear. He knows Mortensen is reading him. "What do you think is going on?"

"You're asking me?"

"Well, you live around here."

"Yeah, but that's crazy."

Mortensen stops well before the shoreline, standing next to Adrian. "Yeah, crazy. That's what I was thinking. We've got someone snatchin' kids right under our noses."

Adrian notices that Mortensen's sneakers are filthy and grins. "So, you think they're out here?"

"Possibly, unless you've got a better idea."

Careful with him.

"I have no idea. Are all three connected somehow?"

Officer Mortensen grins. "What do you think?"

Adrian can clearly see he's no match for Mortensen's antics. He pauses for a minute to look out over the water, then says, "Well, I'm going to head back home for now. I want to bring my kayak around."

"Good. We could always use more help."

Adrian returns to the embankment and climbs it, pulling himself up and over. He sees something out of place in the corner of his eye. It's white, very white.

Holy hell. It's the sewer pipe! I'm an idiot. With all the rain we've been having, DNA is bound to show up in the samples downstream from here and they'll probably end up pinpointing the source directly from the wetlands adjacent to my property. I need to get this covered up at least.

But he can't. Officer Mortensen is almost to the embankment and coming straight toward the sewer pipe.

Adrian panics. "Wait, Detective! I climbed a little farther down that way," he says, pointing to his right. "It's not as steep."

"I don't see much of a difference."

"You can use my foot imprints."

"I think I'm fine," the detective replies. "I'm sure I can hoist myself up easier using that pipe. Wonder what that's doing out here anyway." The officer grabs onto the PVC and uses it to lift himself. "Slippery bugger."

"Yeah," Adrian replies.

Detective Mortensen stands next to Adrian. He sniffs the air. "Did you shit your pants or something?" the detective asks. "Stinks like the devil out here."

"No, sure didn't," Adrian replies.

The detective wipes his hand on his pant leg.

"Must just be the wetland. They always stink," Adrian says.

Mortensen frowns. "Don't remember that smell yesterday, though."

"Maybe you stepped in something. All kinds of critters and dogs out here."

Mortensen lifts his foot to inspect it.

Adrian pulls a tissue from his pocket and wipes at the officer's pant leg a few times.

"Get off me, boy. What the hell are you trying to do?"

"Just trying to help."

Adrian crumbles the tissue in his hand and puts it in his pocket.

The detective wipes his brow with his hand.

Adrian cringes.

He's probably got Wyatt's DNA all over himself!

Mortensen's phone rings. "What's up? What?" He waves at Adrian and without a word, sprints for the woods.

Adrian closes his eyes, relieved that the detective didn't catch on.

CHAPTER

29

W ell, I suppose I'm done now," Adrian says aloud, watching the train go by each of the figurines at the train station. "At least a few of my family members are together again. Except for me, of course." He holds the figurine of himself in his hand. "One day, I'll be adding this figurine, too. I'm not sure how it'll happen, whether they'll accept me in time, but that's a sacrifice I'm willing to make. It'll be my job now to keep them fed, safe, and warm. They won't have to worry about outside influences getting to them. They'll be close, and I'll be there to make sure they have everything they need."

Who are you talking to?

Adrian drops his head.

Just let me have this moment.

This isn't over. There are still police and regular people out there running around. If they find the box, you're dead. You need to make sure to protect yourself. And them.

I know.

Did you find something to distract the dogs?

No.

Did you install cameras?

No.

Are you out there right now assuring that people stay clear of that trap door?

No.

What are you thinking? You can't be in here all reflective and comfortable with that going on out there. Seriously?

I just wanted a moment.

You'll get that moment soon enough. Right now, you better figure out a way no one will ever find that door. I'm telling you.

Shut up! Just shut the fuck up! I'm sick of you!

Oh, that's nice. Just great. I get you through this and you treat me like shit.

You get me through this? You are me. What the fuck am I doing? What the fuck have I done?

Don't think about that.

I've got five people locked away in a box in the ground, three of whom are children who are separated from their parents.

Don't.

And their parents are separated from them. But hell. Do I care? No. I just go right ahead and take their children anyway and throw them down a hole to some strangers. I've got to be the sickest person that ever existed.

Stop the self-loathing. This is going to turn out well. Just get out there and stop them from searching the area.

Adrian stretches his back.

Unless you want to go to jail? Besides, don't you want your whole family together? Why are you giving up?

There weren't any girls out there. I don't think I'm going to have any more chances, and like you've said, I need to make sure I don't get caught.

Adrian rubs his eyes with his fingers, leaves the safe room, and goes into the kitchen. Five containers of chicken and rice are stacked on the counter, meals he prepared earlier. He pushes each of them up his coat and leaves through the back door. The evening air is cool and the sun is setting. He stands on his back porch and listens. He doesn't hear any voices, just occasional chirps from resting birds and the activity of restless insects. He watches the woods for flashing lights or movement but doesn't see anything suggesting someone is nearby. He strolls over to the edge of his yard, then quietly into the trees, being careful not to give away his presence. His black cap and coat help to hide him in the shadows.

He comes upon the small clearing where his family now lives and scans the perimeter of the area, then he crawls to the door, feeling the hard surface under his knees when he's on top of the trap door. He scurries around to find the lock, positioning himself so he can see his family before they see him. An excitement and warmth fill him as he sees a gleam of light peek through as he peers into the box. He can't see anything, so he opens the lid a little further, lying on the ground in amazement. He can see Lorelei is sitting next to Jeremy on a mattress with all the children gathered around her, crossed legs in front of them. The table light on the desk is on behind her, as well as the wall lights on each side of the box. She's reading a children's story, so animated and sweet that they laugh. He's never seen Lorelei this beautiful.

His breathing picks up, though, when he sees Jeremy

bandaged up and spread out on the mattress. He wonders what's wrong with him. Jeremy seems to be having a hard time breathing.

Oh, no! He's hurt. He needs to take better care of himself if he wants to remain as Dad.

Oh, like what are you going to do, replace him?

Adrian snorts at the thought. Lorelei closes the book, her graceful hands moving across the cover, calming Adrian's nerves. "Adrian?" she asks. "Is that you?"

The kids and Jeremy look up also, and all but Jeremy move closer toward the mattress under the trap door. Adrian looks down at them, like a lonely giant peering into a rabbit hole. Adrian's not really a bad guy, is he? He just wants to be friends, right? He misses his family.

Without saying a word, he removes the containers from his jacket and drops them onto the mattress, being careful not to hit anyone. The kids grab the containers excitedly and run to their mattresses to eat. Adrian can see that they are starting to make themselves comfortable. There are clothes, books, and games strewn around. It's truly their home now.

"Adrian, thank you for the food, but why are you doing this?" Lorelei asks.

Adrian is hesitant to respond.

"Tell me the truth. You owe me that, at least."

"You're my family now," Adrian replies.

"I've always been your family. Why all this?" she says, her hands stretched with palms up to show Adrian the room.

"You're precious to me."

"I am? Then why are we not together?"

Adrian takes a deep breath. "I can't live without my family anymore. And it just goes to show that no one watches their children anymore. They leave them alone because their parents are too busy to watch them. They shouldn't let them out alone at night. If I can catch them, then those parents don't deserve to have them when I can offer a safe haven—a place where they won't have to worry about strangers like me anymore."

Upon hearing this, Wyatt pipes in. "You call yourself a stranger to me? Or my dad?"

"It was you who made me see this, Wyatt. When you were alone and fell. Who saved you? I did."

"Are you crazy?"

Adrian's piercing eyes don't leave Wyatt's, his breathing growing heavy, emanating a groan through the box.

Lorelei shushes Wyatt. "Let me talk," she whispers to him.

Adrian's attention returns to her. "What's wrong with Jeremy?"

"He hurt some ribs, we think."

"How did he do that?"

No one answers.

"Probably would have had to have fallen, maybe from some height." Adrian watches their expressions and surmises he's right. "So, you tried to get out by stacking things up, huh? Nice try. You don't think I already made sure that wouldn't work?"

Jeremy attempts to get up, but can't.

"He'll be okay?"

"Should be," Lorelei responds.

"And you? How's your head?"

"Thanks to Jeremy, it's much better."

"Good." Jeremy watches Lorelei, mesmerized by her presence.

Suddenly, Adrian hears a loud cracking sound in the woods. The sounds of men's voices are bellowing through the trees ahead, along with the chatter from others.

"I have to go, but I'll be back," Adrian says.

"But Adrian—" Lorelei replies, running toward the opening. "When am I getting out of here?"

Adrian says, "You're not."

"But I miss you. I've always loved you. Please stop doing this."

Adrian holds back the lump in his throat. "Be with Jeremy, Lorelei. I don't love you that way anymore," he lies.

CHAPTER

30

Adrian runs up the back stairs that lead to the Graystone office, knowing that he hasn't beaten Clark to work so he can peek at any faxes from the forensics lab. He saw Clark's car outside. Taking the time to sneak around the woods that morning to drop the containers by his family's home meant that he arrived at work later than he would have liked. He barrels through the front lobby doors. Rebecca is not in yet, so he hurries to his office to drop off his backpack. Then he quietly scurries by the back-office area to look at the fax machine and sees there are no new transmissions. He stands for a minute to catch his breath and calm down when he notices Clark's office light is on. Once he gains control of himself, he enters Clark's office.

"Hey, Clark."

Clark jerks his head up and squirms in his chair. "Oh,

hey, Adrian. You scared me. You like to scare people, don't you?" Clark flips through a few faxes.

Adrian picks up on the hint of sarcasm in Clark's voice, but ignores it. "So, anything more from the forensics lab?"

"Why don't you stop playing dumb, Adrian. I saw you yesterday while at the wetlands behind your home. I was surprised to see you so close to the crime scene."

"What's that supposed to mean?"

"I don't know. What I do know is that it seems odd that you start a new job that somehow coincidentally is sampling for clues related to your friend's kid and then a few days later there are police looking for two girls missing directly behind your house."

"That means nothing. They started at my house because they hadn't looked there yet."

"I bet this wasn't the ending you'd hoped for. Did you know we were going to be part of the police investigation when you took the job, Adrian? Maybe you wanted some control over the sampling results or at least wanted to see what was going on."

"That's the craziest thing I've ever heard."

"Is it?" Clark watches Adrian for any sign of guilt. "And those visions. All that drama on the bike trail with you and your supposed foresight, convincing Fossie you were a sensitive. All of that was a scheme, wasn't it? You know where Wyatt is, don't you?" Clark shakes his head in disgust.

Adrian stands his ground. "No, I don't."

Clark leans forward and says, "Then why do all the disappearances seem to point to you?"

"Do they?"

"You know, all this time, I actually felt sorry for you?

What with having to deal with the stress of seeing weird visions, your eyes turning red. You had me. Fossie, even worse. She adores you, you know. And all this time, you knew. Did you drag Wyatt off into the water, Adrian?"

"Of course not. I'm very upset over Wyatt."

"Are you? How about the girls. How many are missing now? And they're missing from where? Oh, yeah, some-where near your house. Are you a sick motherfucker, Adrian? Because if you are, I hope you rot in hell. I'm going to have to leave this to the police, but boy, would I love a swing at you right now." Clark's face is red, his nostrils wide. "Get out of my office and stay away from Fossie."

Adrian's heart rate increases and his chest feels tight. He contemplates his words for a few seconds, trying to fig-ure out how he'll convince Clark that he's innocent. When he realizes he can't, he rubs his face to show Clark he's ex-asperated and says, "Fine. Believe what you want."

Clark shakes his head, looking up at Adrian over his readers as Adrian leaves.

Stay cool. Don't let him get to you, Adrian. He really doesn't know anything. He's grasping at straws. Just sit down and relax. Be nice and friendly. Everything is normal, remember?

Right.

Keep yourself collected before you say or do something stupid.

But he's going to tell the police the results.

Well, that's just his interpretation.

I know, but it's going to cause more suspicion.

Just blame it on Lorelei, if it gets too close. She hasn't come back, so it'll be a good story to keep the heat off of you. You're going to have to start telling people that she's missing. Maybe even the police before long. I'm sure Clark is calling the police right now with the results, so you'll be hearing from them at some point.

Shit. I just wanted my family together, and now that I have them, I don't want to let them go.

Adrian holds back a surge of emotion that wants to escape and go wild.

Clark is just doing his job. Stay clear of him for now. Keep your nose clean and just concentrate on taking care of your family. You can handle the rest.

Adrian's not so sure though. All these threats to his family are conjuring up unrest that's been building for years. He never really accepted that his family was gone. He kept the figurines in a box in the side table waiting for the day he could see his family again. He knew the day would come. He knew it wasn't really over. So, he pretended. He pretended that his family was still alive—that they just went on with their lives, going to college, marrying, moving away, growing up to be adults. It was easier to pretend, to not feel the loss. He felt it at first and it brought him so far down, it was the only way he could think to bring himself back up. Lorelei always asked why his family never visited, but he would simply tell her, they were too busy, or too broke, or planned on coming soon. She had no clue they were all gone. She thought it was only Jonathan. He had to tell her that, at least, because he knew she'd feel sorry for him, that she'd accept his weird ways like the nights he'd wake up screaming or the days where he'd spend hours locked away in a small room with a train set. He knows she truly loved him. And now it is time for him to return that love.

It makes sense that she'd be with Jeremy. He even thought he caught them glancing at each other once or twice way back. Maybe there's a spark there, he isn't sure. But what better way to find out than throwing them together under an extreme circumstance? It's like throwing the dice, hoping for a full house—twenty-five points in Yahtzee. Always a good roll. And the chances seem good as well.

He thinks how weird it is that the thought of the two of them together isn't bothering him. Why not? Did he not really love her? That can't be true. So why not a reaction of insane jealousy? He should want to kill the guy, especially being it's his best friend.

It'd be a relief actually. The pressure would be off. No more worries about talks or coming up with excuses for not marrying or reasoning his hesitation away. He can say it out loud now. He doesn't want to marry and have kids. The thought of possibly losing them would be too much. It's bad enough with pseudo-siblings. He couldn't imagine if they were his. Those parents have to be going nuts missing their children right now. How will they handle it when they finally realize they're never coming home? They won't know that their children are happy underground with a warm, loving new family. Lorelei and Jeremy will make great parents. Hell, they may even make a few more of their own.

Finally, his random thoughts subside and he buries himself in his work to make the day go by faster. He's sure the night will hold more questioning from police and sneaking through the woods.

About halfway through reviewing a report, though, he remembers something. The sewer pipe. If the forensics team decide to sample the wetland area behind his house, they might see the pipe and sample the sludge from it.

I can't let them do that. Hopefully, Mortensen doesn't put two-and-two together from the smell yesterday.

He decides to run home during lunch to hide the sewer

pipe with more dirt if he can. Adrian grabs his keys and leaves. No one notices since there are many client meetings behind closed doors today. Adrian races home and sees numerous vehicles parked along his street again. Another search party must be underway.

You need to make sure they're not snooping around in the location of the box. Hopefully, they haven't found anything.

Adrian trudges through the thick vegetation, not caring if someone sees him at this point. He can always say that he's taking some time to look for the kids. He passes by the box without a glance, determined to reach the back of the woods to the wetlands. He doesn't hear anyone around, but he's careful to keep his intentions under wraps. He slowly steps down past the pipe, dragging some plants and dirt with him, which he uses to cover all but the end of the pipe. He pretends to talk on the phone, his back to the wetlands to block the view in case anyone is watching. He's careful not to step directly below the pipe but kicks some dirt under it to hopefully cover it enough so there will be no DNA hits, at least any time soon. He covers the end of the pipe with dirt so no one can see it. He then flies back toward his house. He pauses to take a look into the box, but thinks better of it and continues walking. In the distance, he can see Officer Mortensen talking with a few fellow officers along the roadway. Adrian ignores them and enters the back of his house.

Dread seeps into his veins when he sees two police officers standing in his front yard. One is Mortensen.

Mortensen immediately waves and proceeds over to Adrian, acting excited to see him. "Hey, Adrian! How's it going? Home early, huh?"

"Just for lunch."

"Ah, okay. So, I need your help with something. I got a

call from the forensics lab, and he sent me over this here map. Seems that some of the lab results seem to be pointing upstream from the Corringer crime scene. Do you mind if I search your house again, or do I need to get a warrant?"

"Search my house for what?"

"Oh, let me see. Wyatt, then there was Taylor, then Nadine."

"You are seriously thinking I have all those kids in my house?"

"I have to check it, Adrian."

Adrian sighs. "Fine. Go ahead. I'll be leaving for work in a minute." He doesn't wait for an answer. He goes inside his house to gather his wallet and car keys. He opens the safe room door and puts away the figurines, dropping them in his haste.

If you don't calm down, you are going to give yourself away. Do you want that?

No, of course not. It's just nerve-wracking to have police swarming around all over the place.

They're not swarming. They're just investigating. It's their job.

But they want to search the place.

So, let them. What would they find?

Nothing, I guess.

Do you think they know about the train accident?

Probably. Leave everything as is. Be open. Plant the seed about Lorelei missing tonight.

I don't know. Seems too convenient.

No, it doesn't. Lots of men cover for their girlfriends. He'll probably just suspect you of covering for her.

Guess that's true. Clark is after me, too. I don't think he'd believe it's Lorelei, though.

Who cares what he thinks. The police are the only ones who matter.

I can't calm down.

Adrian paces back and forth in the safe room for a few minutes, then goes to the kitchen to drink some water. He thinks more about the sewer pipe.

If Mortensen puts this together, he's going to think the pipe is coming from my house. If he thinks Wyatt is in here, what does that mean? They'll start tearing up floors?

Well, I guess you could always tell them you have him locked in a box underneath the ground. Would that work?

Shut up.

Stop overthinking this. They'll search the place and then leave because they'll find nothing.

You're right.

Adrian exits his house, walking past Mortensen without a word. He takes off for work, refraining from looking into the rearview mirror to see if the officers are entering his home.

I can't wait until I see my family again tonight.

CHAPTER

31

O fficer Mortensen has been in law enforcement for over ten years. He's not tenured, but he's not a newbie either. And he has a sense about things sometimes. It's been uncanny in the past how right he can be about guilt. He can sniff it out better than any dog, and he's received numerous awards for solving tough cases. At this point, he can't smell guilt. He can just smell that something's not right. He's watched Adrian during the visions on the bike trail a few times, and he thought Adrian seemed genuine, but again, something just isn't adding up.

Mortensen knocks on Adrian's door. He figures he'd better make sure Lorelei isn't home. Her truck hasn't moved in days.

Getting no answer, the officers enter and Mortensen directs them to begin the search. The house is quiet, making him doubt any kids are around.

He enters the kitchen and opens the refrigerator. He's not sure why. Then he strolls over to the safe room. He opens the door and flicks on the light inside. He sees the train set and all the food and supplies. The recliner. The side table.

An officer approaches him. "Man, Vic, this guy is ready for an apocalypse."

Mortensen laughs. "Yeah, guess you could say that."

"That's a pretty cool train set. Wonder why it's tucked away in this room. You'd think he'd want to display it."

Mortensen's lip twitches. "He says it's to keep it out of the way." There's something odd here to him. He turns on the train and watches it go around the tracks. Up the mountain. Over the trestle bridge. Through town. Past the city folk. And back into the mountains again.

"Wasn't this guy in a train wreck? Lost his family or something?"

"Yeah, he lost his entire family. Such a horrendous thing for him to watch, I'm sure."

"He has to have survivor guilt big-time. Or maybe post-traumatic stress syndrome."

"Hopefully, he had some counseling to avoid that."

"Guess he seems normal enough."

"This is just routine. He's one of only a few houses around here. Search the room but leave it all intact."

"Got it."

Mortensen returns to the refrigerator and opens it again. He sees the normal staples: milk, butter, orange juice, eggs, sausage…but then there are juice boxes. He wonders why a grown man would have juice boxes. He examines the contents in the freezer. Meats. Veggies. A lot of it, but nothing uncommon.

He turns around to search the kitchen when he notices a pink phone on the dining room table.

Must be Lorelei's. Strange for her to leave it behind, but then again, where has she been?

He enters the dining room and taps the face of the phone, then a few buttons, but it doesn't turn on.

He heads down the hallway and into the master bedroom. The bed is made. The bathroom is tidy. The shower is dry. No signs of kid's shoes or kid anything.

He turns on his heel and heads back down the hallway. "We've got the wrong place," he says as he rushes out of the front door.

"You still want us to search?"

"Yeah, but you won't find anything. Just do a light sweep."

"You've got it."

Mortensen races to the backyard. He listens to his surroundings. The place is active with swirling birds and the distant dog barking. He turns around, searching for places to keep children like an extra room added on to the back of the house or hiding spots underneath the back porch, but he finds nothing. He hunts for signs of a struggle on the lawn, for a hair tie, for a nine-year-old's bike helmet. But everything checks out. There's no extra room, no hiding spot, nothing belonging to kids.

So, why does he feel so uneasy? He's had this feeling since he started this case, but there have been no major clues. Kid after kid is being kidnapped or killed or something right under his nose. He's not living up to his reputation. That's for damn sure. And he knows it.

Mortensen walks into the woods, trying to stay as quiet as possible. Listening for what, he doesn't know. He never does this. He doesn't usually have to. There's usually some clue. But right now, all he has are his senses. He slows down, stepping around fallen tree branches. All of the kids were taken somewhere in these woods, except Wyatt. Where are they? What's the connection? He traverses farther into the woods, past a clearing, beyond the pine trees, and to the steep incline that leads to the wetlands.

"Uh, sir?"

"Yeah, I'm here," Mortensen says into his shoulder microphone.

"We've got a few angry couples here that want some answers. What do you want us to tell them? They said they're not leaving until you return and give them an update."

"Shit. They just need to let us do our jobs."

"Yes, sir, I'll tell them you're very concerned and will be right back as soon as possible."

"Keep them out of the area, whatever you do. I don't need them messing with things any more than they have already."

"Sure, sir. I'll let them know that this is a criminal investigation and we've got our orders."

"Right."

Mortensen's cell phone rings.

"Officer Mortensen?"

"Yeah, who's this?"

"It's Clark, sir, from Graystone Group. I wanted to know if you would be interested in us sampling anymore?"

"Not sure what good that would do."

"Well, sir, we could do some soil and sediment samples near Adrian's wooded area. We could sample it for organics and if we get hits, I could talk with the forensics folks and perhaps they could check for DNA from the other kids. We could work from the shoreline up to the woods."

"Seems like an awful lot of sampling, and people have been trampling all over the place here. I don't think it's my call. Talk with forensics."

"Okay, sir."

Mortensen slips along the slope and he slides down the embankment. "Goddamnit," he says as he notices mud all over his uniform. "The wife is going to be pissed at me for smelling like dog shit again."

"Are you standing in the muck?"

"Yeah, I guess so. It smells worse here than it did over in the woods behind Jeremy's house."

The detective finds his footing and heaves himself up and over the bank again. "I gotta go. Get with forensics."

He smells his hands.

Thank God, they're not as bad as yesterday. Smells more like dirt.

He wipes his hands off on his pant legs and returns to the uplands, not paying much attention to his direction. He realizes he's veered off a little too far to the left. He passes the clearing on the right side this time and pauses.

I remember this on my left side going down to the wetlands.

He strolls through the clearing. A shiny object hanging from a tree grabs his attention. He moves closer to the tree, barely missing the trap door. "What in the world is a chain doing out here hanging on a tree?" he whispers to himself. He circles around for more chains but doesn't see any.

"Huh," he says.

Twigs and leaves crackle below his feet. Officer Mortensen looks down and two cockroaches flutter across the top of his shoe. He leaps backward with a yelp, missing the trap door again, but exposing a corner of it. Mortensen doesn't notice. He's too busy brushing at his shoes to make sure the roaches aren't finding a way up his pant leg. He cringes, then trots off into the woods again, passing by Adrian's house and into his squad car.

I need a break.

Two sets of parents run over to his car, arms folded in front of them, letting Mortensen know they want answers.

If only he had them.

Later that day, Adrian pulls into the driveway, watching the commotion along his neighborhood street. Several officers are still canvassing the area and search parties are beginning to gather on the sidewalks. Reporters are standing in front of a couple of vans, holding microphones in front of cameras. The place is swarming with people.

Adrian walks quickly toward his house to avoid being seen by the mob, not that they'd have any reason to attack him or at least one they knew about. He notices his door is unlocked.

Nice. They could have at least locked it.

He figures they must not have found anything suspicious or he would have heard. He flicks on the light when he enters his home, rounds the corner, and sees a few Styrofoam coffee cups scattered around in the kitchen. A cigarette butt is lying on a plate with Mortensen's card next to it.

He flings his car keys on the counter and inspects the house to see if anything is missing.

There better not be anything missing from the safe room.

He peers in, but all seems intact, calming his nerves.

I wonder if anything made them suspicious.

You'd be better off thinking about your next steps, Adrian. There are some complications now.

Not now.

Adrian goes to the refrigerator.

Damn, I'm out of Samichlaus. Thank God, I've got some Maduro left.

Adrian pops open a can and sits in the reclining chair. He relaxes for a minute before nagging himself again.

Argh. I just need peace. I'm feeling uptight as it is.

You've got to be on top of your game—stay one step ahead of them.

I know, I know. Or else I'm going to jail. I just need a minute.

The doorbell rings.

Fuck me. Is that Mortensen?

Adrian heads to his living room and peeks through his front windows.

Mortensen and company. This day couldn't get any worse.

"May I come in?" Mortensen asks when Adrian answers the door. A wind picks up behind him, pushing his hair around. Adrian sees some people leaning against the cop cars.

"Didn't you already do that?" Adrian asks as he opens the door. "I told you there weren't any kids here."

Mortensen enters. "Nice train set you have there. Sad about your family. It must pain you to think about it."

Adrian holds back his shock. "Yeah, so?"

"Well, like I said before having a train set hidden away in a room was kind of odd. Were you afraid of some kids getting into it?"

"Funny. No, that's my man cave and the sound of the train relaxes me."

"Really? Wow, I would have thought the opposite."

"Guess you thought wrong."

Mortensen pulls out his pack of cigarettes and notices there's none left. He frowns and says, "You know, I can smell guilt a mile away. That's my reputation." Mortensen pats the cigarette pack against his palm, but none come out. "I'm smelling something, but I've yet to put my finger on it." Mortensen enters the kitchen, squeezes the cigarette pack and places it on the counter. "So, what's with all the juice boxes in your refrigerator?"

"They're Lorelei's. She takes them to the field." Adrian opens the refrigerator. "She's a health nut. See these are 100% fruit juice, no artificial flavors. She takes them in the field all the time." Adrian closes the door.

Good boy. Very clever.

Mortensen nods. "Uh, huh. Makes sense," he replies, watching Adrian's eyes.

"In fact, she should be home any second now. You can ask her yourself."

"At first, I thought it was kind of funny that she forgot her phone at home today, but then I noticed it was dead."

"She did? Crap. Well, at least she's with the student. I worry about her all by herself in the wetlands. She's been researching them for years, but I still have to know where she is every day. You just never know."

"Where was she going today?"

"Well, she didn't say this morning since she left before I got up, but last I heard, she was taking samples at Colt Creek again."

The officer writes down this information in his notepad.

"Why are you writing that down?"

"Just a habit, I guess. I tend to forget things otherwise."

Adrian frowns at him. "There's no reason to be taking any notes about Lorelei."

"I'll take whatever notes I feel necessary. Got it?" He doesn't wait for Adrian's answer and says, "Tell Lorelei I want to speak with her when she gets home. I've already asked this once. Now, I'm telling you."

"Yes, sir," Adrian replies as he escorts the detective out of the front door.

That might be kind of hard to do, Adrian thinks to himself, grinning.

CHAPTER

32

Adrian rinses his razor and returns it to the stand on the bathroom counter. He gazes into the mirror, remembering when he used to be afraid he'd see the vision—the one where Wyatt is being kidnapped by someone he didn't know—the one where he found out he was actually looking at himself, or a modified version of himself with huge arms and shoulders. All of those creepy shadows lurking in corners and the corner of his eye were actually just his subconscious mind giving him hints about his own disgusting deed. *I am loathsome. I know it. But now, I can't help it. I can't stop. I know this is wrong. I know I should let them out, but if I do, I will lose everything—my girlfriend, my best friend, my siblings. I will be all alone.*

You're already all alone.

Who are you anyway? The evil side of me?

The practical side.

Practical? No, I don't think so. I think you're my inner de-mon. You're always pushing me toward the bad. Why have you come?

I'm just trying to reunite you with your family.

Because?

You want it to be so. I'm helping you.

Adrian rocks back on his heels, not sure he needs the help or wants it for that matter. He grabs his coat and leaves out the back door with the morning meal. The thought of seeing the family has him excited. Every time he opens that trap door, it's like a reunion. He just can't believe that before long, he'll be a part of the family too.

Adrian unlocks the door and lifts it a smidge, as usual, wanting to get a peek at them before they notice him watching them. It's been two weeks since Wyatt came. Now, with more family, it's more active inside—active with kids and parents who have already instituted routines. Perfect.

Inside, the air is cool but not too cool. Adrian lifts the door a little more to get a better view. Adrian backs away and scans the woods around him to assure himself that no one is close by. Then, he returns. Lorelei is moving around. She spies him and immediately sits up. The kids turn around to look at him, too.

"Adrian?" she asks.

He doesn't answer.

"I see you."

"I can see that," he replies in his raspy voice. His pulse is racing.

"Why do you sound so different now? You're scaring the kids."

He pushes the containers out of his coat and drops them onto the mattress. "I really can't explain it, Lorelei," he continues.

"Are you really Adrian? Or has someone else taken over?"

"Guess it's the new me."

There's a wheeze, and he realizes it's Michelle. She's holding onto the mattress with one hand, trying to catch her breath. "Where's your inhaler?" Lorelei asks.

"I've got it," she replies, then inhales the medicine, calming her down. "He freaks me out," she says, glancing back at Adrian. "He really is a monster." She starts to cry, which makes her symptoms worse.

"Adrian, she needs medicine. Prednisone and more inhaler. She has asthma."

Jeremy starts to stir, then opens his eyes. He sees Nadine pull the inhaler from her mouth. He jerks up but immediately recoils. "Argh, these damn ribs."

Lorelei whispers, "Adrian is here."

Jeremy lifts his head toward the opening. "Hey, buddy. You see this? You see what you've done? You're causing misery to this little girl, and this one, and, oh, wait, this boy. I figured out what you're doing. We can't be your family replacement, you sick, son-of-a—" Jeremy stops himself, glancing at the kids. "All these years I've known you. I would have never pegged you as someone who would hurt kids."

"They'll be happier in time."

"No, they won't. Besides, your so-called family-to-be isn't for real anyway, right?"

"I'll squash you like a bug," Wyatt says.

"Wyatt..." Jeremy warns.

Adrian chuckles, a deep-throated half laugh from the gut. "You had your chance at me, Wyatt. Besides, you're

Jonathan now, and he wouldn't hurt me."

"He's not Jonathan," Jeremy says.

"To me, he will always be Jonathan. Maybe you should watch your kid better so he doesn't get stolen."

The veins in Jeremy's neck protrude and he rises. "Maybe sick men like you shouldn't be walking the streets so we don't have to worry about our children being stolen. *You're* the one who is wrong in this. Not me. My nine-year-old should be able to ride his bike home from his friend's apartment without being tied up and stolen. I can't believe you did that to him."

"I don't have to listen to this. I'm out of here." Adrian slowly lowers the lid to keep it quiet.

"Don't forget the meds for Nadine!" Lorelei yells.

"You mean, Michelle?" he replies, then closes the lid and locks it.

Later that morning, the mist from the morning dew coats the water as Clark kayaks his way through puffs of clouds. Numerous cranes and other birds are nestled in trees and bushes, their beaks resting between their feathers. A soft glow fills the sky as the sun slowly breaks through the horizon. Fish burst up through the water, quickly retreating and leaving bubbles behind.

Clark has always loved this time in the morning. It's peaceful—so much a different world than at other times of the day. He paddles lightly, not wanting to interrupt the morning awakening and rounds the corner to the back side of Adrian's property. The forensics team hasn't requested his assistance again. He just wants to snoop around a bit.

He hikes up to the embankment and notices a pungent smell. He's worked in numerous wetlands in his day, and he's never smelled anything quite like it. It's the kind that burns the inside of your nostrils.

He grabs a bandana out of his pocket and places it over his face. His eyes are tearing.

Holy cow, what is that?

He digs around in the dirt to examine its consistency but doesn't notice much out of the ordinary, other than it's causing the smell to become even more atrocious. Clark gags a few times, almost hurling his breakfast, but manages to keep it down. He sees a white pipe sticking out of the embankment. He steps up to it and peers inside. A gust of air escapes from it right into Clark's face. He slips and falls into the muddy concoction. He jumps up, disgusted by the mud covering him and grabs onto the PVC pipe again. He can now see the sludge that is coming from inside of it and dripping onto the ground.

That has to be a sewer line. If Wyatt's DNA is in there, it could mean he's alive at Adrian's house, but why would the sewer line dump into the wetland? That's not permitted. Very strange for a house.

Clark starts walking toward the kayak when he hears a noise from the woods. It sounded like a soft voice, perhaps from a child. It was faint as if carried by the wind. He stops, moving closer to listen.

He hears it again and jerks his head toward the left side of Adrian's property. Clark climbs up the embankment and enters the woods. Watching his footing, he enters the dense forest, attempting to listen quietly.

He hears chatter again—a woman's voice.

He carefully steps toward it, gently maneuvering around the plant debris on the ground. Then stops to listen again.

Clark's heart is beating so fast, he has to cover his chest with his hand to remind himself to calm down. He has a heart condition, one the doctors have said is benign, but who believes doctors anyway? To him, they're all a bunch of crooks.

He sees someone's head passing through the trees, then arms and legs as a person rushes toward a narrow path through the woods. Clark stands behind a tree, then turns his head and slowly peeks around the side of it. He sees that it's Adrian.

Wonder what he's doing out here so early in the morning.

Clark treads lightly toward the area of the woods where he saw Adrian. He's close to the box, but he doesn't know it. He doesn't hear anything further or see anything unusual. He ducks down for a few minutes to make sure Adrian doesn't see him, then runs for the kayak. He might be sixty-six years old, but he can still sprint when needed. Heart condition or no heart condition, he wants out of there. He slides down the embankment, leaving plenty of space between him and the pipe, and darts to the shoreline. He jumps into the kayak, wasting no time in leaving, rounding the curve along the shoreline swiftly.

There's something wrong going on in those woods. I knew there was something odd about Adrian from the first day I met him, but the visions were the dead giveaway. It was him on that bike trail. He was seeing himself. Why he was sharing that with all of us, I don't know, but what I do know is that there are human feces and urine coming out of a pipe in the middle of the wetlands. If that's Wyatt's, we've got Adrian. There's no way Adrian will be able to talk his way out of it this time. But whose voice did I hear? Sounded like a regular conversation. No screaming. No crying. Just an everyday morning talk. It doesn't make sense. Maybe it was Lorelei.

He shakes his head.

Clark rounds the corner and paddles past the apartment complex and toward the original crime scene. He can still see the tape the police wrapped around the trees.

Seems like forever ago.

He pushes onward and turns toward the coastline. And there, standing up on the trail with his eyes focused on Clark is Adrian.

It can't be. How did he get here so fast? I had to be paddling faster than he could walk.

Clark does everything he can to not look startled and continues to paddle. When he gets closer, he jumps out of the boat and secures it.

"What are you doing here?" Adrian asks, his arms crossed.

"Guess I could ask you the same."

"Were you trespassing on my property again?"

"No, I just went for a ride."

"I saw you, Clark. You were cleverly hiding behind a tree," Adrian replies with a sneer.

"Oh, well I thought I heard someone. A woman's voice."

"Yeah, so?"

"Seemed unlikely it could have been Lorelei's that far away from the house."

"She was on a walk with me."

"I didn't see her."

Adrian doesn't answer.

"And what about that sewer pipe? Where does it connect to? Your house? You know that's illegal for it to discharge into a wetland, right?"

"What sewer pipe?"

Clark smiles. "It better not connect to your house or soon the police will have all the evidence they need once forensics samples from there."

"On your suggestion, of course."

"Of course. I always try to be helpful to my clients. It's routine."

"Just stay out of it, Clark."

Clark marches up to Adrian and sticks his finger in his face. "It was you that you were seeing here on the bike trail, wasn't it?"

Adrian frowns, looking unsure of what Clark means.

"The visions. It was you. You are the kidnapper, aren't you? Admit it!"

"Old man, I think you need to stick to the facts and stop conjuring up stories that don't make sense."

Clark throws his hands up. "Like I said, I'm just calling it like I see it. I hope I'm wrong." He then heaves his kayak up over his head and grunts as he stumbles down the trail toward Jeremy's house and the work van.

Adrian follows him.

"Why follow me, Adrian? I—ahhh!"

Adrian grins when he sees Clark fall to the ground, tripping on a thin wire Adrian tied tautly around two trees on opposite sides of the trail. The kayak flies forward and skids across the grass. Adrian scans the area around him, then removes some rope and duct tape from his jacket.

Clark is lying on his stomach, his arms stretched outward. He had no warning the fall was coming and landed with the full force of his weight and nothing to soften the blow. Adrian slithers up behind him, pausing to assess the best way to tie him up. He leans forward, but stops when a voice calls out.

"Hey! What happened? Everything okay?"

Adrian sees a policeman running his way from Jeremy's house. He waves with one hand while hiding the rope and tape with the other.

"So glad to see you," Adrian says. "He suddenly tripped and fell forward. I was behind him, thank God."

Clark stirs, moaning from pain in his hip. One side of his face dug into the dirt from the fall, leaving cuts on his cheek.

"Here, let me help you," the police officer says to Clark.

Clark sits up, confused by how he tripped. "I didn't see a thing when I was walking, not even a root or stump."

"You probably just lost your footing. Can you get up?"

"I...I...think so." Clark uses a hand to steady himself, then stands. He limps across the yard. "Damn, that could have been bad," he says.

"For sure, Mister." The police officer grabs part of the kayak and pulls it along as he helps him. "You're one lucky man."

Clark glances back toward Adrian who stays behind on the trail.

"I think you're right."

CHAPTER

33

T his whole thing is imploding and you just sit there.
What else am I supposed to do? Clark is on to me, and he's not going to give up.

Well, maybe the forensics team won't want to sample behind our place. Think of that? Have faith.

He's going to show them the discharge pipe sticking out of the embankment. I should have done something different with the sewage.

Too late to worry about it now. Just concentrate on your family.

I almost took him, too.

I know. That was stupid.

Well, how else can I keep him quiet?

I don't know, but putting him in that box would have either killed him or helped them to get out.

Adrian slumps. True.

I've been on you about this before. Make sure you plan before you make a move.

Well, sometimes I gotta think fast.

Just don't be an idiot about it.

I'm not.

Adrian places his figurine next to the others at the train station.

Pretty soon. Be patient. Don't rush it.

I just want to be out there with them, not cooped away in here.

I know. Your time will come. Glad you got the meds for Michelle.

Yeah, they'll last for a while. It was pretty easy at the walk-in clinic. Pretending to wheeze was stupid, but the doctor seemed to think I was coming down with something. Better to be safe than sorry with my so-called asthma condition. So gullible. I'll need to remember that for future meds they may need.

The doorbell rings, startling Adrian. He gets up and peeks around the safe room doorway to the front door. It's Gentry. Adrian sighs in relief, glad that the police aren't there to ask him more questions.

Adrian heads to the front door and opens it. "Hey, Gentry. How's it going?"

"Not great, but I'm hanging in there. Can I come in for a minute? I need a break from all the goings-on at the house."

"Sure. Come on in."

"Any news on Wyatt?"

"No. How about Taylor?"

"Nothing. The nights are getting longer with the wait."

Adrian can tell that from the bags under Gentry's eyes.

"Do you want anything to drink? Water, beer?"

"Beer sounds good."

Adrian pours him a glass and stands across from him at the kitchen counter.

"I guess I just needed some normalcy. It's not such a madhouse here. I think they've finished the sweep on this side of the woods and are focusing behind my house now."

Adrian nods. He hangs his head for a minute, then looks at Gentry. "I'm really sorry this has happened to you. You don't deserve it."

"You're right, but it's happening. I've lost my little girl."

"Don't give up hope."

"Why? Are you still hoping for Wyatt to be found?"

"Realistically, I don't know. It's been three weeks. But I keep hoping anyway."

"Three kids. How in the world do three kids disappear? And with the exception of Wyatt, both taken from our neighborhood?"

It's really five with the two parents but...

Adrian shakes his head but doesn't answer.

"I think they suspect you." Gentry waits for a response from Adrian.

"I know. They've searched my house twice now. You can, too, if you'd like. Go right ahead. There are no kids here."

"No, of course not. I just hope they're not all dead," Gentry says, wiping his eyes.

Adrian closes his eyes for a second. "Don't say that. I'm sure they're not."

The doorbell rings again. Adrian sees it's Officer Mortensen.

Shit.

He opens the door and immediately steps back to let him in. "Hello, Detective."

"Hi, Adrian. Mind if I come in?"

"No, Gentry is here, too."

"Oh, good."

"Hi, Gentry. I don't have any further news, really. We've done a full sweep in the farthest woods behind your house and nothing has turned up. Even the dogs have come up dry. One thing we're going to do is take soil samples out back beyond the woods behind Adrian's house." He watches Adrian. "Your coworker, Clark, felt it could give us some clues."

"Why?" Adrian asks.

"Well, you know that pipe that's sticking out through the embankment out back?"

"Yeah."

"It seems there's sewage coming out of it. So, he just wants to rule out the possibility of Wyatt's DNA being in there."

Adrian nods but keeps his cool.

"Gentry, I'd like your permission to add Taylor's DNA to the analyses. In fact, I'm going to ask Nadine's parents also."

Adrian's palms grow instantly clammy.

"We're going to have to figure out who that pipe belongs to anyway since it shouldn't be discharging sewage, or anything for that matter, into a wetland."

Gentry nods. "Of course. Just let me know what you need."

"Good. Would you mind if I spoke with Adrian alone?"

"Umm. No, sure."

Gentry leaves, shutting the front door behind him.

"I, ah, was talkin' to Clark this morning, and he says he saw you in the woods out back doing something. What was that, Adrian?"

"I always walk in the woods."

"Instead of the neighborhood sidewalks?"

"Yeah, why would you want to look at concrete and half-built houses instead of the beautiful trees in the woods? He probably did see me."

"Didn't know engineers were nature lovers."

"Some are and some aren't."

"Awful spill Clark took this afternoon. He's lucky he didn't break his hip. I understand you were there, too."

"Yeah, I was stopping by to see if I could help one of the search parties, but no one was around. Then I saw Clark rowing up toward the bank."

The officer studies Adrian's expression.

"Well, guess I'll be on my way. Just wanted to let you know the latest."

As soon as the detective leaves, Adrian runs for the safe room and sits in the recliner, grabbing onto its sides.

Stay calm. Breathe.

They are going to find everything out. If they sample for all of their DNA, this whole thing is ruined. I should have done something about Clark earlier.

Like what?

Thrown him in there too. I could have.

Again, that would have been a stupid move.

They're going to dig up that sewer line and see that it goes to the box. What do I do?

First off, stop panicking. Think. What would help besides going after Clark? You can't do that.

Well, I don't know. I'm not an environmental scientist.

Think.

Clean it up and shut it down.

How about cutting the pipe and taking out about ten to twenty feet of it, so it doesn't connect? They'd think it was an old piece of pipe from way back that's not being used anymore. You'd have to figure out a way for the ground to handle the sewage though, moving forward.

I don't have time to put in a septic system. Plus, that'd be obvious, but I do like the idea of cutting out a big chunk of pipe. I'm sure I could do that without disturbing the ground surface much. Maybe if I just dug a big hole and put a metal plate over it, then covered it with dirt, it could act as a semi-septic. I'm just afraid it'll back up.

You may have to pump it out every once in a while.

I don't know. I'll figure it out.

Adrian grabs his jacket and a few containers of soup he prepared earlier and heads out the back door toward his shed. It'll be nightfall soon, so he knows he needs to get going. He flicks on the light and puts the containers to the side. Then he searches for anything that he can use to modify the sewer line. He decides on a hacksaw, shovel, PVC pipe, and an old metal barrel. He pushes holes in some of the PVC pipe with his drill, modifies the barrel, and hurries into the woods to make the only change he can think of that'll save him and his family from being discovered.

On the way, Adrian stops by his "parent's house" to check on them. As usual, he opens the lid slightly to peek in first. He's always taken back by the wonder of it as he lifts the lid. It's like looking into a different world, especially when it's dark outside and the light streams from the container and into the woods as if elves or centaurs lived inside. Tonight, his family is quietly sitting on the mattresses, each reading, playing, or resting. There's not much to see, and he knows he needs to get going, so he lets the containers go and they land on the mattress below him. Everyone turns to look at the food first, then up at Adrian. Wyatt gets up and gathers the containers, ignoring Adrian.

Adrian says, "Hi, Jonathan."

Wyatt doesn't respond. He passes out the meals and returns to bed with his own. Lorelei passes out spoons in silence and they all begin to eat. There's no begging or crying or laughing or yelling. There's no shouting his name or telling him to let them out.

Adrian drops the medicine inside the box.

They all look over to it but don't get up to retrieve it.

Adrian observes Michelle, but she's concentrating on eating.

"What's going on?" Adrian asks in his raspy voice.

No one answers.

"So, you're ignoring me now?"

Silence.

"Fine."

He shuts the door and locks it, looking around him for others. Seeing no one, he battles the brush and tree limbs until he makes it to the embankment where he finds the pipe. He steadies himself and starts digging out the soil around the pipe, letting it drop to his feet. He saves the plants he removes for later. Once he's cleared several feet, he saws through the pipe, separating it from the main pipe and removing it from the ground. He then digs a hole large enough to fit the small plastic drum. Once the hole is dug, Adrian places a foot of gravel at the bottom of it and pushes the container into place followed by some of the soil from the embankment. He pats it evenly, then adds the plants he dug out earlier, as well as twigs, leaves and other debris to hide any sign that it was disturbed.

Now all I have to do is clean out the separated pipe.

He tugs at the pipe until it comes loose, then brings it down to the wetland and washes it out. He grabs a handful of wetland muck and coats the inside of it, then pushes it back into the embankment a little farther away from the previous location and packs it in with the dirt until it doesn't look disturbed. He stands next to the shovel admiring his handiwork, proud that he's left no way to detect the disturbed soil without inspecting it closer.

He treks back to the house swiftly, moving toward the shed with his tools. He hesitates at the edge of the woodlands before stepping into his yard, looking around for any searchers or police officers. Seeing none, he quickly returns the tools to the shed and speeds through the back door of the house, locking it behind him.

Maybe now, my family will have half a chance.

CHAPTER

34

T here are police swarming everywhere," Adrian says to himself aloud. He watches from his bedroom window as they rush into the woods, between his house and the empty house next door. "There must be something up. God, I hope they didn't find the septic line cut. Or even worse—the box."

He looks at his watch.

Damn, it's almost time for me to give the family their break-fast. How am I going to do that with the police everywhere?

Adrian slides on his jeans and shoes, then opens the sliding glass door. He scans the area around his house to see if anyone else is coming. A police officer is running his way.

"Hey, what's up? Did you find them?"

"If there are any updates, we'll let you know," she replies. "Just go back into your house for now. There's nothing to see."

Ugh. This is bad.

Adrian's world circles around him as he turns to figure out what he should do next. He stands in his yard until she's out of sight, then runs to the opposite side of the yard and enters the woods, far enough away so they won't see him. He jogs toward the clearing where his family lives, keeping his distance when he sees it. No one is there. He winds around the clearing toward the sewer line, but no one is there either. He relaxes a bit. Then, he sneaks down toward the wetlands, staying in the trees. The police are gathered along the shoreline. It appears like they're talking with Clark and the forensics team. They're showing them papers. Adrian sees Fossie standing next to him.

He must have gone in early to work today and talked her into coming with him. They must be helping with the DNA samples. What do I do?

Watch them, for now. Just relax.

Right.

Adrian keeps his head down and watches the forensics team follow Clark to the soil sampling locations. He's pointing at certain ones as he reads off the paper. Mortensen has his hands on his hips as Clark is talking. Adrian sneaks around to the side to get a better view. He sees Clark pointing at the sewer pipe, then at the woods directly behind Adrian's house. Mortensen takes a forensics investigator aside and Clark begins collecting more soil samples.

I'm so screwed.

You don't know for sure. Just keep one step ahead of them.

I do know. It's the only thing that makes sense.

Driven by pure panic, Adrian takes off for the box.

They can't have my family.

Before he enters the clearing, he stops and squats behind some bushes.

You don't look guilty or anything.

Shut up.

Get back to the house and leave for work. Do everything you normally do. Hopefully, the severed pipe will stump them.

Adrian cannot control his breathing and sweat forms on his forehead.

I can't let them take my family. I lost them once. I can't lose them again.

You need to relax.

I can't relax.

Adrian's senses kick into high gear again. He hears the soft fluttering of butterfly wings and their legs landing on delicate petals. He hears the ruffle of leaves floating along the ground. He smells the rotten decay of a log with its center disintegrated. His breathing is heavy. His extremities feel tingly. But he feels strong.

They can't have them. I will not let them.

Adrian turns toward the trap door.

I should warn them that they shouldn't leave. That they made that mistake before when they all got on that train, and they all died. That they should stay in the box where it's safe. That I love them all. That I only wanted my family back. That I'll find the rest of the family soon.

He tries to catch his breath.

I've got to get the ladder. If I get caught, they'll be stuck down there.

No, that's a bad idea.

Why?

They'll just get out and leave. Adrian, you need to stop and think. You're going in fast motion.

You're right. Why would I get the ladder?

There's no reason to. If you get caught, we'll worry about it then.

Right.

Adrian calms down more. He leans his head against a tree and closes his eyes.

"We've got you, Adrian."

He opens his eyes, but there's no one there. He scans the surrounding bushes but doesn't see anyone nearby. His breathing increases.

Who was that?

He leans forward and peeks over the bushes. Police officers are walking toward his house. He sees Mortensen walk by too. It must have been one of them that said it.

Okay, just stay calm.

They know.

They might know that there's suspicion related to the woods behind your house, but they have no idea that you have your family in a box underground.

They can't prove anything right now. It may not even be the DNA test results. Those take weeks to come back. You probably have time to plan.

I need to see them.

Your family?

Yes.

Not now. The police are everywhere.

They just left.

Adrian, just go to work.

I have to see them. It may be the last time I do.

Don't say that. You're getting carried away.

Adrian crawls on all fours toward the clearing. His arms are shaky, but his legs hold him. He leans down on his elbows and unlocks the door. His eyes well up just with the thought of seeing his family.

Officer Mortensen knocks on Adrian's front door, noting that Adrian's truck is there. Getting no answer, he marches around to the opposite side of the house and bangs on the back door.

"Adrian? This is Officer Mortensen. Open up. We need to talk."

He walks behind the back of the house to the sliding glass doors and looks in.

An officer greets him. "Anything, Vic?"

"No. It doesn't appear he's home." Mortensen pulls on the sliding glass door, and it opens.

"Adrian?" he calls out.

He and his partner walk through the house, finding no sign of him.

Mortensen sees Lorelei's phone in the same spot he saw it the other day.

Why would she not even move the phone? It doesn't make sense.

He goes over to the refrigerator. There are fewer juice boxes.

Mortensen turns to his partner. "He's got them somewhere. The kids, Lorelei, maybe even Jeremy. What the hell is going on?" He leans on the counter as he contemplates the case, then turns to an officer and says, "Where's the file?"

His partner radios for them to bring the file inside.

Soon, an officer hands it to Mortensen.

Mortensen opens the file and reviews Adrian's history. "How old are the missing kids?"

His partner pulls out the other files. "Wyatt is nine, Taylor is seven, and Nadine is twelve. What difference does that make?"

"All the difference in the world," he replies.

"He's replacing his family members. I just hope they're alive."

"But we've searched his house. There's no sign of them."

Mortensen pulls out the search party maps. Map after map shows search grids everywhere. "They searched out back, right?"

"As far as I know."

"The containers," Mortensen says. He looks over to his partner. "He's been cooking up all kinds of food for the search parties. But they weren't for them. They were for his new family. Search the woods. Search it now."

"Sure, Vic."

Word spreads amongst the police officers to gather at the edge of the woods. Mortensen leaves the house.

"Damn. Those kids were easy targets for Adrian. I knew this whole thing didn't add up, somehow," Mortensen says to an officer standing by.

"Well, you don't know for sure yet. Don't beat yourself up. If nothing else, the DNA samples should help."

Mortensen nods. "Yeah, but the results won't be back for weeks. I can feel it in my gut now, though. I couldn't feel it before."

"Well, your gut is usually right. So, we'll check it out. Do you want to search too?"

"No, I think I'll wait inside the house, but keep it quiet. Adrian's probably out in the woods someplace. He told me he likes to walk out there."

There's the sound of the front door opening and then Gentry's voice. "Hi, Officer Mortensen. Find something?"

Mortensen gets up and walks over to the front door. "Oh, hi, Gentry. No, nothing yet on Taylor."

"Are you searching behind Adrian's house?"

"Yeah, we're doing a sweep again, just to make sure."

"Well, it's a waste of time. Adrian's my friend."

"I know, but I think it's best to start here and look again."

"Shouldn't you be trying to find the bad guy here? I'm telling you, this is a waste of time. I want you to find my daughter, and I want you to find her now. This is not helping."

"Let's walk, Gentry."

Mortensen and Gentry walk down the driveway, leaving the others to get started on the search.

"It's been over two weeks now. How long can she live without food and water, if she's even alive? I hope she hasn't been suffering, cold and alone. If so, it's on you, Mortensen."

"I'm well aware, Gentry."

The parents of Nadine walk up toward Mortensen. He knows they'll want answers. He knows they'll be disappointed because he doesn't have any.

And he knows they'll blame him.

CHAPTER

35

Adrian doesn't hear the officers searching the woods several hundred feet away. His mind is on his family. He wants nothing else in life. He lost them. He saw them fall from a train. He won't lose them again.

He pulls up the trap door an inch or so, just wide enough to see inside. Lorelei is combing Michelle's hair and Taylor is lying next to her, holding a juice box. He wants to get a better view, so he lifts the door a little more, but all he sees is a big yellow blob. Searing pain shoots through his nostrils as a pencil plunges through his nose and into his sinus cavity. The surprise hit sends Adrian reeling backward. He tries to cover his face with both hands, but his arm becomes wedged in the door.

"You spineless bastard!" Jeremy screams and grabs Adrian's arm, pulling him forward. Pain surges through Adrian's forearm as it's stabbed with another pencil.

Adrian's hand shakes while Jeremy wraps the rope around it and pins his hand. Adrian can't see what's going on, because the door is in the way, so he pushes it open with his free hand and flings it over to the other side. He then punches Jeremy square in the jaw. Jeremy jerks backward, barely hanging onto the sheets that have been used to make a hammock near the opening.

Adrian becomes furious. He feels bigger than life now, his senses overreacting. He broadens his shoulders and his neck veins bulge.

Jeremy yanks on the rope to pull Adrian in. He steadies himself on the hammock, ready to plunge another pencil through Adrian's eye, but Adrian has better leverage and is too fast for him. He grabs the pencil out of Jeremy's hand, breaking Jeremy's finger in the process. Then he reaches for Jeremy's neck and shoulders to push him out of the hammock.

Lorelei screams from below. Wyatt cheers his dad on. Taylor and Nadine are huddled in a corner.

Jeremy holds onto Adrian's arm, but the force from his own weight is too much, and he plummets to the mattresses below him. Adrian's breathing is loud, echoing in the room. Lorelei sees him for the beast he really is, for the first time. She runs to Jeremy.

"As long as I'm alive, you will not be leaving!" Adrian yells. He begins to speak again but is cut off by a rope that's twisted around his neck and being pulled from behind. Clark yanks it as hard as he can, using his feet for leverage. He pulls harder and harder, forcing Adrian out of the opening and onto his side.

"I heard something over there!" a police officer yells from the woods. He's followed by a couple more. Adrian panics and pulls on the rope, burning Clark's palms. Adrian attempts to run for the woods, but Clark shoves his arm into Adrian's ankle. Adrian flies forward onto his stomach, giving Clark a moment to jump onto his back and grab the rope from his hand. He wraps the rope around Adrian's neck once again and Fossie screams for him to stop, punching at Clark's shoulder.

"Fossie, stop! This is his doing! I—"

Clark is hit on the side of the head by Adrian's elbow. He drops the rope and falls backward. Adrian jumps up and runs toward the woods. Police officers are running through the clearing, making their way toward Clark.

An officer stops and peers into the box, bewildered by what he's witnessing. "They're here! They're all here!" he says to the others. Another barrels at Clark with handcuffs.

"No, no, wait. It was him! Adrian!" Clark yells.

"Right. Of course, it was someone else. They all say that." The officer handcuffs Clark and jerks him to his feet.

"No, I'm telling you. He—" Clark glances into the woods behind him, but Adrian is gone. "I'm telling you, you need to get him!"

"We'll sort that out later."

The officer hands Clark over to another officer, takes his sunglasses off, and peers into the box. "I can't believe this," the officer says, waving another officer over to peer inside.

Another officer calls Mortensen. "We found them. We found them all."

Gentry and the other parents are soon running out of the woods and into the clearing. Mortensen sprints ahead of them, warning them to wait until the police assess the situation, but they pay no heed, dodging every which way to find their loved ones. Finally, they see the officers in the distance.

A ladder is brought in from Adrian's house and lowered into the box.

Mortensen puts his hand up. "Everybody stop! Just stop for a minute! I know you want to see your kids, but let me assess things down there first. I'll send them up as soon as possible. If not, I'll make you go back to the house. Understand?"

The yearning parents reluctantly wait close by while the officers hold them back.

"What is that in the trees overhead?" one of the parents ask.

"What do you mean?" Mortensen replies.

"Up there!"

Mortensen and the officers circle around below it.

"Bikes," one of the officers says. He shakes his head.

Mortensen climbs down the ladder. He catches his partner's eye on the way down. He slowly steps downward and turns around to see inside the box. His mouth drops open. "Oh, my God," he says.

Lorelei is clinging to the girls, while Wyatt is standing behind Mortensen with his dad.

"Lorelei?" he asks.

"Yes, officer," she says, tears streaming down her face.

"Did Adrian put you in here?"

"Yes," she replies.

Mortensen calls to the officer standing near the box. "It was Adrian. Find him." Mortensen steps forward, then squats so he doesn't look so enormous to the kids. "Are you all okay?"

They nod.

"Can you climb up the ladder with me? Your mommy

and daddy are up there," he says with a smile.

Mortensen helps Nadine climb the ladder and hands her off to his partner. He hugs her and brings her over to her parents who scream in relief, praising God. Nadine clings to her parents and rests her head on her mother's shoulder. Her dad hugs them both.

Gentry watches the other parents.

"Where's Taylor? Maybe she's not in there!"

There's a pause and then a shimmering blonde comes through. Gentry is taken aback when he sees her. She appears scared, searching for him. When they lock eyes, she screams and runs for him, tears running down her face.

"She's alive!" he yells. Audrey weeps into her hands.

Last out are Lorelei, Wyatt, and Jeremy. Lorelei closes her eyes when she feels the breeze on her face and the organic smell from the woods she loves. The paramedics arrive and chaos ensues with the commotion from having to assess each survivor.

They didn't realize someone was watching—watching from the corner of the woods where darkness can hide things.

The paramedics move Jeremy to a stretcher for assessment, but later decide that his ribs are just bruised. They push on his chest, feeling for punctures, and Jeremy grabs Lorelei's hand. She squeezes his hand to let him know it'll be okay, perhaps better than okay now that this is all done. They also splint his broken finger.

The police continue their discussions with Clark who is still handcuffed. Fossie is fit to be tied at this point, yelling at them to let Clark go—"That he's a good man—an outstanding citizen who works for the public good and doesn't deserve this terrible treatment."

Clark describes what happened when he saw Adrian leaning into the box and points in the direction in which Adrian took off, opposite of where Adrian is standing now.

Gentry marches toward Clark. He can't believe what he's hearing. "Are you telling me that Adrian did this? My friend took my little girl?" He falls to his knees. An officer assists him and guides him back to his family. Distraught, he asks, "He knew where she was all along? He lied during every one of my visits to his house?" When the realization hits, Gentry turns toward the officers, face red as the crimson sky, and screams, "You need to find him! He needs to rot in hell!" The officers hold Gentry back from joining in on the search for Adrian, trying to calm him down.

Wyatt, angry and wanting revenge, overhears the conversation. He struts over to Officer Mortensen who's comforting the other families. "Excuse me, sir." He yanks on his shirt a couple of times. "You mean to tell me you didn't catch Adrian? He's free?"

"They're looking for him, son. They'll find him. No worries."

Three weeks of torment and a broken Dad foster a reaction in Wyatt. He turns around and storms past everyone.

"Wyatt?" his dad asks. "Where are you going?"

Wyatt doesn't answer.

"Hey! Hey you!" Jeremy yells to an officer. "You need to get my boy! Hey!"

But the officers are too sidetracked with the others.

Wyatt suddenly sprints to the woods. He jogs passed old oaks with crooked arms, he runs by stumps sticking out of the ground, past pine trees, the smell of which remind him of being carried through the woods, not knowing where he was going, not knowing if he'd survive, not knowing what was happening. The tape. The rope. No vision. No voice. He was absolutely, positively at the mercy of Adrian—the man who is running around free.

Wyatt passes a few more trees when he's abruptly stopped by Adrian's arm. Wyatt fights with everything he has, trying to gouge Adrian's eyes, trying for his groin, trying to bite, scratch, and kick, but the hand over his mouth and the power of Adrian's strength is too much and he feels like the wayward ant in a spider's web who fights and fights but cannot and will not escape. Before he knows it, Adrian lifts Wyatt to his shoulder and hurries toward the shoreline. Instantly, Adrian is grabbed from behind and a fist is planted into the side of his face. He recoils, gathering himself for a second, when he sees another fist coming from Jeremy and ducks. Wyatt tries to push himself off Adrian's shoulder, but Adrian holds onto Wyatt's arm with his left hand while he blocks another punch with his right arm. A blow to the head again rocks Adrian forward and he struggles to hold onto Wyatt. Adrenaline shoots through Adrian's veins. His senses kick in, hearing Jeremy's breathing, seeing the distress in Jeremy's eyes. Adrian feels his body grow stronger. Adrian whips around toward Jeremy as he feels Wyatt being pulled away and the palm of Jeremy's hand pushing into his shoulder.

But Adrian remains strong and holds onto Wyatt tighter. He can taste the blood on his lips. His face is throbbing. Rustling sounds coming from the bushes behind him let Adrian know others are moving in. He pulls a chain out of his pocket, the same one that was hanging from the tree a few minutes ago. Despite his pain, he rears back and with every ounce of force he can muster, whips it hard into Jeremy's already bruised ribs. Jeremy winces, losing his breath, and Adrian runs, careening down the side of the embankment as fast as he can, and flings himself and Wyatt into Clark's kayak. Adrian holds Wyatt down with his legs and paddles as fast as he can into the deeper water of the wetland.

Jeremy screams for Wyatt as he flies into the water which immediately slows him down. He takes huge steps, then flops into the water to swim toward them but the friction from the water and agony of his bruised ribs prevent him from reaching Wyatt. Jeremy screams at Adrian to let Wyatt go, but Adrian continues to row away.

Adrian turns around and yells, "Maybe if you could keep your son safe, men like me wouldn't be forced to keep him safe for you. This is all on you, Jeremy."

Adrian then notices Lorelei running up to the shoreline. The woman he still loves.

She runs into the water. "Please, Adrian. Come back. Don't leave! We'll work this out. I promise I won't go. I'll stay with you and marry you. We'll have our own kids. You don't need Wyatt. Let him go!"

"She's right, Adrian." Officer Mortensen yells, running down to the shoreline near Jeremy and Lorelei. "We can make a deal. This can all go away if you just come back now with the kid. You know you don't want to do this." Adrian sees Mortensen talking to his shoulder and assumes he's calling for backup.

Adrian stops paddling and grabs Wyatt, flinging his arm around his neck and placing his palm on the side of his head. He locks Wyatt down with his legs even tighter. "Come closer, and Wyatt is dead! Keep your people back, Mortensen!" He knows he'd never kill Wyatt, but they don't.

Wyatt yells and jerks around, trying to free himself from Adrian's stronghold.

Other police officers and parents swarm in along the shoreline, followed by Clark and Fossie. He watches their expressions, long faces of despair. Adrian hears Mortensen tell his men to stand back.

Adrian then focuses in on Lorelei. What he wouldn't give to be with her again. The smell of her skin. The tenderness of her caress. The bed they once shared.

I love her. Adrian looks down around him. *What am I doing?*

Adrian. Stay with me. You'll never have your old life back with Lorelei.

No! I can't do this. I've told you this over and over. This is not me!

Sorrow takes over his emotions. He locks eyes on Lorelei and her expression softens.

If you do this, you will lose everything. You will be alone. You will live a life in jail forever. It's too late, Adrian. She no longer loves you.

Jeremy runs back to Lorelei and hugs her out of excitement. Lorelei's expression grows concerned and Adrian hears her tell him to wait, but his exuberance makes him swirl her around in the water as they embrace.

Adrian blinks.

See what I mean? She has moved on. Take Wyatt. You can still have a life with him.

"Come on, Adrian. It's okay." Officer Mortensen says.

Lorelei pulls out of Jeremy's arms.

"It's too late," Adrian yells, his senses piercing through him. "It's all too late."

Adrian tries to push the evilness aside, but he hears the

drip from the paddle plop into the water, smells the putrid organic decay, and feels the smoothness of the plastic between his fingers.

Adrian jerks his head left and right, trying to push out the beast that has once again taken hold of his mind.

But he loses himself.

He lets go of Wyatt, grabs the oars, and frantically rows toward a marshy area on the other side of the wetland.

Good, Adrian. Escape. They have no right to be part of Jonathan's life.

Adrian hears Mortensen yell to his officers to fan out. He then hears splashing he assumes is from people swimming toward him.

Wyatt punches at Adrian's legs and wiggles around, trying to free himself.

Adrian pushes forward and locks his legs around Wyatt's waist. "No worries, Jonathan. You're where you should be now. You're family. We'll find another home soon, I promise. You stay with me, and your dad will live a long, healthy life."

"No!" Jeremy screams, plunging into the water once again. Tears flow from his eyes as he watches the kayak move away. "I will find you, Wyatt! I promise!"

"Get him!" Mortensen yells to his men.

They're kidding themselves. You know these woods better than anybody. You know where to go. Where to hide. Protect your brother.

Adrian flies into the tall grasses of the marsh and heads to another shoreline, his arms aching and chest heaving. He covers Wyatt's mouth with a twisted shirt, and drags Wyatt out of the kayak. Adrian winces from the pain in his face as he takes a deep breath and flings Wyatt onto his shoulder.

Then Adrian runs into the woods, the sound of Wyatt's muffled screams dampened by the mossy limbs of ancient trees and extinguished by the chorus of chattering insects as Adrian and Wyatt once again disappear into the depths of Green Swamp.

CHAPTER

36

SIX MONTHS LATER

H i, Mr. Weber. Hi, Jonathan."
A refreshing breeze pushes by Adrian's skin, relieving him of the stifling humid air still lingering in September. They both wave back at the young girl riding by on her bike along a neighborhood sidewalk in an old Florida town known for moonshine and a good place to blend in. A place where no one asks questions.

"She looks to be about twelve years old, doesn't she?"

"I would say so," Jonathan replies.

"Why don't you go for a bike ride, too, Jonathan."

Jonathan goes to the garage and pulls out his bike and helmet. He grabs some rope and tape too, just in case.

"You better go get your sister. She'll be late for dinner."

"Okay. I'll meet you there."

THE TAKINGS

Adrian closes his eyes as a rush of adrenaline runs through his veins with the thought of another family member coming home. Though he goes by a different last name now, it's close enough. Webster, Weber, what's the difference? He hasn't changed it officially, of course, since that'd spark suspicion. The last thing he needs is Mortensen crawling down his back again, especially after all the effort moving has taken. He sighs when he thinks about how he's had to restart his life, but at least he has Jonathan, and perhaps soon he'll have Michelle back as well.

Adrian heads inside and stops by his new trainset for a minute. The train is rounding the track and makes it safely over the trestle bridge once again. Though new, he was able to find similar buildings and accessories to bring back all the memories. He grabs a velvety sack. He waited months for them to leave the back door open and was able to grab it from the side table late one night when Lorelei and Jeremy were sleeping in his bed, her head on Jeremy's arm.

Perhaps that was where Lorelei was meant to be all along.

He pulls out a figurine that reminds him of Michelle and places it at the train station.

So glad she'll be home again. I've missed her.

Soon you'll have them all back again, Adrian. Patience, my friend.

You are no friend. You are my inner demon, and I hate you.

You can stop this any time you'd like, Adrian, but you choose to continue. That's because you are me and I am you. There's no split between us anymore, no me making you do anything. No evil side. You are just plain evil. Admit it.

All I want is my family back. That is not evil.

Taking others away from their loved ones to do that is evil.

I don't know, Jeremy and Lorelei seem happy enough. Their

experience kindled love. It's so nice seeing them together. Soon they'll start their own little family, I bet.

You don't think they're yearning for Wyatt every night?

Lorelei has what she needs. She can take care of Jeremy. Now I need to get back to what I need.

You're doing just that. And best of all, you're not doing it alone this time.

Isn't that perfect?

Why, yes, it is. On that, we can agree.

Now go get your sister!

Acknowledgements

Thank you to my son, Michael, for sitting with me on a beautiful December evening at an Orlando restaurant and spending hours hashing out this story. I was stuck, and you helped me move forward again. That night made this book happen.

Thank you to my husband, Charlie, and son, Tom, for the countless times you listened as I pieced this work together. The writes, the rewrites, the texts – the list goes on. You were both always there with love and patience.

Thank you to my editors, Heather Whitaker, Christina Kaye, and Margit Crowell. You were all essential in making this book professional. I'm so happy I had the opportunity to work with all of you.

Special thanks to all of my readers and virtual promotions team for the tremendous support over the years and always helping me spread the word on my new book releases. I appreciate your time and endless posts and tweets. You rock!

Sandie Will is a multi-award-winning author of psychological thrillers/horror. She loves tapping into our fears to scare us all and make us cringe.

She lives in the Tampa Bay Area, and works as a geologist by day and a writer at night. Her down times are spent with her husband of over 30 years, family, and pets.

Road trips with Sandie should be avoided as she's been known to demand endless stops at road cuts to satisfy her geology cravings and teach her companions everything they never wanted to know about the Earth.

Sandie especially loves finding little bookstores and antique shops, tasting new wines and coffees, learning histories and cultures, exploring the Appalachians and Rockies, and writing in her back room nestled in the arms of an old oak.

Awards & Recognitions:

The Caging at Deadwater Manor

2020 Top Shelf Magazine Awards: First Place - Young Adult Horror

2018 Florida Writers Association Royal Palm Literary Award: First Place - Young Adult/New Adult Fiction

2017 Readers' Favorite Book Awards: Honorable Mention - YA Horror

The Takings

2020 Florida Writers Association Royal Palm Literary Award: Finalist in Blended Fiction

For more information on her books visit:
www.sandiewill.com

CONNECT WITH SANDIE WILL:

Facebook: @authorsandiewill
Twitter: @sandie_will
Instagram: @sandie_will

Made in the USA
Columbia, SC
12 May 2022

60323341R00219